THE
FRANCHISE
BABE

ALSO BY DAN JENKINS

NOVELS

Slim and None
The Money-Whipped Steer-Job Three-Jack Give-Up Artist
Rude Behavior
You Gotta Play Hurt
Fast Copy
Life Its Ownself
Baja Oklahoma
Limo (with Bud Shrake)
Dead Solid Perfect
Semi-Tough

NONFICTION

I'll Tell You One Thing
Fairways and Greens
Bubba Talks
You Call It Sports, but I Say It's a Jungle Out There
Saturday's America
The Dogged Victims of Inexorable Fate
The Best 18 Golf Holes in America

DAN JENKINS

THE FRANCHISE BABE

A NOVEL

DOUBLEDAY

NEW YORK • LONDON • TORONTO • SYDNEY • AUCKLAND

DD

DOUBLEDAY

PUBLISHED BY DOUBLEDAY

Copyright © 2008 by D&J Ventures, Inc.

All Rights Reserved

Published in the United States by Doubleday, an imprint of The Doubleday Publishing Group, a division of Random House, Inc., New York.
www.doubleday.com

DOUBLEDAY is a registered trademark and the DD colophon is a trademark of Random House, Inc.

Library of Congress Cataloging-in-Publication Data
Jenkins, Dan.
The franchise babe : a novel / by Dan Jenkins. — 1st ed.
p. cm.
1. Sportswriters—Fiction. 2. Middle-aged men—Fiction. 3. Women golfers—Fiction. 4. Midlife crisis—Fiction. 5. Golf stories. I. Title.
PS3560.E48F73 2008
813'.54—dc22
2007041088

ISBN 978-0-385-51910-6

PRINTED IN THE UNITED STATES OF AMERICA

1 3 5 7 9 10 8 6 4 2

First Edition

Always for June.

Heart of my heart.

THE
FRANCHISE
BABE

It doesn't take any great effort to work up
a healthy dislike for those ladies and gentlemen
of the Press who shape our destinies.

—BRYAN FORBES, *The Rewrite Man*

RANCHO TRUSTO FUNDO

1

All it took to bring out the Texas in me was one look at the lady in the jacked-up mini standing by the ninth green. I thought, man, if this is a golf mom, you can dip my ass in batter and fry me for dinner.

The jacked-up mini was bright blue, the legs were tan. They were toned and shaped and it was a good guess she could kick a hole in the ceiling of a motel room if she was on her back doing what it looked like she could do best. I might add that she was also first-team upstairs in a formfitting, sleeveless, scoop-neck white top— and if those were store-boughts, she damn sure got her money's worth. But all this was merely the opinion of Jack Brannon, white man, forty-seven, sportswriter, and spiritual person of great depth, which was me.

I was at this tournament for chicks. You could say I was trying to change my luck. Or you could say I'd grown tired of writing Tiger Woods, comma. For more than twenty years I'd been covering the PGA Tour, but in the last ten or twelve years all I'd done was write about Tiger whipping up on a bunch of slugs—in his sleep, blind-folded, with one endorsement contract tied behind him. I needed a break from watching him beat guys who all dress the same, get rich for finishing tenth, and couldn't give you a good quote if you stuck a shoehorn down their throats. There's a joke in the press-rooms now that the tour should be known as Black Jesus and the Dwarfs.

So I decided to check out the ladies. See if the rumor was true that the LPGA Tour was suddenly interesting, more heterosexual

than it used to be, and even halfway glamorous. There was supposed to be a surprising batch of young babes out there now—a
new wave of Lolitas—who could solid play the game and were good-
looking along with it.

Anyhow, it was a warm day at this tournament, and the jacked-up
mini was behind the gallery ropes with a leather bag slung over her
shoulder. Her streaked blond hair was falling open in the middle like
the showstoppers on Fox News. She wore tinted shades. I watched
her glance up at the big scoreboard on the veranda and then back
down the fairway.

For all I knew, she could have been a golf aunt, a golf sister, or a
golf cousin as easily as she could have been a golf mom. What I did
was, I decided to ask one of the obvious golf moms about her.

I had choices. The ladies over by the putting green were obvious
golf moms. I could tell. How? Because they looked like middle-age
flight attendants and were in possession of chair seats, binoculars,
and pairings sheets. What else could they be?

I strolled over to a lady who looked pleasant, helpful. Ann Wendell she said her name was. Fortyish. Adequate brunette. I pointed
to the jacked-up mini and asked if she knew the person's identity
and wittily wondered why security hadn't called for backup.

Ann Wendell ignored the attempt at humor and looked at me like
I'd been living in Antarctica or Oregon and said the woman I was
inquiring about was Thurlene Clayton, of course.

Of course?

I said, "Excuse me, but why am I supposed to know who Thurlene
Clayton is?"

She said, "That's Ginger Clayton's mother, for goodness' sake!"

"No fooling?" I said.

I did know who Ginger Clayton was. She was one of the reasons
I was out there. I'd read about Ginger Clayton, seen photos. She
was the newest child star in women's golf. A fiery eighteen-year-old
blonde who could launch it and putt it. She was from North Cliff,
Texas, which I was familiar enough with to know it considered itself
a suburb of Dallas and had the freeway traffic to prove it.

Ginger had turned pro last year and won an LPGA event and a

million and a half dollars overall. She'd already been second twice this year and scooped $200,000. And I knew one more thing. If Ginger was eighteen, the jacked-up mini couldn't be more than thirty-eight—and could play younger.

Ann Wendell said, "That's an interesting statement Thurlene is making with the Vuitton shoulder bag she brought to the golf course. It must have cost her daughter fifteen hundred dollars."

Headline: Man Finds Jealous Woman Among Golf Moms.

I casually asked if there was a Mr. Jacked-Up Mini around. I hadn't seen a guy in a muscle shirt anywhere with gold shit around his neck.

"They're divorced," Ann Wendell said. "He isn't here."

I thanked Ann Wendell and walked away, thinking that the sight of Thurlene Clayton had begun to change my mind about women's golf.

In my wholesome life as a sportswriter and recreational golfer, all women's golf had meant to me was four plump ladies in shin-length skirts, cardigan sweaters, and floppy hats directly in front of me, and playing so slow and squatting so long behind so many putts that they'd force me to yell, "Pick it up, Doris—it's good!"

I decided the jacked-up mini needed to meet me, since I was in a position to help her daughter's career, owing to the literature I turned out regularly in the magazine I wrote for.

If you wanted to attach an ulterior motive to why I wanted to meet her, you could start with the fact that I'd been single for three years, the result of two losses in the marriage game. My first wife, Carolyn, the magazine reporter, left me for a stockbroker for the same reason that my second wife, Renata, the real estate agent, left me for a gel-hair lawyer.

I took a philosophical view of it. Stockbrokers and lawyers, pound for pound, made a shitload more money than journalists. So I wrote it off as one of God's mistakes, like not letting dogs live longer.

I'd stayed friends with Carolyn. She was a nice person, had a good heart, and I didn't blame her much for wanting a husband who made more money than I did and wasn't always out of town in a bar or a pressroom.

Renata, on the other hand, was a different package. She was attractive, fashionable, and inquisitive, but that was the disguise I fell for.

She turned out to be a humorless, screeching, spend-with-both-hands, life-sucking bitch who could throw a clock radio into a wall mirror harder and straighter than Tom Brady could throw a football.

The gel-hair guy was welcome to her. He's the only lawyer I've ever pitied.

2

This was early March. I was in a part of Southern California I didn't know existed. I was at an exclusive new country club and real estate development that was advertised as an "enthralling resort destination." This was despite the fact that it was located in a vast desert somewhere between Indio and El Centro and populated by happy throngs of illegal aliens at work and play in their quaint regional costumes.

I'd flown from New York to L.A., spent the night at the Hills, dined on the McCarthy salad, and rented a Lincoln the next morning. I'd spent six hours driving. The first three hours were for enjoyment. The last three I felt like I was in a desperate race to reach the Wadi Zim Zim ahead of Rommel's Afrika Korps.

The tournament was the Firm Chick Classic. Firm Chick was a skin cream, I was excited to learn. And I was always impressed when a golf tournament declared itself a classic in the first year of its existence.

The first round was already under way on this Thursday in the kind of LPGA tournament where the winner makes page nine in the sports sections but could be a nail-biter if you were a golf mom or a golf dad and had a precious princess in the hunt.

The fifty-four-hole event, a ladies thing, Saturday conclusion, was taking place at the Enchanted Villa, which was the name of the "resort destination."

I'd checked in at the front desk, received a press credential and a press packet of info, dropped off my bag and laptop in my room, freshened up, and gone out to case the joint.

According to the press guide, the Enchanted Villa was owned by Toppy and Connie Pemberton of La Jolla. They had realized their lifelong dream when they built Enchanted Villa and hired Burch Webb, the "world famous architect," to design thirty-six holes of golf. Villa was the "championship course," where the tournament was being held, and Cottage was the shorter, easier course.

I didn't need to look at the two layouts to know they'd feature fake waterfalls, dirt-shoved hills, phony ponds, rows of palm trees flown in from Kauai, and here and there a copycat golf hole.

Ah-ha—the eleventh at Merion. And what have we here? I do believe it's the eighth at Pebble Beach.

Nor did it take much imagination for me to conclude that Toppy and Connie Pemberton were born-rich golf nuts and the place should be called Rancho Trusto Fundo.

But now I was standing there peering at the jacked-up mini again and wondering if Ginger Clayton's mother would think "Rancho Trusto Fundo" was as funny as I did when I put a breath mint on my tongue and went over to make my move.

It was tempting to open up with an old standby and ask the lady if she was as interested in poetry and art as I was, but I only smiled and said, "Golf is my life—how about you?"

When she turned to look at me, I said, "Hi, I'm Jack Brannon with *SM* magazine. My investigative talents have uncovered the fact that you're Thurlene Clayton . . . Ginger Clayton's mother."

She offered me her hand. "I *am* Thurlene Clayton. Who did you say you were . . . are?"

"Jack Brannon. I write for *SM. The Sports Magazine.*"

"You're Jack Brannon? The writer? Really?"

"You read?"

A little humor there. Got back a look.

"You certainly don't have to," I said.

Got another look. Then she said, "I do read and I've read your books, as a matter of fact. I read *Excuse My Free Drops* first. Isn't that the name of it? The short stories?"

"Collection," I said. "Stuff from the magazine. It sold like a collection of stuff from a magazine."

"I read your novel too."

"The title of which was . . . ?"

"*You Can Bet Me*. How am I scoring on the test?"

"I'm surprised you found a copy of it. Oprah never saw it. Hollywood never called. And the publisher's idea of promotion was to put it outside the door of every room at the Comfort Suites in Shreveport, Louisiana."

She pulled her shades down on her nose and squinted at me.

"Hey, I'm flattered you know my name," I said. "Usually people can't find my stuff in *SM*—they get lost going through Myrtle Beach or exploring Florida's new gated communities."

I was referring to those multipage ad inserts that piss off readers so much. They vary between golf destinations that promise to improve your game and marriage and the "hot lists" that tell you what's new in the zany world of golf equipment.

She said, "If you don't mind my saying so, I can't always tell if you're serious when I read you. Are you writing a new book?"

"I'm always serious and very deep," I said. "Yeah, I'm creeping up on something, but the muse doesn't seem to be in a hurry. As far as the magazine goes, people don't know what they read or where they read it. Guys come up to me and say they saw my piece in *Golf Digest*. I say, No you didn't. They say, Okay, it must have been *Golf World*. I say, No it wasn't. They say, Okay, *Sports Illustrated*, and I say, Yeah, that was it, hoping to end the conversation. Then they ask what I do for a real living."

"You mostly cover men's golf, don't you? The PGA Tour and all?"

"I have for a long time, but it's no fun anymore. I decided I'd try Lolita golf for a while."

"*Lolita* golf? Is that what you said?"

"Aren't there a lot of young babes out here with talent?"

"Yes, there are. Maybe we should promote it more. Come to the LPGA, follow Lolita golf."

"It got me out here."

"Why aren't the men fun anymore? I would think . . ."

"I'm over-Tigered."

"You don't like Tiger Woods? He's awesome."

"I like him fine. But he happened to come along at a time when he has no competition. It's the slugs that have worn my ass out. They think they're celebrities even though they don't win squat. Meanwhile, for some reason, the tournament sponsors slobber over them, pamper them, lust to have their pictures made with them. America used to reward winners."

"Slugs? You call them *slugs*? Players good enough to make it on the PGA Tour?"

"What PGA Tour? It's Tiger and a bunch of guys playing pushover courses the tour sets up. There used to be a lot of good players who could win tournaments and do that incredibly difficult thing of talking to the press at the same time. Nicklaus, of course. And Trevino . . . Crenshaw, Curtis, Lanny, Fuzzy, Watson, Nick Price. Some others. They even played tough courses now and then. But this was before the slugs came along. These guys get rich for not winning . . . and this is while they're criticizing the golf course, *and* the clubhouse food, *and* telling the sponsor they may not come back next year. They don't even know each other, much less the press. They only know their agents, swing coaches, sports psychologists, and TV anchors. It's a boring, dreary period in American pro golf. The worst since 1911 or 1912, before World War One, I'll argue. When the only star we had was good old Johnny McDermott."

She said, "Why do I think I've read that somewhere?"

"You have," I said. "I wrote it in the magazine three weeks ago— and lived to tell it."

3

Looking proud of herself—or her memory—she said, "You wrote that the PGA Tour needed to have a nervous breakdown and start over. I laughed, not really knowing what you meant, but now I understand you were serious."

"That was good," I said. "You almost quoted it exactly."

"Why are you so bitter, Mr. Brannon?"

"It's Jack. Please. And I'm not bitter. Am I cynical? Guilty. It goes with the job. And I'm amused. If you want to know why I'm amused, it's because I'll still be covering golf long after these slugs have disappeared on the senior tour and can't understand why nobody recognizes them or wants their autograph in Dump City, Arkansas."

She looked at me for a long moment, like she was trying to decide something, then gazed down the fairway. "Oh, here comes 'Lolita' now, my kid. Looks like she has a five-iron."

Ginger Clayton, the kid, was about 180 yards away. The player she was paired with was in the rough. One of the dozens of Asians on the LPGA Tour these days. If you looked at a list of LPGA scores in a newspaper, you'd think our ladies were being invaded by Chinese takeout.

Ginger took a smooth swing and the ball came right at us. It hit the front of the green softly and rolled up to three feet of the flag.

"All right!" the golf mom yelled, clapping. "Way to go, Gin!"

They looked more like sisters. That's what I thought when Ginger Clayton walked up on the green. A showstopping young lady, is what she was. Tall, built, attitude.

"Your kid," I said. "She looks like she can wreck homes if she gets tired of golf."

"I assume that's a compliment."

"Big one in my league."

I was pleased to see Ginger carrying a sane putter, a Scotty Cameron blade, as opposed to a trendy but idiotic design. Every new putter today reminds me of a showerhead or a gardening tool.

The kid was outfitted in short red shorts and a white collarless shirt that exposed her belly button on the follow-through. Ginger was all business as she rapped in the three-foot putt for the birdie. She did a little fist gesture and marched off the green and headed for the tenth tee without acknowledging her mother's presence. Game face. Focused.

The mom reached into her shoulder bag and took out a pack of slender king-size cigarettes. Capris.

"I only smoke when she makes a birdie," she said.

"You call that smoking?" I said, taking the Bic from her and lighting her Capri, which was about as thick as a strand of angel hair pasta. "Back in my Hall of Fame smoking days, I went with Marlboros. They were the best friends I ever had. They saw me through divorces, deadlines, most dinners in most restaurants. I never ordered anything I couldn't eat with one hand. I'd have smoked in my sleep if I'd lived next door to a fire station."

"Why did you quit?"

"The cigarette police wore me down. I live in New York City and it's too much trouble now. You have to go down to the street and freeze or melt if you want a smoke. I could have moved to Europe— they arrest you in most European cities if you don't smoke. But Europe has its drawbacks too. Soccer, for one thing."

She said, "You're welcome to try a Capri." She offered the pack to me. "They're very mild."

"No thanks," I said. "But I hear they do cure emphysema."

She laughed. Good sign.

"I may want to write about your daughter," I said. "Who's she signed with? CSE? IMG? William Morris?"

"We haven't signed with anyone yet."

"Really?" I was surprised. "You must be fighting them off with hand grenades. You have a franchise on your hands here. But you need to be careful. One thing agents know, athletes are naive . . . gullible . . . even stupid when it comes to money. Like writers. Does Ginger have a swing coach?"

"Me. I'm the entourage."

"You . . . ?"

"I was a pretty good golfer once . . . The agents who hound us the most are Howie Daniels with CSE and Sid Lasher with LTG . . . Logos to Go. Do you know them?"

"I know them. Howie the Dart and Smacky Lasher. People learn to hide their wallets when they come in a room."

"Howie offered us a million dollars over three years if Ginger would go pro when she was sixteen. It wasn't easy to turn down, but we did. We took the gamble. We gambled on Ginger's confidence in herself and our confidence in her. Her father represented her. He thought he should be Ginger's agent and manager—for her own protection. That didn't work out too good, although he did arrange some 'what-if' deals when she was still an amateur with Nike, Mastercard, Wild Honey Cream."

"Is he here?" I asked casually.

"Pete Clayton?" she said with a frown. "Hardly. We've been divorced for two years. It should have been sooner."

"You guys divorced while he was handling Ginger's career?"

She said, "It's more accurate to say we divorced while Pete was stealing our daughter's money. Listen, I'm going the back nine with 'Lolita.' It was nice meeting you, Jack Brannon."

"In those?" I said, looking down at her shoes. They were wedge-heeled sandals with an ankle strap.

"Oh," she said. "I guess I would have noticed eventually. I was at a luncheon for parents in the hotel." She pulled a pair of sneakers out of her shoulder bag and changed into them.

"How did you know who I was, by the way?" she asked, bracing herself with a hand on my shoulder while she changed shoes.

"That lady over there told me." I pointed to Ann Wendell.

"You asked *Ann Wendell* about me?"

"I think that's her name," I said, detecting a note of displeasure. "Is there a problem?"

"She's Debbie Wendell's mother. Debbie and Ginger came out of the academy at the same time. They've been rivals forever."

"How good is Debbie Wendell?"

"She has potential. But she's on the small side . . . and she only has one speed. She can't take anything off of it."

Golf lingo. Debbie couldn't hit three-quarter shots.

"It sounds like she's not in Ginger's class."

"Not even close. Ann Wendell knows this and hates it. Debbie's a year older but she's never beaten Ginger one time . . . amateur or pro. And Debbie is envious as hell. That's why the little brat tried to poison my daughter last year!"

4

Your basic journalists come in two categories. There are the point-missers, who seem to be multiplying, it's sad to report, and there are—I think I can say this without sounding too boastful—the rest of us.

If a point-misser had heard Thurlene Clayton say Debbie Wendell had tried to poison her daughter, the point-misser's immediate question would be, "How long has Ginger played Callaway clubs?"

When Thurlene walked away after dropping that news on me, I called after her and said we needed to chat some more on the subject.

She said, "You're staying here in the Villa, aren't you?"

"Yeah," I said. "The cactus and I."

"We'll chat," she said, and jogged off to catch up with the kid.

How so many point-missers manage to get into the business of sportswriting is a good question. Maybe some of them learn it from their university professors in more or less the same way that others learn to become left-wing radical anti-American commie socialists. I speak of the academic loons who prefer to call terrorists "freedom fighters" even though terrorists hate golf, football, barbecue ribs, and enchiladas, and want to cut off our heads.

But that's a subject I only think about when I'm shouting at a bearded academic loon on TV who's blaming America instead of Grantland Rice for pestilence, famine, death, and destruction.

I first heard the term *point-misser* from Jim Pinch. That's when he was at *SM*. Jim was my guru, my godfather, in the profession I'd always wanted to be part of.

I grew up reading Jim's stuff the same way I grew up reading my other sportswriter heroes—Damon Runyon, John Lardner, Red Smith, Jim Murray. I still reread their collections even though they're reminders of how inadequate the rest of us are. I smile at . . .

Jim Pinch saying, "If Arnold Palmer took the game of golf to the people, John Daly takes it to the people in the RV parks."

Runyon saying, "Al Capone was quietly dressed when he arrived at the courthouse this morning, bar a hat of pearly white, emblematic, no doubt, of purity."

Lardner saying, "When the Giants won the pennant Leo Durocher's license to think was renewed for two more weeks."

Red saying, "Rocky Graziano stirred up a bobbery in fight circles by not mentioning not taking a hundred-thousand-dollar bribe before not throwing a fight that was not held."

Murray saying, "Willie Mays's glove is where triples go to die."

And I grew up reading my dad, Jackson Brannon, a general columnist for the *Fort Worth Light & Shopper* for twenty-five years. He wasn't the first guy to say that politics was showbiz for unattractive people, but he was the first I ever read say that politics was where failed lawyers go to wear ugly suits and let the government pay their rent.

Jim Pinch and I were both from Fort Worth. Jim had read my stuff in the *Light & Shopper*, his old paper, and recommended me for the job of golf writer at *SM* when Cloyce Windham retired.

That was twenty-two years ago. I was twenty-five. It was four years after I'd graduated from the University of Texas, where I wallowed in the successes of the Longhorn gridiron gladiators and left Austin before the loon-dancing professors could turn me into a deep-fried liberal.

The idea of replacing Cloyce Windham was intimidating. His name was identified with golf. But Jim said I'd have no trouble. He guaranteed that despite Cloyce's knowledge of golf history and precise use of the language, he was the high priest of point-missers and a master of burying the lead. Jim liked to cite the time that Jack Nicklaus won the '78 British Open in dramatic, last-round fashion but the top half of Cloyce Windham's story rambled on in high literary style for 1,500 words about the marvelous day four centuries ago when the storms and seas and other forces of nature created the Old Course at St. Andrews.

The Firm Chick pressroom was off in a wing of the Enchanted Villa. I was drinking coffee and had finished my conversation on the phone with Gary Crane, the latest managing editor of *SM*.

"Jackie-boy," he said when I reached him. "What's going on? Where are you?"

"I'm out here in California at the ladies golf tournament I told you I was going to," I said.

"You did? When did you do that?"

"Two weeks ago. I'm checking out the babes."

"Women's golf?"

"The LPGA Tour."

"I wonder if anybody reads women's golf?"

"I wonder if anybody reads *anything*. Listen, I think I'll stick with the ladies for a while. There's a young babe out here who can really play. She's hot. Think lingerie model plays golf. This girl could make a cover. She's eighteen. Her name's Ginger Clayton."

"Ginger," he said. "Ginger . . . Ginger. Good name. Might give us a catchy cover billing. Ginger. Rhymes with *danger*."

"Almost," I said.

The managing editor had to run. Another lunch with some members of Old Port Country Club. He was close to being invited to join after four years of proving to the members that he wasn't black, Jewish, Spanish, crippled, or in debt. Old Port was in a serene, manicured, leafy part of Connecticut that screamed money at you. It consisted of a charming old-fashioned golf course, a beach club, and a harbor where the wait to obtain a slip for your boat was ninety-five years.

The conversation with Gary Crane made me dwell on how good my life was when Nell Woodruff ran the magazine.

Gary was as qualified to be m.e. as any other guy who learned his journalism from a college professor with a beard. He'd been a big-time point-misser as a staff writer on the magazine. He covered the NBA in the winter and track and field in the summer. It was Gary who wrote that he wouldn't trade Dennis Rodman for Michael Jordan. It was Gary who wrote that Shaq would never make it. And it was Gary who wrote that slalom kayaking was the most exciting event in the Summer Games.

He was the third m.e. I'd suffered since Nell Woodruff retired. The other two were Roddy Burke and Parker Trace. They'd climbed to the top the same way Gary had. They'd worn three-piece suits and looked deeply concerned when they carried clipboards down the hall—as if on their way to a vital story conference instead of the coffee bar.

For their efforts of not totally ruining the magazine by ordering dizzy layouts and hiring more point-missers to write for it, Roddy Burke and Parker Trace had each been rewarded with promotions to loftier titles and higher salaries within the company. Gary was trying to follow in their footsteps and doing it quite well.

When I'm not on the road I work in a different Manhattan skyscraper than the one I started in—the TPG Building on Sixth Avenue and Fiftieth Street. This was because *The Sports Magazine* and the other holdings of the Padgett Group—TPG—had been bought by SDC, another conglomerate.

SDC, which stands for Sandford, Davenport & Camp, owns thirty-six newspapers you've never heard of, seventeen other magazines you've never read, all of them targeting teenage girls and celebrity publicists, and fourteen radio stations you've never listened to because they specialize in talk shows on which sportswriters with jagged hair yell at each other about crap that doesn't matter to anybody but the scary people who paint their chests and faces in team colors and wear animals on their heads.

I did like the renovated tower that SDC had acquired and moved us into. It was the old Time-Life Building on Forty-eighth Street that borders the ice rink. Not many people today can name the ten original tenants of Rockefeller Center in the 1930s, but I can. In a bar, for money.

They were Time-Life, RCA, Associated Press, RKO, Eastern Airlines, U.S. Rubber, Sinclair Oil, Radio City Music Hall, and Roxy Theater.

In a bar for money I could also give you Ben Hogan's first name (William), Byron Nelson's first name (John), Jimmy Demaret's middle name (Newt), Gene Sarazen's real name (Eugenio Saraceni) . . . I knew Babe Zaharias's birth name was Mildred Ella Didrickson, and Mickey Wright's was Mary Kathryn Wright.

I could name every U.S. Open golf champion and the course he won on without missing Alex Smith in 1906 at Onwentsia in Lake Forest, Illinois. I could name all of the PGA winners and where they won without missing the tough one, Tom Creavy in 1931 at Wannamoisett in Rumford, Rhode Island.

I could even stray into baseball, not my strength, and position the great Brooklyn Dodgers lineup defensively: Duke Snider, Carl Furillo, and Gene Hermanski in the outfield. Gil Hodges at first, at second number 42, the incomparable Jackie Robinson, Pee Wee Reese at short, and the flawless-fielding Billy Cox at third. Campy behind the plate, Branca on the mound, and we're set to deal.

I'd dwell on such trivia in my twelfth-floor office with a view down to the ice rink on days when I'd be having trouble getting from one paragraph to another on a feature that would immortalize yet another athlete who was going to make more money by waking up in the morning than I would make in a year. I'd be having trouble on the piece because I could no longer rely on Marlboros—and the Milk Duds, sour balls, and chewing gum weren't doing it for me.

The pressroom was the first one I'd been in where I didn't know anybody. But people introduced themselves.

I met a gentleman with a white handlebar mustache who claimed he wrote for the *Palm Springs Desert Sun*. I met a radio guy who said he was "the voice of the Valley." A strange girl named Tisha introduced herself as a writer with *Golf for Women*. A guy came in lugging his golf clubs. He shook my hand and said he was on the staff of *Golf World*. I didn't meet the guy from AP. He was busy on the phone, cussing.

All the others were PR and publicity women who were alarmingly thin and wanted to tell me about Firm Chick skin cream, or the LPGA, or a new sand wedge with a double-angled sole, or the Enchanted Villa.

The one who represented the Enchanted Villa was in her thirties. She said her name was Allison. That's all. Allison. Period. It made me recall reading somewhere that young people stopped using last names in the sixties and seventies—it was asking too much of somebody who was stoned or wired to remember last names. Allison of PR handed me an invitation to a reception in the hotel that evening.

I made a habit of ducking those affairs when I was covering a classic on the PGA Tour. The last one I'd attended, the only fun I had was picking on certain sportswriter friends who'd made themselves look foolish a while back over Tiger Woods . . . when they fell into a trap of tour propaganda and wrote rhapsodizing stories about Tiger winning seven tournaments in a row.

But the streak spilled over into two calendar years and was interrupted four times by Tiger losing foreign tournaments he entered.

I'd point out that when Byron Nelson won his record eleven in a row in 'forty-five, it occurred in one year, and Nelson happened not to have lost any other tournaments while he was at it.

Sometimes my very own media embarrassed me.

I said to Allison of PR that I might be busy working, but then I accepted the invitation after she informed me that most of the contestants and their families would be attending—and so would Toppy and Connie Pemberton.

5

Two chunko South Koreans shot inscrutable 66s and led after the first round of the Firm Chick Classic. Kim Yim Yum and Soong Sang Sung. Close enough.

Thurlene Clayton was pleased with Ginger's four-under 68, which left the kid only two strokes back, but Ginger herself said the round was a piece of shit and the greens ought to be chopped up and fed to the homeless.

Words to that effect.

We were at the reception. It was in the Villa's grand ballroom, which may have broken the world record for tall ice sculptures. They rose up from buffet tables of unidentifiable party food, except for the rich man's caviar, to which I did serious damage, on toast squares.

In the far wall of the grand ballroom as you entered there was a bandstand and a dance floor. A small tuxedo-clad orchestra was at work, and I was instantly taken with the agility of the couples on the dance floor, who must have been in their seventies, minimum.

Close friends of Toppy and Connie Pemberton from La Jolla, I guessed. The men were deeply tanned, gray-haired, brightly blazered. The women were hickory shafts with leather headcovers for faces, but their gold lamé frocks sparkled.

I enjoyed watching them swirl around the dance floor, recapturing their moves from the swing dance and jitterbug days when they did the Lindy hop, the Hollywood shag, and the Harlem shuffle.

They kept up with the beat of the band and the husky voice of a buxom, middle-age redhead vocalist who explained through the lyrics of the number that she was most assuredly sittin' on top of the world, just rollin' along, just singin' a song.

Thurlene Clayton looked exquisite in a pale blue cocktail dress and heels. She found me almost immediately—with her daughter in tow.

I'd gone with my standard uniform for social occasions. White open-collar button-down shirt, black double-breasted blazer with gold buttons, gray slacks, cordovan loafers.

Thurlene acted as if it might have been an accident that we ran into each other, but it was my belief that she wanted the kid to meet the golf writer from *SM*. Over the years I'd found that the calling card of a national magazine did have its advantages.

"Hi, I'm Ginger," the kid said before the mom could make an introduction.

Ginger had a look that combined mischief with confidence. Her eyes were radiant. Her hair was down, longer than her mom's. She was suited up in white slacks and a tight-fitting cream-colored V-neck designer sweater that struck me as better-looking than most golf togs.

It didn't take me long to conclude that if there was a prettier babe in the room than the mom, it was the daughter.

They grabbed us a table in a corner while I went to one of the five, six, or eight bars and fetched our drinks. A white wine for Thurlene, a Coke for Ginger, and a straight-up Bombay Sapphire gin martini for me, rocks, with four green olives.

I had no intention of getting boxed that evening, but I did want to factor in wit and brilliance.

"Four olives?" Ginger said, wrinkling her nose.

"Old habit," I said. "I do it out of fear there might not be anything on the menu but a wounded sparrow on a clump of fern."

"What does that mean?" She tossed her long hair. Good for tossing.

Mom said, "There might not be anything he likes on the menu."

"Thanks," I said to Thurlene.

"I still don't get it," the kid said. "What's a wounded sparrow?"

I said, "If it's not cooked in bacon grease, it's not worth eating."

She sped past that and said, "Mom says you have a sense of humor . . . but I don't see how anybody can have a sense of humor and write about golf at the same time."

I smiled. "I have readers who would agree with you."

"You do?"

"They think golf is a religion. You're not supposed to make fun of religion."

"Do you make fun of religion?"

"No. But given the opportunity I might make fun of atheists."

"Why would you do that?"

"I guess because of what my grandmother used to say. One day your atheists are going to be all dressed up and nowhere to go."

"Are you a religious person?"

"I think so. I don't go to church too often, but I believe there has to be a higher power in this life than managing editors. What about you?"

The mom said, "We're Christian."

"As opposed to Muslim?" I said. "That's a relief."

Thurlene said, "No, Jack Brannon. Not as opposed to Muslim. We're members of the Magnolia Christian Church in Dallas."

Chewing an olive, I tried to inject another bit of humor into the conversation, saying, "I was raised a Whiskeypalian."

Mom grinned. Daughter stared.

Ginger said, "Golf is hard work, Mr. Brannon. To be good at it. You agree with that, don't you?"

"I do."

"So why make fun of it?"

I looked at the mom. "Help me out here."

"He's a wiseguy, Gin," Thurlene said.

"But shy and likable," I said. "Tell me about your round, Ginger."

"It sucked," Ginger said.

I said, "It's been my experience that most sixty-eights don't suck."

"Yeah, well. You ought to throw down a sixty-five on this shitty track. There's nothing out there but birdies."

The mom said, "Excuse her language. But she did miss three makable putts on the back nine. Three short putts spun out . . . They hung right on the lip."

Ginger said, "Man, I got *so* margarita-d. I'm like, Where's the *salt*?"

I announced to Ginger that I was originally from Fort Worth.

"Yeah?" the daughter said. A glance at Mom. "He can't be all bad."

Back to me, she said, "I love Colonial. I've played it three times. Were you there when Annika played in the Colonial with the guys?"

"I covered it. Great two days. Everybody was pulling for her."

"I was there! I was twelve. Mom took me. Annika's the greatest ever."

"I don't know about that," I said. "Babe and Mickey must have been pretty good."

"Annika was seismic. She would have handled 'em."

"I suppose you think Tiger would handle Ben Hogan too, huh?"

"Sure."

"Well, we'll never know, will we?"

"I know."

If this was a debate, I declared myself the loser. I smiled at mother and daughter and sat back in the chair with my martini.

"Oh, here you are!" a voice behind me said. It was Allison of PR.

"Toppy and Connie are on their way," Allison said. "They'll be coming in any moment. They're dying to meet you."

Allison of PR asked Thurlene and Ginger if she could borrow me.

The kid said, "What for?"

Thurlene said, "I believe the Pembertons would like to meet Mr. Brannon, Gin."

"They very much would," said Allison of PR. "Perhaps you're not aware that Toppy is a major stockholder in Firm Chick."

"Oh, sponsors," Ginger said. "Go for it, Jack."

6

They seemed to float in out of nowhere. Suddenly, as if on cue, the orchestra and vocalist stopped what they were doing and launched into a rendition of "Baby Face"—and here came this bandy-legged, white-haired gentleman in a red and white checkered sport coat, white slacks, and white shoes, and with him was this woman with platinum hair and a frozen smile. She wore a short hoopskirt, a glistening top and vest, and silver high heels. The guests made room for them and the couple went quickstepping onto the dance floor.

People applauded vigorously. I could see and hear the woman with the platinum hair singing along with the vocalist.

". . . there's not another one to kick your taste . . .
My old head is thumpin'
You done did do with somethin'."

Those couldn't be the right words. I wondered if Junior Alzheimer was doing the singing.

"I didn't light a stove,
I'm just dumb in love
dip his silly baby paste."

After controlling her applause, Allison of PR said to me, "It's their theme song. Connie chose it. The orchestra is instructed to play it when they enter to dine and dance every evening. It's rather become a tradition here at the Villa."

Allison of PR didn't look so stiff when she favored me with the hint of a smile. And she was generous enough to tell me all I'd ever care to know about Toppy and Connie.

Toppy's full name was Topham Clewis Pemberton III. He was heir to a large chunk of the Sinclair Oil fortune, and once a year he liked to celebrate this fact by putting on a dinosaur costume and parading through the streets of downtown La Jolla. Many of the residents and shopkeepers looked forward to the annual event.

Connie Shaughnessy came from showbiz. Toppy met her sixty-three years ago in New York City at Bill's Gay Nineties in the fading heyday of Fifty-second Street. She was part of a popular trio called Cholly, Connie, and Solly.

She and Toppy fell in love and married quickly, and just as quickly Connie hired Cholly and Solly to work for them. Cholly was their personal limo driver and banjo player for many years until he died, and until Solly died he was the head of security and the piano player at their 30,000-square-foot home in La Jolla that overlooked the Pacific Ocean and the comings and goings of the United States Navy.

Toppy and Connie became interested in golf in the seventies when they met Dinah Shore in Palm Springs. It was during the Colgate–Dinah Shore, which would be ordained a major championship by the LPGA even though it would be renamed the Kraft Nabisco. It still resides in the same high-rent category as the U.S. Women's Open, the Women's British Open, and the LPGA Championship. One of the Big Four.

Connie and Dinah became friends that evening. Dinah was entertaining guests at the party with songs. When she asked if anyone knew the words to "Smiles," Connie seized the moment, and the two of them roared into a medley of old favorites.

The Pembertons took up golf the next day, and ever since they'd been dreaming of one day sponsoring their own tournament.

While I was learning all this, it was hard not to notice that Connie had gone up on the bandstand and was doing harmony with the vocalist. We paused for a moment to hear . . .

"There are styles that have a numbing stinking
that the files of me you bet can pee . . .
But the styles that flip my heart with poopy
are the kikes that you lift to me."

I was led past two ice sculptures to the table where Connie was returning from the bandstand. Toppy was sitting with two other couples, who were forced to shift around and make room for me.

"Connie . . . Toppy . . . everybody," Allison of PR said. "This is the famous author and golf writer from New York . . . Jack Brannon."

"Do they get to vote on famous?" I said.

Having done her chore, Allison of PR backed away and was gone.

"The old scribbler," Toppy said, sounding like Dean Martin, although maybe not intentionally. "What would the old scribbler be drinking?"

An Oriental waiter was hovering.

I said I didn't want to get boxed, but I might do with one more Bombay Sapphire martini on the rocks with four olives.

"Hear that, Kato?" Toppy said to the waiter. "You and the Green Hornet get on it. I don't mind getting boxed. Bring me another Scotch."

Connie inched close to me, squeezed my arm, and softly sang, "I've bought a crush on you, sweetie who . . . all the night and morning, hear me coo."

I judged her to be in her high seventies. The jewelry on her neck, ear, wrist, and arm could light up all of La Jolla if a brownout occurred.

In the brochure for the Enchanted Villa I was alerted to the fact that among its many luxuries it offered an opportunity for ladies to visit the resort's "Academy of Body Sculpturing" and allow the academy to put its experience to work on them.

Among the "contouring procedures" available were "liposuction, breast augmentation, belly button approach, tummy tucks, arm lifts, buttock implants, fat transfer, vein treatments, and facial rejuvenation."

A shrewd observer might guess that Connie had experienced all of it.

Smiling, I said, "I understand you used to sing professionally."

She sang softly to me again. It could have been lyrics from "I've Got a Crush on You," but maybe not. Could be she forgot the rest of the words as she let go of my arm and drank the rest of her glass of vodka.

Vod and Junior Al. Great combo. There was the answer.

If this was a nostalgia night, I wondered if it would do me any good to request a little Bruce, some Ray Charles, some Bonnie Raitt?

A man across the table said, "Brandon . . . Brandon . . . New York City . . . Manhattan . . . Any relation to my good friend Wild Bill Brandon? Goldman Sachs? Yale 'sixty-five?"

"Nope," I said.

The man's blazer was yellow. His pants were maroon. The other man's blazer was green. His pants were pink.

"Jumpin' Jimmy Brennan?" he said. "Morgan Stanley? Yale 'sixty-seven?"

"Missed me again," I said.

"Shipwreck Shep Benton? Lehman Brothers? Princeton 'seventy-one?"

"Sorry," I said.

The two couples lost interest in me. I reached that conclusion when they never spoke to me again.

My cocktail arrived and I was trying not to gulp it when Toppy leaned over and said, "I'm pins and needles, scribe. What do you think of my golf course?"

I said, "I haven't seen all of it yet, but I will tomorrow. It looks interesting. I understand it's well bunkered and there are plenty of water hazards. But there were some low scores today, weren't there?"

"Yes, there were," Toppy said. "It made me sick."

"It did?"

"I hire Burch Webb to build me a championship golf course and what do I get? The women tear it apart. Women! Little girlies! They go out there and gnaw on it like puppies."

I said, "It's hard for any course to hold back today's equipment.

You've got a nuclear shaft, a steroid golf ball, custom fitting, square grooves. Match the technology with the golf swing, it's a new world."

Toppy said, "Eight million to build it. Two million for the idiot to design it. What made Burch Webb famous? He can't design a toilet."

I said, "These young girls are raised on titanium . . . graphite . . . composites . . . the new technology. They've never seen a wooden golf club. They think persimmon is a town in France."

"Do what . . . ?" Toppy said.

"Nothing," I said. "It was just something I said that was wildly hilarious."

Connie stood up. She grabbed her small shining purse that could well have been covered with diamonds. I ascertained she was headed for the restroom because she quietly sang to the table:

"Chowder your face with moonshine,
  put on a floozy pile."

I could have sworn that when I heard Dean Martin sing it one time on TV he'd said "powder your face with sunshine." Nevertheless, the other two women at the table went with Connie.

"How'd the little girlies get so good?" Toppy asked me.

I said, "As I understand it, Mom or Dad start them out young now. There are financial incentives today that weren't there yesterday. A kid shows some talent, she can become a family meal ticket. Golf academies contribute. College programs are getting better all the time. Young girls with ability are coming along every year now. The good news is, a lot of them are cute. The better news is, I'm told, they're straight. Only one player in the top ten money list last year that was on the Other Team—so to speak."

Toppy slumped in his chair. We sat in silence for a while. I savored my cocktail, ate an olive, looked around the room.

I noticed a group of the older, established stars sitting together at a large round table. From their photos I recognized Jan Dunn, Marian Hornbuckle, Linda Merle Draper, Suzy Scott, Peaches Crowder.

I saw Ann Wendell and what must have been Debbie at a table with another mom and daughter. Debbie was on the small side, and I could see where she might give up considerable distance to Ginger Clayton and therefore want to poison her.

I didn't count them all, but most of the forty or fifty South Koreans on the tour were scattered about. Through ace reporting I uncovered the reason there are so many now. They turn pro at fourteen in South Korea. They start competing in Asia. Thus, they arrive in the USA with four years of professional experience already behind them.

I broke the silence with Toppy. "Quite a resort you have here. My room is terrific. I can see Tucson from my balcony."

He said, "It was a great place till Burch Webb designed me a sack of shit for a golf course."

I said, "I'm not prepared to judge it on the basis of one round. There was no wind today. If the wind blows and the greens firm up, it could be a different story."

Toppy said, "No, it's ruined. I'll have to rename it. Change it from the Villa to the Sack of Shit. How's that for a sales tool? Come to the Enchanted Villa, buy a four-million-dollar lot, play golf on Burch Webb's Sack of Shit."

Toppy lapsed back into a slump in his chair. I sat and drank.

Presently Connie and the ladies returned to the table. A waiter appeared at Connie's shoulder.

"Another vodka rocks, Mrs. Pemberton?" the waiter asked.

Connie looked up at him.

"Anytime you're sneaking bonely," she sang, wiggling her empty glass. "Anytime . . . you're slipping through."

The waiter hurried off.

She took my arm and kept singing. "Anytime you shame . . . you kick me in the thing . . . that's the chime I'll bundle up to you."

I yawned, reclaimed my arm, glanced at my watch, stood up, said I was glad to meet everyone, I'd see them on the course tomorrow, I had work to do in my room.

I retraced my path past the ice sculptures to look for Thurlene and the kid, but they weren't at the table where I'd left them, or anywhere else as far as I could tell. They'd retired. Early tee time.

I made the long trek to my own room in the Villa, a variety of old songs ringing in my head.

Headline: Man Survives Lawrence Welk Reruns.

7

Ginger Clayton birdied the first five holes of the second round and took over the lead in the tournament. I said to Thurlene that her daughter did it so quickly she probably gave the chinks a head cold. Thurlene said the Asian girls weren't chinks. They were South Korean. I said I meant *chinks* in the best sense of the word.

For my information, Thurlene said, the name of the player I'd been calling Kim Yim Yum was Jin Hee Soong, and the name of the player I'd been calling Soong Sang Sung was Su Lee Kim. She said they lived in the United States now.

I said that would make them South Korean Americans. The politically correct loons had already given us Native Americans, African Americans, Japanese Americans, and Asian Americans. Now they were hard at work on giving us Illegal Alien Americans, Terrorist Americans, and Suicide Bomber Americans.

One of these days, I said, your law-abiding, English-speaking, tax-paying Americans will have to find another planet to live on.

"I know how to slow down the terrorists, if you're interested," I said. "Give every Praise Allah a thousand dollars and a list of sports events to bet on. Then the suicide bombers among them would only blow themselves up when the Patriots and Colts don't cover."

"You must share that with the White House."

"Nuke them before they can nuke us. That's my political position. Only way to save the planet and the future. I'd nuke every fanatical lunatic in the world if we could scrape 'em into one pile."

She sighed. "No point in trying diplomacy, huh?"

I said, "Oh, you want to *talk* to them? Okay, I'll try that. How you doin', Abdul? Got a minute? What can we do to keep you from trying to wipe us off the map? Want to blow up some more of our buildings? Have at it. I know we deserve it because our toilets flush, we like cheeseburgers, and we wear jeans. Sure, we'll get rid of our military for you. No problem. How about this? We'll all kneel down and hum a bunch of shit and thump our heads on the carpet. Will that help? By the way, can I have my head back? How can I reason with you people when my head's rolling around down here on the floor?"

"That's absurd."

"Yeah, it is. I have to stop watching the news. Want to take a terrorist to lunch?"

She said, "My Uncle Otis used to say you could add five years to your life if you never listened to the news."

"My Uncle Will used to say he'd like to kill every Jap on the face of the earth. He was a marine in the Big Deuce. He hit the beach at Okinawa. I don't feel that way myself, you understand . . . except when I hear a Jap holler 'Fooka Babe Ruth!' "

"Humanitarian traits run all through your family, do they?"

"My grandparents were Democrats, like everybody else's in Texas. It went back to that FDR thing. But I started to lean conservative when I went to work at the paper and saw how much the Democrats took out of my paycheck every two weeks."

"I see. So tell me, Senator. What should we do about the environment? Shall we nuke that too?"

"We don't have to worry about the environment."

"No? What exactly are your views on global warming?"

"You mean aside from the fact that it's bullshit?"

She may not have looked amused. It was hard to say.

Thurlene was dressed more tamely today. She wore a pair of white slacks that fit to my satisfaction. Her golf shirt was pale green with a little collar. Her hair was held by a wide white ribbon.

I was walking with Thurlene down one side of the sixth fairway.

On the other side were a dozen fans of Jan Dunn, Ginger's playing partner for the day. Jan was a slender woman in her thirties. Tour vet.

All of Jan Dunn's fans were mature ladies as well. Some were in shorts and hiking boots.

Pointing them out, I said, "Looks like the Other Team has us out-numbered. Do you prefer 'Other Team' or 'the Dark Side'?"

"In Jan's case 'friend' will do. She's a sweet person."

I said, "Hey, I won't bring it up again. You think I want those women over there to beat the shit out of me?"

She said, "Jan has never been anything but nice and helpful to Ginger. She's befriended her, introduced her to other players, helped her learn the ropes, how to deal with the media, travel tips . . ."

I said, "Well . . . I'd keep a sharp eye on it, if I were you. I daresay more than one cupcake's been turned around out here."

Thurlene said, "If anybody tries to 'turn Ginger around,' as you put it, they'll have to fight Trey Bishop."

Trey Bishop was Ginger's regular caddie. Handsome young guy. Athletic-looking, somewhere in his late twenties.

"It's a romance thing, is it?" I said. "Ginger and Trey?"

"Moms don't know everything," she said. "I do know they like each other. They go to movies and dinner and play video games together. It may be friendship only. She relies on him, trusts his judgment on the golf course."

"Most parents would say their ideal choice for a daughter's boy-friend would not necessarily be a caddie."

She said Trey Bishop was a good golfer himself. He played col-lege golf at Georgia. He tried to make it on the tour, but he couldn't get through the Q-school. Failed six times. So he turned to caddy-ing. "His first job was with Mimsy Buck," she told me. "But Mimsy paid him a little over ten percent of her winnings. When Ginger came out she liked Trey, thought he'd be right for her. We offered him eighteen percent and he jumped at it."

"Sounds like Trey's doing okay in the money department."

"He is indeed. He made two hundred thousand last year. He's already made over forty thousand this year."

"Maybe I can get a bag," I said.

I made the joke only a few seconds before Ginger rolled in another birdie. Her sixth straight.

I couldn't help wondering if Topham Clewis Pemberton III was
keeping up with the scores, and if so, what type of agony he was
planning for Burch Webb, the famous architect who'd given him a
sack of shit for a golf course.

Thurlene lit a cigarette. Only her third during the round. The
birdies had come so fast, she couldn't keep up.

She said, "This isn't the first time Ginger made six straight birdies. She did it in the Molly Reynolds Cup at Lost Goose Country
Club . . . when she was fourteen."

"Where is Lost Goose?" I said. "I don't know it."

"It's almost close to Atlanta, like everything else around Atlanta.
She shot a sixty-three that day—from pretty far back. She did it
again when she was sixteen, when she won the Girls Junior Nation-
als at Swarming Ivy in Philadelphia."

"I played Swarming Ivy once," I said. "My ball kept winding up in
somebody's portfolio."

Conversation was put on hold over the next three holes as the
mom sweated out Ginger's struggling to make pars.

The kid played too boldly and found trouble in the rough and
bunkers and barely saved her round with the putter. When she
holed a twenty-foot putt for par on the ninth green, she didn't even
complete the high five Trey offered her. She was too hot at herself.
Steaming.

I followed Thurlene to the tenth tee and we found a spot against
the gallery ropes right at the tee markers. Mom gestured a happy
thumbs-up at the daughter. Ginger came over to us, still looking
pissed.

"What a round, Gin!" said the mom. "Thirty! Six under!"

Tight-lipped, Ginger said under her breath, "Damn, I wanted that
twenty-nine. I was so lame on seven, eight, and nine. Shit . . . *shit.*"

"You're leading by three, Gin."

The kid said, "This tournament is *so* over, man. They can't catch
me the way I'm swingin', way I'm rollin' it."

The kid and Jan Dunn smacked their drives and walked off down
the fairway.

I said I'd let Mom handle the back nine. I wanted to track down two or three players and talk to them about Ginger.

"I don't want to seem pushy or anything," I said, "but are we going to talk about Debbie Wendell trying to poison Ginger—if that's what actually happened?"

Thurlene said, "Oh, it happened. Believe it."

"Fine," I said. "When do I get to hear about it?"

"Are you free for dinner?"

8

T he kid threw down a course-record sixty-four and was ush-
ered into the pressroom to answer questions about her round
and her life. Right. Like somebody eighteen years old, who's
never done anything but hit golf balls—who's not allowed to have a
car yet—could have lived a life.

There were new faces in the pressroom. Three new girls. Two
tall, one hefty. The tall ones were from Los Angeles and San Diego.
The Whataburger queen worked for an obscure weekly. A guy from
the Golf Channel I'd never seen before kept walking around, sizing
up the place, holding his on-air duds on a hanger. Loud sport coat,
striped shirt, dotted necktie. A half dozen Asian fellows were now
present, all of them weighted down with cameras, lenses, tripods.

Thurlene, looking a little moist, came in to hear Ginger's interview. She stood by me in the back of the room. I never ask questions
in group interviews. Most of those who do either are point-missers
or like to hear their own voices.

"What a round, huh?" the mom said. "She made four more birdies
on the back . . . but she bogeyed twice. She got greedy. It cost her.
She really wanted that sixty-two."

"How'd she bogey?"

"Flew the greens. Pin hungry. Pitched badly coming back."

Allison of PR came up to us. She was in a black pantsuit and white
shirt with a big collar. She was definitely looking more and more like
one of those sexy blondes on Fox News.

"Hi," she said. "Can I fetch anyone something to drink?"

"I would love a bottle of water," Thurlene said.

"What about you, Mr. Brannon?"

"No thanks . . . and it's Jack, if you don't mind."

Allison dashed away and was back in a flash with the Evian.

She said, "Anything you need in the hotel, Jack?"

"No, I'm good," I said.

"You'll let me know, though?"

"Absolutely."

"We want you to enjoy your stay. First impressions matter a great deal to us. I live here as well as work here. So I'm always on call. Toppy and Connie like it that way. I live in one of the bungalows along the first fairway. You've seen them . . . on the right?"

"Convenient," I said.

"Very much so. Holler now if I can do anything for you."

She gave my arm a squeeze as she left.

Thurlene grinned at me.

"What?" I said.

"You just took a hit."

"I what?"

"You got hit. I see blood."

"What do you mean?"

"Come on."

"You think that skinny woman was hitting on me?"

"She's not that skinny . . . and I know a hit when I see one. I've been a hitter myself."

"You haven't hit on me."

"I haven't had to. You've been hitting on *me*."

"That's what you think I've been doing?"

"Please."

"All I'm doing is working on a story."

"Yeah, right."

"I *am*."

She elbowed me.

"Be quiet," she said. "I want to hear Gin."

Up behind a table and a microphone on a platform, Ginger had been going through her round, hole by hole, revealing the length of her birdie putts. She was sitting next to a snooty LPGA press rep whose job it was to conduct the interviews with the tournament leaders.

The name of the LPGA press rep was Monique and she was remindful of the person at the door of a fashionable restaurant who relishes telling you it'll be a forty-five-minute wait for a table even though the place is half empty.

"What are your general thoughts about your round?" Monique was now asking Ginger into the microphone.

"It rocked," Ginger said.

"Perhaps you could be more descriptive," Monique said.

Ginger said, "I was bomb squad with the tee ball. My irons were cooking. I had the harpoon going on the greens. But I did two flip-wads. I gunched the wedge twice. It cost me the bogeys at fifteen and sixteen. I was trying to throw down a sixty-two."

Monique looked at the audience.

"Questions?" she said.

Somebody asked Ginger to go through her bag. What equipment was she using?

Ginger said she hadn't signed any club contracts yet. Her bag was a mix. She was carrying a nine-degree Callaway Armageddon driver. An Adams Destroyer three-metal. Her hybrid was a twenty-one-degree S-flex Ping Tormenter. Her irons were the Callaway Monsters, four through nine. "But my seven is really a five and a half—like the men," she said. Two Titleist wedges. A fifty and a fifty-six degree. And her Scotty Cameron was the putter she'd had since she was twelve.

Somebody asked Ginger if she'd made six straight birdies before today. She said yeah, twice, as an amateur, at Lost Goose and Swarming Ivy. She described the events.

Somebody asked her to talk about the experience of being in a golf academy in Florida.

"I wasn't there like most of the kids," Ginger said. "It's expensive. I was only enrolled in the summer when school was out in Dallas . . . from when I was twelve through, uh, sixteen. The academy was great. I had good teachers. I was around a lot of terrific athletes. Some have gone on to college. Some are out here now. Some are good friends. I almost went to college instead of going pro. I had full-ride offers from Duke, Texas, OU, Tulsa, Chapel Hill, Arizona State, TCU . . ."

Somebody asked if she still lived in Dallas. She said part of the time but she and her mom had bought a condo in Palm Beach, Florida. Her mom was her manager, her "keeper"—and best friend—although her mom wouldn't let her have a car yet.

Somebody asked what her future schedule looked like. Ginger said she was playing in New Mexico next week and she'd come back to California for the Kraft Nabisco. Maybe a week off here and there later on.

Somebody asked about her father.

Monique said, "That's a private matter. Next?"

A voice said, "You have a four-stroke lead. Do you think you can hold up over a strong field like this for one more round?"

"Sure," Ginger said.

The voice belonged to the AP guy. He looked tired, thirsty, hungry, overworked, underpaid.

He said, "What posters are on your wall?"

Ginger said, "Gee, let me think. Matt Damon's up there . . . Leo . . . Brad Pie used to be . . . Kelly Clarkson—she's from Texas."

"Who do you listen to? What rock groups? Rappers?"

"I'm not into rap. I'm a Texas girl. I like the honky-tonk angels, the heartache chicks. LeAnn Rimes is great."

"What's your game plan for tomorrow?" somebody asked.

"My game plan?" Ginger rolled her eyes. "Like, I mean, go out and try to lay down another good one. Let 'em know how bad I want it."

The tall woman from L.A. said, "You were quoted in *Golf World* saying one of your goals is to be the number one player in the world. Did you really say that?"

Ginger looked around. "Well . . . yeah, I said it. There are lots of great players out here. Lorena, Paula, Britt, Tricia, Morgan, Penny. They tease me about the quote. But I'm a competitor. I say things."

The tall woman said, "You're eighteen, Ginger. You've only been on the tour a year. Isn't that setting your sights a little high?"

"What am I supposed to say?" Ginger grinned. "My goal is to be the *number three* player in the world?"

Laughter filled the room.

"She's good," I said to the mom. "She's real good."

Ginger kept talking.

"I have lots of goals. I want to win tournaments. I want to win majors. I want to make Solheim Cup teams. I want to play on *winning* Solheim Cup teams. And . . . someday I know I want to marry and have children."

The handlebar mustache from Palm Springs hollered out, "You want to make a swimsuit commercial?"

Ginger shot back rapidly. "Want to be my agent?"

More laughter.

Monique, looking grim, spoke into the mike.

"This interview is concluded."

9

The thing I root for the hardest when I'm adventurously dining in a fancy restaurant is that my entrée doesn't come out looking like the Eiffel Tower sitting on a bed of garlic mashed potatoes.

I announced this to Thurlene after Count Dracula, the maître d', seated us in Connie's Corner, the "gourmet" room at the Villa. The room was stocked with antiques and Oriental rugs, and a little card at our table said we could thank Gavin & Brice of San Francisco for the decor.

Ginger was invited, but she'd made other plans. She and Trey Bishop were going to eat in the coffee shop, the Sips and Dins, then go to the video game room in the hotel and kill droves of Al Qaeda.

Our waiter looked like he'd been deeply touched by the life of Alexander Godunov. His name was Dorian. He recommended a white wine for Thurlene and brought a bottle to the table along with my martini.

I'd been thinking for years that it was all over for garlic mashed potatoes. But evidently that news hadn't reached the chef at Connie's Corner yet. I also noticed on the huge leather-bound menu that tortilla soup was still alive and kicking.

"I wonder if they have any unblackened fish or beef," I said, more to myself than to Thurlene.

She closed her menu. "I'll have the mixed green salad, house dressing, and the chicken breast."

"You're in luck," I said. "They say it's free-range chicken."

"I'm so relieved."

"I'm torn," I said. "Should I go with the line-caught salmon or the Pacific Rim tilapia?"

"That's a tough one," she said, and sipped her wine.

I said, "Where did tilapia come from? We've been invaded by tilapia. I can remember when there were only four kinds of fish. Trout, Dover sole, catfish, and fried shrimp."

"Don't forget canned tuna."

"Canned tuna's not a fish," I said. "Canned tuna is lunch meat."

We were on coffee. We'd finished our free-range chicken and line-caught salmon and neither of us wanted to order the restaurant's highly praised, prize-winning dessert—tiramisu.

I spent a while telling her about myself. How I'd arrived where I was at this stage of my development. How my track record in the marriage game wasn't admirable. How I liked my work almost as much as I used to like smoking. Eventually I got around to saying it was time to talk about what I wanted to talk about.

Thurlene said, "First, you have to understand that these young girls lead a sheltered life. They start being sheltered as soon as they show any promise and want to work at the game . . . with the idea, you know, of earning a college scholarship or having a pro career. A parent starts off thinking it would be great if the daughter could get a scholarship. Especially if the parents are people with average incomes, which most of us are. I've watched dads see it as an excuse to quit their jobs and devote full-time to 'managing' the daughter. I was married to one."

"What kind of job did he quit?"

"Pete was a salesman. But what he mainly did was gamble on the golf course. His specialty was losing. The last job he quit was calling on pro shops to sell them ugly golf shirts."

"Why did you marry him, if I may ask?"

She shrugged. "I thought he looked like Nick Nolte in *Under Fire*. He thought so too, incidentally."

I laughed.

She continued. "It didn't matter to us so much when Pete quit his job. He had a better gig. Creative Sports Enterprises—CSE, your man Howie Daniels—put him on the payroll when Ginger was fourteen. Howie figured she'd get an LPGA waiver to turn pro at seventeen, which she did. Howie saw her as a hot property even at fourteen, and he thought this was a way to lock her in. CSE paid Pete seventy-five thousand a year as a 'junior talent scout.' He was supposed to file reports on players at the junior amateur tournaments we took Ginger to play in. It's a scam, but the USGA says it's legal. My problem started with Pete over that money. It was supposed to go into a savings account for Ginger, which was what we discussed. She was the one earning it. But most of the money wound up in Pete's pocket and eventually in somebody else's pocket on the golf course . . . I don't want to talk about him anymore. Why did you hook up with those two all-stars you married?"

I said, "Carolyn Reese was one of the first people I met when I went to *SM* in New York. She was a reporter at the magazine. She was cute, put together. I was naturally attracted to her because she liked to drink and smoke and cuss and laugh and hang out as much as I did. But as soon as we were married, she didn't like to do any of that anymore. I hear this happens often. What Carolyn wanted was a home and security and a husband who didn't travel. We were married two years. When I came back from the Masters in the spring of 'ninety-three, I discovered she'd farmed herself out to a stockbroker."

"What about number two?"

"That would be the elegant Renata."

"Renata?" she said. "You married a *Renata*?"

Like I must have been asking for trouble, right?

I said, "Renata Schielder. The name alone strikes fear in the hearts of man. She was a real estate agent. She talked me into renting a two-bedroom apartment on Park Avenue I couldn't afford . . . and moved in with me and we got married. She was stylish, very pretty, sophisticated. But the sense of humor martinis made me think she had never surfaced. I think she saw us as a New York City 'power couple'—I had a byline in a magazine and knew restaurant owners. She fancied herself as the real estate agent to the stars. But one day it dawned on her that I wasn't ever going to be rich, and worse than that, I didn't care. I liked my job too much to worry about it."

"That did it, huh?"

"No, the thing that did it was the gel-hair Wall Street lawyer she met while she was trying to find *him* an apartment. You may be entertained by the way she left me. In the last year of our marriage—while she was secretly getting it on with Gel-Hair—I inherited some money when my Aunt Alma died. Aunt Alma left me twenty-five thousand dollars. I stuck it in the bank and didn't think anything else about it. But Renata did. She told me the reason our marriage was in trouble, a little rocky, was because I'd never given her a proper wedding ring. I had 'diminished' her. I said okay, let's go pick one out for you. So we did. We went to Tiffany's and she spent twenty thousand of what my aunt left me on a ten-carat diamond ring. *Then* she left me. A week later."

"That's a horrible story. What a cunt!"

"I love that word, don't you? Actually, baseball players love it more than we do. They like to yell, 'Hit him in the cunt!' "

Thurlene said she would be smoking a cigarette if it weren't a felony to smoke indoors in California. She wondered if I could pay the check so we could continue this outside . . . take a stroll or something?

I made a gesture at Dorian to bring the check. He came over and said the evening was compliments of Allison in PR. All I had to do was sign.

"I can't let Allison do that," I said. "My company won't allow it. I'll have to insist on paying myself."

"Certainly, sir," Dorian said, and handed me the check.

It was for $737.50. I stared at it.

Dorian said, "It was a very nice Montrachet."

"I wish I'd tasted it," I said. "Tell you what, Dorian. Maybe I'll make an exception in this case and let Allison handle it." I signed and we left.

Thurlene laughed her way through the lobby. We were barely out the front door of the hotel when she lit up a Capri.

Out of casual curiosity I asked what her maiden name was.

She said, "If you had gone to Woodrow Wilson High when I did you would have known me as Thurlene Kay Robertson. I grew up in old east Dallas . . . Lakewood. It was an upper-crust neighborhood at one time. My folks say it was Highland Park before there was Highland Park. You're not with a Highland Park chick tonight."

"Another bad break . . . but I knew that."

"How did you know that? I'm not wearing enough jewelry?"

"You're thirty-eight and you haven't had any work done yet."

She smiled. "That's funny because it's so true. Thanks for the compliment, but I'm forty. Want to take it back?"

We were still strolling.

She went on. "I was always athletic. Fairly good at tennis, but better at golf. I went to SMU on a golf scholarship. Thank God I got one. I guess my parents would have scraped up the tuition somehow. I was the number two player. But I worked too. I always had jobs. I was a part-time waitress in college. I worked in a jewelry store. When I graduated I took a job at a bank in Arlington. I stayed in banking. I became a loan officer at Sunset Bank in North Cliff. It was a good job. I liked it. But . . . when Ginger made the choice to go pro instead of college, I felt I should resign and so I could travel with her, for a year or two anyhow."

I said, "I understand you have a place in Palm Beach."

"A little south of Palm Beach proper. About eight minutes from Worth Avenue. Fifteen minutes from the airport in West Palm. Very convenient. On the ocean . . . it's lovely. I wish it were paid for."

"Tell me more about the kid."

"It starts for these girls when they're eleven and twelve. I'll bet you don't know that when eleven- and twelve-year-olds play in tournaments the parents can't gallery. Unless they volunteer to work on the tournament, they have to watch through fences. That's good, I think."

"I agree," I said. "No sideline coaching from Mom and Dad."

"Generally it's the father who drives the kid too hard. Working a kid too hard can result in burnout by the time a kid is sixteen. But when Ginger was sixteen, she was already dedicated. She'd go out and hit practice balls in bad weather, while most of the other girls were at the mall, buying things they didn't need, and eating junk that wasn't good for them."

"And flirting with boys."

"Of course."

"Doesn't make them bad people," I said. "Is all this leading up to Debbie Wendell, by chance?"

"It is," she said.

We sat on a bench in a hotel garden. Tall cacti surrounded us. I was tempted to try one of her Capris, but being a person of great inner strength, I let the idea pass.

She asked if I'd heard of something called dushuqiang. That's how it was spelled. She pronounced it "doo-shoo-chang."

"Doo-shoo-chang," I said. "Goes good with egg roll?"

"Not particularly," she said. "It's a Chinese rat poison."

10

Thurlene said I'd probably never heard of a young golfer on the LPGA tour named Tang Chen. I said she was right. I'd never heard of a golfer on the LPGA tour named Chen . . . Deng . . . thing.

"Tang Chen is from Beijing," she said.

"I would hope so."

"She and Debbie Wendell became friends on the tour last year."

"The Chinese girl speaks English?"

"Good enough."

"Why did they become friends? Debbie Wendell is a self-appointed goodwill ambassador?"

"I'll get to that."

"Is Tang Chen in the tournament? She could be in the field and I wouldn't know it—unless you told me to look in the scores between Mao Tse-tung and wonton soup."

Thurlene looked at me the way a person would look if the person was saying, "Do you want to hear this or not?"

Then she said, "Tang Chen is *not* in the field this week. She relies on sponsor invitations and hasn't come over yet. She will be watched closely when she *does* come—you can count on it."

I said, "Hard-hitting reporter that I am, I'm sniffing a scandal here. Debbie Wendell is envious of Ginger Clayton. Debbie Wendell is friends with Tang Chen. Tang Chen is Chinese. There's a rat poison that comes from China called doo-shoo-chang."

"You may be sniffing, but you can't write it."

"I decide what I can write and what I can't."

"You can't write this. Not yet. It hasn't been written, and you can't write it."

"Who's going to stop me?"

"The LPGA."

"The LPGA?" I said with a chuckle. "You must be kidding. The LPGA can't stop hand-holding."

"The LPGA with the help of the United States of America."

"Oh, them."

"The United States doesn't want to embarrass a Chinese athlete, particularly since there's no solid proof she's done anything wrong."

I said, "Why don't you walk me through this so I'll know exactly what we're talking about? And give me a damn cigarette."

Grinning, she handed me a Capri and her Bic. I lit up, took a drag.

"Jesus," I said. "These *will* cure emphysema."

Thurlene lit a fresh Capri for herself, crossed her legs, and said, "All right then. Last September at the Good Grub Classic in Oklahoma City—"

"Wait, wait, wait," I said. "The *Good Grub* Classic?"

"You've never heard of Good Grub?"

"If it happens in September and doesn't have anything to do with the Ryder Cup or college football, I don't hear about it."

"Good Grub is a new restaurant chain. It's very good."

"What kind of restaurant? Like a Taco Bell? The Alamo was the first Taco Bell, in case you don't know. That's what made it worth dying for."

Ignoring that, she said, "Good Grub is like, uh . . . I would say it's in the same ballpark with a Cracker Barrel. The food is down-home wonderful. I've bought stock in the company for Ginger."

I said, "Okay, you're at the Good Grub Classic in Oklahoma City. What golf course?"

"A new one. Grain Hills Country Club."

"The Good Grub Classic at Grain Hills Country Club. Hard to go up against that for charm."

She leaned back on the bench, smoked, and waited for my full attention. Satisfied that she had it, she related how Debbie had introduced Ginger to Tang Chen and said the Chinese girl was lonely and needed friends on the tour. She asked Ginger to be nice to her. Ginger said sure.

Ann Wendell, Debbie's mother, had taken the three girls to dinner a few times on the tour. Sometimes Thurlene went along, and she recalled listening to Debbie and her mother try to make conversation with the Chinese girl. And although she thought nothing of it at the time, she was now certain that she overheard Tang use the word "doo-shoo-chang" in conversation with them.

Ginger had been leading the Oklahoma City tournament after the first round by two strokes over—I might have guessed—Debbie Wendell. And that evening Thurlene took the three girls to a movie at a theater in the Cowbarn Mall, which wasn't far from Grain Hills Country Club. Thurlene drove them in the courtesy car the sponsor provided for the contestants. Ann Wendell had left the Oklahoma tournament after the first round for some business reason, which was unlike her. It would usually take a death in the family to drag Ann away from a tournament where Debbie was a contender.

In any case, the girls went to a movie Thurlene didn't care to see, and Thurlene went to a different movie in the same theater complex.

I said, "Let me guess. The girls went to the riotous high school comedy where Kelli, Meghan, and Stacie tell their parents to fuck off and their boyfriends to eat shit and die."

"That's the one," Thurlene said dryly.

I said, "But you went to the grown-up movie . . . where the rooms are dark, you can hardly hear the dialogue, and you still can't understand why Julia Roberts would want to screw that scruffy asshole."

"May I continue?"

"If you would."

She said, "I wasn't in my seat twenty minutes before Debbie found me and told me Ginger was really sick in the ladies' room. I rushed in and there she was, curled up on the floor with a burning fever and having spasms and vomiting."

It looked like it might be food poisoning. What had she eaten? Debbie said Ginger had a Coke and popcorn. They all had Cokes and popcorn.

Instead of calling an ambulance, which might have wasted time,

Thurlene obtained directions to the O.U. Medical Center in Oklahoma City. She drove Ginger to the hospital, to the emergency entrance, and in something of a crazed state managed to demand immediate assistance from a group of trauma people who were not as recognizable as the doctors, interns, and nurses you see on TV but were helpful nonetheless.

They did all the IV and EKG and blood pressure and suppository things to Ginger that emergency rooms do. They got her resting easily, out of danger, and took the liberty, while they were at it, of zapping the hysterical mom with a jumbo antianxiety pill.

Twenty-four hours later, Ginger was on the road to recovery, but she had withdrawn from a tournament she was leading, leaving the contest to Debbie Wendell and others.

To this day it delighted Thurlene that Ginger's withdrawal hadn't done Debbie Wendell any good. She didn't come close to winning the Good Grub Classic. Peaches Crowder came from behind in the last round to edge Suzy Scott by two strokes. Debbie choked badly and finished in a tie for seventeenth with Su Lee Kim.

Meanwhile, back at the hospital, a doctor concluded that Ginger had been poisoned.

With what, he wasn't certain, but tests showed traces of strychnine and what sounded to Thurlene like "mono flora tetra metha motorhome." Words that nobody understands but doctors.

The doctor had said, "It could be rat poison, but I can't imagine how she would have been exposed to it."

The mom could imagine it, but kept it to herself.

Thurlene researched the rat poison later and found that it came in the form of white powder, was easy to acquire in China, a cinch to smuggle into another country, and was odorless and tasteless. And it didn't take much of the dust to make a person ill, and not much more to kill someone.

I said, "Nobody else who ate the popcorn in the theater that day or night got poisoned?"

"Nope. I made sure of it."

"You were alone. That must have been a terrible night for you."

"It wasn't the best night of my life."

"When did you get in touch with Ginger's dad?"

"I tracked him down the next day in Dallas. He happened to have his cell with him while he was getting picked like a chicken on the back nine at wherever he was. Do you know what he said when I told him what happened? He said Debbie wouldn't do a thing like that. Ginger must have eaten something that didn't agree with her. He was relieved Ginger was okay, but he said I shouldn't blame Debbie or her mother for what happened. Ann Wendell was our good friend, our *dear* friend. We had all been so close for so long. How could I forget that? Guess what? That's when I realized the sorry bastard had been screwing Ann Wendell for at least three years."

I said, "Well, he did look like Nick Nolte."

11

e weren't through talking and smoking. As we sat on the
bench and watched other hotel guests walk by and ad-
mire the cacti, a slow-moving waiter appeared. He asked
if we needed anything. He looked like someone whose surfing days
might not be over if he could only get back to the beach.

"You're the writer, somebody told me," he said.

"Guilty," I said.

"See, that's what I want to be," he said. "I've got these really good
ideas for books and movies. Any advice you can give me?"

I said, "You want to write, get a job on a newspaper, go from
there."

"That's it?"

"That's it."

He limped away, looking injured, confused.

Thurlene said, "You blew him off quick enough."

"Yeah, well, most people who say they want to write would rather
talk about it than do it," I said. "You were saying you went to see the
commissioner about the poison deal?"

She said Ginger left the tour for three weeks. Thurlene took her
to their condo in Palm Beach, where the kid recuperated. They did
beach time and Worth Avenue's shops and cafes, and Ginger practiced at Emerald Dunes, the club they'd joined. While they were in
Florida, Thurlene drove up to the LPGA headquarters in Daytona.

It was easy to find. If you took away the palm trees and windows, it
looked like the one-story office building in Dallas where she would
go to see her dentist or dermatologist.

Thurlene let the commissioner in on the scoop that the tour had two dangerous young girls on its hands. One American, one Chinese.

I interrupted her to ask who the LPGA commissioner was these days. I didn't keep up with it. The last one I remember was some guy, but it seemed like there'd been two or three since him.

"Marsha Wilson. She's new. She's been in the job a year. She replaced Karen Bassler."

"What happened to Karen Bassler?"

"She resigned to become Queen of Norway . . . I'm sorry. Bad joke. The players never liked Karen. They could see from the start she was only using the job as a stepping-stone to something bigger."

"Did she find it?"

"I don't know where she is now."

"Where did Marsha Wilson come from?"

"Marketing. She's supposed to be a marketing whiz."

"What did she market?"

"I understand her greatest success was selling the world's biggest driver for Callaway. Bertha's Hindenburg."

"She did that? I remember the slogan. 'There'll be a hot, hot time on your country club course when your Hindenburg lands today.' Some marketing people have it, some don't."

The commissioner had listened patiently to the tale of poison and intrigue. She took notes. She said it was hard to believe, but she conceded that the circumstantial evidence was worth considering.

It was a delicate thing, the commissioner said, one of the girls being Chinese. The commissioner would "float a balloon" through her legal department to see what the lawyers thought, and since she had friends in Washington, D.C., she would "stick her toe in the water" around the State Department and hear their "soundings" on the matter.

The commissioner ended the meeting by saying the situation was something they needed to "keep an eye on."

I said, "You should have reminded the commissioner that 'they needed killin' is a valid legal defense in Texas."

Thurlene said she wished she'd thought of that. She also said I didn't have to walk her to her room. She was tired. A little woozy from the wine. Tomorrow was a big day. And she wasn't in the mood to be hit on.

I said I had no intention of hitting on her. She and her daughter were merely the subjects of a story to me. I never mixed business with pleasure.

"Ginger needs this one tomorrow," she said. "It would be her first win since . . . you know."

"Since that thing I can't write about."

"Yes."

"I have to confess something," I said. "I'm meeting Ann Wendell for breakfast in the morning. I want to interview her. I hope this doesn't make you hot."

"It doesn't in the least. I'm sure Ann will be polite and pretend that we're good friends. If you have a chance, ask her about the Estee Lauder Classic last spring."

"Why would I ask her about the Estee Lauder Classic?"

"That's where Debbie blew a five-shot lead over the last nine holes and lost to Marian Hornbuckle. She was this close to winning her first tournament out here, but she cratered. She shot a forty-five on the back."

"It doesn't sound like a pleasant subject to bring up."

"I'm not finished. Ann was so furious at Debbie, she stormed into the locker room and pushed her up against a wall and started slapping her own daughter in the face. Can you imagine? She should have been barred from the tour for a year . . . or forever."

"Were you there—in the locker room?"

"No, but Jan Dunn and Linda Merle Draper saw it."

"Did this make print? If so, I must have missed—"

"Ha! Guess again. It was covered up for 'the good of the tour.' Our new commissioner saw to that. Putting the lid on it was Marsha Wilson's first big decision. The players weren't happy about it, but Marsha convinced them that covering it up was in the best interest of the tour. The tour would deal with it 'from the inside.' But Marsha never did. She must have thought it would go away on its own."

We were at the door to Thurlene's room. She put a key in, opened it slightly, and turned back to me with a smile, and said, "Even if you were hitting on me . . ."

"Which I'm not," I said.

"But if you were, and if I wasn't minding it . . . I couldn't ask you to come in."

"Why would that be, hypothetically?"

"Ginger and I are sharing a suite."

"Is she a sound sleeper?"

Thurlene laughed and shook my hand.

"Goodnight, Jack. I enjoyed tonight. See you on the tee?"

"I'll be the guy with no logo on his shirt," I said.

I considered treating myself to a nightcap in the pub, which was called the Nightgown. In printed matter it boasted of a margarita called Take Me I'm Yours. I thought better of it, the same as I thought better of buying a pack of Marlboros and renewing old friendships. Instead, I voted to reward myself with a good night's sleep.

Which didn't happen. You could say I was startled, amazed, and otherwise astounded when I entered my room and found Allison of PR waiting there.

Right there in good old Room 423. She was sitting in a chair on my balcony, a bottle of champagne iced down in a bucket on a table next to her, a glass of champagne in her hand. She wore a pair of low-slung designer jeans and a slipover top.

"As you can see," she said, "I take my public relations job seriously."

She stood, came over to me, and drenched my mouth with a kiss.

I said, "Is it going to make any difference that I'm not married?"

She whispered, "It'll be less fun for me, but I'll deal with it."

Soon enough, Allison of PR was slipping out of her duds, then helping me slip out of my duds, and we went tumbling onto the bed.

There on the bed, while she was completing the rest of her PR chores, the lyrics of an old song kept going through my head.

Maybe I was justifying my sordid, weak-willed actions, but whatever the case, I kept hearing, "It was just . . . one of those things . . . just one of those crazy flings . . ."

12

The next morning I woke up to find Allison gone and a note by my pillow. The note said, "We'll always have 423. Compliments of the PR Department. Enjoy the rest of your stay."

As I shaved and showered and dressed I realized I didn't need to know Allison's last name if I decided to put her in the lineup with Ruth, Gehrig, DiMaggio, and Mantle . . . or maybe I should say in the shootout with Hogan, Nicklaus, and Tiger.

Ann Wendell was waiting for me at a table by a large window that looked out on a fake waterfall when I went down to meet her in the Sips and Dins. She was having coffee.

"I apologize if I'm late," I said, taking a seat, doing a quick study of her. I determined that she was on the high side of forty. Nice-looking in a nominee for Best Supporting Actress kind of way.

"You are right on time," she said. "Coffee?"

"Hmm," I said, holding up my cup. She poured from the pot that was on the table.

I announced that I was starving. She announced that she was only having a toasted English muffin. When our blond, sleepy-eyed waiter named Dale acknowledged my presence and wandered over—another surf bum in action—I ordered two glasses of V-8 juice, a large glass of ice water, a fresh pot of coffee, the biggest breakfast steak available, four eggs over medium, hash browns, sliced tomatoes, white buttered toast, and honey.

"My, you must have missed dinner last night," Ann Wendell said.

I said I'd done more or less the same thing. I'd eaten in the gourmet room.

I couldn't tell whether it registered or not.

Trying again, I said they should call this place Rancho Trusto Fundo.

No luck there either.

As we waited for our order, she asked if I was going to the Speedy Arrow Energy Bar Classic in Ruidoso next week.

I said I was considering it.

It was a new tournament on a new golf course—Mescalero Country Club. Commissioner Marsha Wilson was urging all the players to show up. She was taking the credit for creating it, and deserved the credit.

"We must support the commissioner," Ann Wendell said.

I hadn't been to Ruidoso since I was a lad in Texas, but I assumed it still had a quarterhorse racetrack and its share of trailer parks.

"Not the ideal schedule," I said. "You're in California, you go off to the New Mexico mountains, then come back to California—to Palm Springs—for the Dinah Shore. I mean, the Kraft Nabisco. If the Nabisco weren't a major, the top players might skip it."

She said, "I hear more people call it the Dinah, and yet it hasn't been that for years."

I said I would get right to it. My goal was to get Ginger Clayton on the cover of *SM* and pronounce her the next great lady golfer. Would that be overstating it, in her opinion?

Ann Wendell said, "Ginger is a talented young lady and she is very ambitious. But calling her the next great player might be going a little too far. There's a good deal of competition out here."

I said, "Let me tell you what I see. I know a great golf swing when I see it. Ginger has one. She has as good a natural grip as God ever gave a human being. She has size. What is she, five-ten? She has an athletic body . . . If she were a man, you'd say she has the physical stature of a Tiger Woods. That's going to be hard for the other young ladies to compete with. The way she goes about everything is picture book. She doesn't stroke a putt until she's ready. She says she's never missed a putt in her mind. In other words, she's mentally tough. On top of it all, I'm convinced she wants it bad—the fame and glory. Something tells me she wouldn't mind carrying the burden of number one at all. She would relish it."

"Her mother couldn't say it better," Ann Wendell replied. "But Thurlene is a mother, isn't she? We're all proud of our girls."

"You *are* friends, right? You and Thurlene?"

"Heavens, we've been 'golf moms' together for seven years. My Debbie and her Ginger are very close. They've known each other since they were eleven."

I was momentarily distracted by the sight of Allison passing through the Sips and Dins with an armload of stuff. She was pant-suit perfect. The anchorwoman in stride. Spotting me from a distance, she tossed a quick smile and a finger wave—me, the casual acquaintance—and continued on about her business.

"Isn't Allison wonderful?" Ann Wendell said. "I have never encountered a hotel person who tries so hard to please the guests. All hotels and resorts should have someone like her."

"They certainly should," I said.

My massive breakfast arrived and I started to inhale it while I conducted the interview.

We didn't speak for a moment or two. Then Ann Wendell said, "It's a shame about Ginger's father."

"What do you mean?" Mr. Innocent. Slicing up the fried eggs at the same time.

"Surely Thurlene has told you they're divorced."

"She has. But she seems to think she's well rid of him. Why is it a shame?"

"Ed and I always thought Pete was a wonderful man and a good father. Ed is my husband. He doesn't come out here much. Our three hardware stores keep him busy."

"Where are your stores?"

"All around Houston. We have a home at Champions."

"I read where you were from Houston in the press guide."

"We moved to Houston from Wichita, Kansas, when Deb was five."

I said, "Talking about Pete Clayton and Thurlene, I guess there's always two sides to every story. Except in my two divorces. There was only one side. Mine."

No laugh. Blank-faced Ann Wendell said, "The tragic thing about Pete . . . he's missing out on Ginger's success. It was Pete who started Ginger in golf. Oh, I can't tell you how hard that man worked with his daughter when she was eleven, twelve, thirteen. I don't know any father who has made more sacrifices than he did. Ed and I often talked about what a splendid father Pete was."

Good old Pete.

I said, "This isn't for my story by any means, but Thurlene is of the opinion that Pete was mishandling their daughter's funds. I suppose that's one way to put it. Did she ever speak to you about that?"

"She did . . . and I don't believe it for a second. I don't mean for this to sound the way it's going to sound, but the fact is, I don't think Pete Clayton, sweet man that he is, would be, well, *smart enough* to know how to steal anything. Do you understand what I'm saying?"

"Uh-huh. Sure."

"The other thing is, anyone in a family-owned business will tell you there's a fine line between mishandling money and making an honest error in bookkeeping. Now, that's all I'm going to say about it."

She sat back in her chair.

I tried to look as though I understood what she said. I nodded as I dwelled on one person's theft being another person's bookkeeping error, and how this went right in there with a loon-dancing professor saying one person's terrorist is another person's "freedom fighter."

"One more thing," I said. "I hesitate to ask you about this, but intrepid journalist that I am, I have to. Two different sources have told me about you and your daughter having a little dustup at the Estee Lauder Classic last year. I'd like to hear your side of it."

She laughed ho-ho-ho. "Lord of mercy, is that old rumor still going around? I must say! Some people have nothing better to do."

I waited.

"Jan Dunn and Linda Merle Draper were completely mistaken about what they observed. Debbie was bitterly angry at herself for the way she gave the tournament away. She let the bad breaks get the best of her, and believe me, she suffered one bad break after another. When I went in the locker room to console her, she was beating her fists on the wall. All I did was restrain her before she injured herself."

I said, "Jan Dunn and Linda Merle Draper apparently thought enough about what they saw to report it to the commissioner."

Ann Wendell said, "Yes, well. I probably shouldn't say this, but I think before you accept Jan and Linda Merle's version of what happens regarding anything at all, you might want to consider their . . . sexual orientation, shall I say?"

Later on, when I was halfway down the first fairway with Thurlene and we were waiting for Ginger to tee off in the final round, I reported my conversation with Ann Wendell as best I remembered it.

Thurlene couldn't help it. She laughed out loud three times.

13

Why so many sports agents have been allowed to become part of the human race is still something of a mystery. Nevertheless, they are here, they've been here, they're multiplying, and two of the finest liars and thieves among them joined us in Ginger's gallery as the kid was finishing the front nine three under par and turning the tournament into cake.

They were a rare sight on the golf course. Two guys in dark suits, sweating, ties loosened, slipping around in street shoes, lugging briefcases, punching on their BlackBerries.

They looked like they'd dropped out of the sky. Maybe it's more accurate to say they looked like they'd jumped out of an American Airlines 767 and flapped their arms enough to land safely.

Howie (the Dart) Daniels, the one with bushy black hair and a thick mustache, had been a top thief at Creative Sports Enterprises, CSE, for a decade. Sid (Smacky) Lasher, completely bald and five-two, had been a reliable crook for ten years with LTG, Logos to Go.

If the two agents had cared about anything other than money, they would have admired Thurlene's outfit for the day. She wore what I would swear was a tennis ensemble. Her white top was sleeveless, showed an expanse of back, and was cut dangerously low in the front. The white skirt was mid-thigh. Another jacked-up mini.

I remarked on how much I liked her tan. Oh, and nice outfit.

"You're very observant," she said. "You must hear that often."

What I hadn't said was that a man who didn't know she was forty years old would swear that she couldn't be more than twenty-five. But somehow I had an idea she knew this.

Her outfit brought something else to mind. Lady golfers were dressing more like tennis players now. Showing more skin. Maybe the next step in their progress would be to dress like gymnasts. Show their legs up to the crotch. Then in their final marketing—branding—step they could dress like topless dancers in a T&A club. It was only a thought.

In other news, it was a handy thing that Ginger Clayton had the Firm Chick Classic under control—she was seven strokes clear of the field going to the last nine holes. That's because Howie and Smacky were determined to occupy Thurlene's time.

As we walked down the tenth fairway, Howie the Dart said to Thurlene, "Why is he with us?"

Meaning me.

She explained that I was doing a piece on Ginger for *SM*. The kid might make the cover.

"We can do better," Howie said. "I can get *Sports Illustrated, ESPN, Golf Digest, GQ, Esquire*. I've got 'em all right here."

He showed us a fist.

"That's a lot of magazines for only one hand," I said.

Howie said, "I thought I was talking to the lady. Do you mind if I talk to the lady? I'm here to do what's best for the Clayton family, and the last time I looked, sportswriters didn't know crapola about finance."

I said, "You can't guarantee a cover, Howie. It doesn't work like that, and even if it did, you don't have enough stroke to get it done."

Howie said, "Tell me something you don't know, Jack. There must be something you don't know anything about. What is it?"

"I'll tell you something I read once about agents," I said. "Ben Hogan said you always say no to the first three offers."

Howie said, "Ben Hogan, huh? He was, what, sixty years ago? Wow. He must have made a hundred grand in those days. What do you make, big-time golf writer? One seventy-five? Two bills? Yo! My watch and car cost more than that."

Smacky jumped in. "I go in a different direction. I get her *Vogue, Teen Vogue, Glamour*. We turn the kid into Twiggy."

"*Twiggy?*" said Howie the Dart to Smacky Lasher. "What decade are we in here?"

Smacky said, "I say we go glitter all the way. LTG slides her into fashion. Fashion and sports have a head-on. We're talking hot mix here. We're talking Sharapova plays golf. Know what I mean? The Russian babe? Blonde? Legs up to here? It rains money on her. We do the same thing with Ginger. Good looks and golf talent on the fast track to Coinville. Open the vault, here we come."

Thurlene said to both agents, "My daughter needs to win this golf tournament before she does anything else. If you don't mind, I would like to concentrate on the tournament."

Howie said, "The stove is hot, Thurlene. It may not get any hotter. I have a deal memo with me. All we need is your signature, we put on catcher's mitts, they start throwing it at us."

She said, "Guys, Ginger's going to New Mexico next week, then she's playing in the Nabisco. We're not making a decision until after Palm Springs. If she does well in the Nabisco, well . . . you guys are familiar with arithmetic."

Way to go, Thurlene, I thought. Stick it right up there where agents can understand it.

Smacky retreated. He walked over to find a little shade in a palm grove and toyed with his BlackBerry.

Howie stood there, studying a message on his own BlackBerry.

"Just curious, Howie," I said. "Is that from John Dillinger or Bonnie and Clyde?"

As it often happens when somebody tries to nurse a lead, the back nine turned into a thriller. The combination of two overcautious bogeys by Ginger and three birdies by Suzy Scott left the kid with only a two-shot lead as they went to the treacherous seventeenth hole.

Burch Webb, the famous golf course architect, had thrown all of his artistic skills into the design of the par-three seventeenth hole at the Villa. He'd copied the twelfth at Augusta National.

There were only two differences. This seventeenth hole was thirty yards longer than the twelfth at Augusta. It was 185 compared to 155. And the backdrop at the Villa was a fake waterfall instead of bunkers and bushes. Everything else was the same. Water front and right. Shallow green. Today the position was front right. Same as it always is at the Masters for Sunday's final round. A nerve-tester.

We pushed up against the ropes at the tee markers before Suzy Scott and Ginger hit their tee shots, Ginger looking a little shaken by the swift turn of events. Howie and Smacky were off to the side, away from the gallery, discussing various crime sprees.

The mom was grousing, mainly to herself. "Suzy Scott," she was saying. "She's not a good putter, never was, but today—*naturally*—she starts rolling in no-brainers!"

"The kid needs to get it over the water," I said.

"No shit."

Suzy Scott stepped up to hit first. She was a dark-complexioned woman in her thirties. A consistent money winner. She wore Capris. Not the cigarettes, but what I would call bullfighter pants and my mother would call pedal pushers.

Suzy put a three-quarter swing on a lofted hybrid and played a steer job to the left edge of the green. It was puttable, if a long way from the cup, but safe and dry.

Truly relieved to have cleared the water, Suzy Scott playfully clutched her throat with her hand. She smiled and did a little stagger at the same time. This was for the crowd as well as for herself. The crowd rewarded her act with applause and laughter.

Ginger paid no attention to it. She was discussing her club selection with Trey Bishop, looking from her golf bag to the green, golf bag to green, thinking, measuring, trying to eliminate guesswork.

This day she was wearing a white golf shirt with short sleeves and a flat collar, a white visor, and her short little blue skirt barely covered what it was supposed to cover front and back. For my taste, her legs ran a dead heat with her mother's for Best Wheels in Golf.

The look on Ginger's face was cold, calculating.

Ginger took out a seven-iron, addressed the ball, waggled the club.

Thurlene grabbed my arm tightly, breathed the words, "Jesus . . . is that a seven? It's not enough."

I recalled Ginger in her press conference saying her seven was actually a five and a half.

"It's enough," I said, "if she pures it."

Ginger took a smooth cut at it and the collision of clubface and golf ball made that familiar swish-crack sound. Sweetest sound in the game. Golfers know it when they hear it. It's the sound that says you've nailed it, clubfaced it.

The towering shot seemed to hang in the air forever, but it was headed for the flag—if the distance was right.

"Go, ball!" Trey hollered.

"It's enough!" Ginger said.

"Sit!" Trey called out.

"Grab a chair!" Ginger yelled at the ball.

The ball landed on the front edge of the green, took a big hop, put on the brakes, and spun over to within a foot of the cup. Gimme birdie.

The roar of the gallery might have made the cacti shudder, but I wasn't looking at the cacti.

"Yes!" screamed the mom. I squeezed her around the waist. She gave me an excited kiss on the cheek.

"I'm sorry," she said. "Did I overcelebrate?"

"Was that as good for you as it was for me?"

She blushed a trifle.

We watched the kid calmly hold out a palm for her caddie to slap, which Trey did. Then the two of them went off on their triumphant march to the green.

"The hunt's over," I said jovially. "They can piss on the fire and call in the dogs."

Thurlene grinned, eyes wide. "My granddad used to say that!"

I said, "*Everybody's* granddad used to say that."

When Suzy Scott two-putted the seventeenth green for a par and Ginger tapped in the birdie, it gave the kid a three-shot lead going to the last hole, which was an easy par five. A no-water, no-boundary Burch Webb sack of shit. She put it on in two—driver, five-iron—and made an easy birdie and won by four shots.

Cake with icing.

"And to think," I said. "I could be at Doral this week watching Tiger Woods beating Rod Pampling, Fred Funk, and Tom Pernice by fourteen strokes."

"Why does that sound like a recurring theme to me?"

"It's one of them. More fun here, though."

"I'm glad you think so."

"Much better scenery," I said.

14

The party Saturday night for the winner of the Firm Chick Classic was in the grand ballroom again, but it was casual attire this time, which was why Connie Pemberton dressed down. In her white silk pants and yellow silk shirt and four-inch-heel sandals, she wore only one heavy-duty emerald necklace, six gold bracelets, her lightbulb-size wedding ring, and her diamond and emerald earrings that didn't appear to be any bigger than Titleists.

It appeared that every hotel guest had been invited. Pink blazers and lime slacks bloomed everywhere. Most of the players had left town, the "names" faster than others. They hadn't performed well. They had split for outings and exhibitions and would eventually make their way to Ruidoso, the next tour stop.

Debbie Wendell and her mother had departed. Debbie had finished in a tie for fifty-eighth with Hung Ju Kim and Jang Jo Yung and pocketed $3,043.

The thoughtful Ann Wendell went to the trouble of coming into the pressroom to tell me goodbye. "I gather we'll be seeing you again in New Mexico?" she said.

I said they would.

She said, "Ginger played beautifully, didn't she? She's such a lovely girl. I can't remember. Did she miss a putt all week?"

The sports agents had vanished.

Howie the Dart hustled back to New York to be nursemaid for an NFL client—Novocain Washington, the esteemed linebacker for the Giants. Novocain was refusing to sign a one-year contract for $38 million because it didn't state that he'd never have to piss in a bottle for the trainer.

Smacky Lasher was off to Sacramento. He was hoping to sign Days Inn Lewis, the seven-foot-two, 295-pound high school basketball player. Days Inn was going to skip college and go straight to the NBA if he proved he could walk through a room without breaking furniture.

Days Inn's older twin sisters, Radisson and Ramada, who were six-five and 250, were already playing basketball at UConn. How Radisson and Ramada got from California to Connecticut was a mystery known only to the women's basketball coach of the UConn Huskies.

Toppy was already boxed when I bumped into him at a service bar, but he looked dapper in his white Hogan cap, navy blue cardigan, red golf shirt, light gray slacks, and fleece-lined brown suede house slippers.

Connie was up on the bandstand, chatting with the orchestra leader while Toppy and I visited. At the same time I ordered drinks for Thurlene and Ginger and myself.

Earlier Toppy had posed for a photograph with Ginger as they stood at opposite ends of a huge replica of the $225,000 first-place check. The amount was still a fair distance from what a winner on the men's tour receives, but it was an improvement over the old days of the LPGA. In those days, it's said, Babe and Mickey and Kathy and Betsy and them used to play for pots and pans and cans of peas.

"Goddamn the goddamn," Toppy babbled. "The little girlie shoots fifteen under par right here on my 'championship' golf course . . . sixty-eight . . . sixty-four . . . sixty-nine. Burch Webb should have put the greens where the tees are and the tees where the greens are. That's all I can figure. It's a good thing the asshole's not here tonight. It would give me a world of pleasure to stick a bamboo shoot in his ear."

Toppy closed his eyes for a moment, rocked back and forth on his heels, and came alert again when a young gentleman joined us. A guy about my age. He wore a loud green and gold plaid blazer and tasseled loafers.

He was Harvin Goodger, the tournament director, a marketing vice president at Firm Chick skin cream. I hadn't laid eyes on him all week. Apparently nobody else had either.

Toppy wheezed with laughter as he introduced Harvin Goodger to me. "Jack Brannon, I don't believe you've met our capable tournament chairman, Ensign Pulver."

Harvin Goodger didn't get it. I did—but held the laugh.

"By golly, we brought it off, didn't we?" Harvin Goodger said, smiling, holding a glass of club soda on ice, which had been daringly loaded with a slice of lemon. "I saw a lot of good things this week."

"Like what?" Toppy said rudely.

Harvin said, "Oh, you know . . . a little of this, a little of that. The fans, the spectacle, how it all came together . . . the golf course."

"The golf course is a sack of shit," Toppy said.

"Precisely the point I was going to make," Harvin said. "It's been on my mind throughout the week that . . ."

I collected our drinks and scurried to the table reserved for the champion. On the way I passed Allison of PR. She was at a table chatting intimately with a handsome new hotel guest.

I nodded a greeting to her. She ignored me. Must have been that sportswriter's salary thing.

Ginger had bathed and slipped into a pair of seven-hundred-dollar jeans and a cropped sweater. She had finished all of the winner's chores. The press conference. The interview with the Golf Channel. The interviews with radio and TV stations from L.A., San Diego, and Palm Springs. The slow process of autographing programs and golf caps for the tournament volunteers.

The mom had soaked in a tub and changed. She was now in a pair of dark blue hip-hugging pants, a gray and white striped shirt with a turned-up collar, and a light blue blazer.

It occurred to me that we should have invited Trey Bishop to join us, but when I brought it up I learned that Trey had already hit the road. He had taken Ginger's golf clubs with him and was off to Ruidoso. On the drive he planned to stop and spend a couple of days snowboarding in Taos.

Snowboarding. Another adult sport.

"Trey will meet us at the El Paso airport Tuesday," Thurlene said. "It's a two-hour drive from there to Ruidoso."

I said, "Why not Albuquerque instead of El Paso?"

Thurlene said, "Albuquerque is a four-hour drive to Ruidoso. You don't know much about geography, do you?"

I said, "I know Columbia, South Carolina, is closer to Augusta, Georgia, than Atlanta. I know Raleigh is closer to Pinehurst than Charlotte. What else do I need to know?"

The mom said, "We would have gone to New Mexico from here, but this gig came up in L.A.—in Redondo Beach, really—and it was too good for Ginger to pass up."

"What gig?"

"Ginger's doing a commercial Monday. It's for Luxury Palace Hotels. There will be three other people in the commercial with Gin. All are connected to golf. They'll discuss aspects of the game. Garrett Hicks will be there. He's the biggest name. Happy Stoddard from the senior tour . . . and some comedian I've never heard of."

Ginger said, "*Booty Grimmett*, Mom! Jesus . . . he has his own TV show! He plays in the Hope every year."

I said, "Garrett Hicks is a big name in golf. He leads the PGA Tour in stupidity. He leads the PGA Tour in eating with his mouth open. He leads the PGA Tour in farting in front of galleries. What agency arranged this?"

"No agent arranged it," Thurlene said. "The director—director of the commercial—called me out of the blue two weeks ago. He said they needed a 'hot babe' who plays golf for the 'shoot.' He wanted Ginger. He offered fifty grand. I said a hundred. He said done . . . Hey, why don't you come with us? You might pick up some material for your story. Can you? I'll tell them to reserve a room for you. You can fly with us to El Paso Tuesday. Does that sound like a plan?"

I was considering it when Ginger said, "They're calling you, Jack. They want you up on stage."

I hung my head.

"The orchestra leader is introducing you. The 'famous golf writer.' Whoa! All the way from New York City! You have to go up and say something, Jack."

I grudgingly shuffled up on the stage. At the mike I congratulated Ginger Clayton on her victory. I congratulated everyone who helped run the swell tournament. And got off after telling the only golf joke I could remember from the past year.

I said, "So this guy gets in a violent argument with his wife about playing too much golf, and he's arrested for beating her to death with a golf club. The homicide detective says, 'How many times did you hit your wife with the golf club, sir?' The guy says, 'Aw, I don't know . . . let's see. Four, five, six . . . seven . . . Just gimme a six.' "

Toppy wheezed and coughed. I heard him.

When I returned to the table I said to Thurlene, "Book the room for me. I'm there."

"Will do," she said, looking pleased about it.

The evening turned a little rowdy before it ended. Connie Pemberton took over the entertainment. She dedicated a number to "all the boys and girls in uniform who serve our country so proudly and protect us from the foreign slimeballs."

With that, the orchestra went into a bouncy number from days of yore. Connie swayed her hips and sang:

"If you don't love the stars in Old Glory.
If you don't like our red, white, and blue.
Go down to the dock in a hurry.
There's a boat there waiting for you!"

People in the audience spiraled into roaring applause and shouted and stomped their feet. There were even those among them who knew the words and began to sing along as Connie ripped into several more patriotic verses.

As we were leaving I stopped off to tell Toppy it was a pleasure meeting him, and not to worry about his golf course. There was nothing wrong with the layout a bulldozer couldn't fix.

He shook my hand warmly, and through a wheeze, a cackle, and a coughing spell, he said, "Just gimme a six."

PART TWO

STRONGER
THAN LAUNDRY

15

Imagine my surprise to find out it takes five thousand people to make a TV commercial. But of course I never could have guessed how many doughnuts would have been required for the crew.

Joking, joking. A rough guess is there were only two hundred crew members in all. Not as many crew members as there were wires and cables strung everywhere on the hotel mezzanine floor. Most of these wires and cables were outside the conference room where the "shoot" was taking place.

Shallow World was the name of the ad agency making the commercial. Luxury Palace Hotels was a client of Shallow World. Shallow World was headquartered in Leakage Park, New Jersey, a suburb of Newark. Shallow World used to be headquartered in Manhattan, but Ray Shallow, the man who founded the agency, moved it to New Jersey after a bitter argument with his New York City landlord. Unfortunately, Ray Shallow died last year of a heart attack while watching two liberal midgets discussing politics on CNN. The agency was now owned by Ray Shallow's widow, Mopsy, who rarely questioned anything to do with the business. She let a group of workers she referred to as "the little people" run the agency while she lived full-time in Nantucket and pretty much kept to herself, her pharmacist, and her deckhands.

All that pertinent information came to me from Rick, the director of the commercial, and Crystal, the assistant director.

Rick was in his forties, wore dark glasses, and looked like he hadn't shaved in four days. Holes were worn in his sneakers, and the message on his soiled gray sweatshirt said:

Would I Be Doing
This Shit If I Were
Steven Spielberg?

Crystal wasn't bad-looking, a chick in her thirties. Maybe a tad fleshy. She wore ragged, loose-fitting jeans, a sloppy T-shirt, and a red bandana around her head. Strapped around her waist was a tool belt with cell phones and walkie-talkies and pill bottles clipped on it. She was draped in wires and earplugs.

Numerous members of the crew, particularly the younger ones, seemed to be afraid of her.

Under his breath to a coworker, I overheard an older technician say to another older technician, "Look out, here comes Katie Couric again."

And a moment later Crystal came storming down the hall, barking into one of her phones:

"Where the fuck are you, Kevin? Talk to me! How fucking long does it take you to run a fucking errand, you fucking dipshit? You and that clueless little bitch Rachel better get your fucking asses back up here now, do you fucking hear me!"

The sponsors of the Firm Chick Classic had been thoughtful enough to arrange a limousine to transport Thurlene and Ginger from the Enchanted Villa to the Luxury Palace Hotel in Redondo Beach.

We didn't do a motorcade. I left earlier in my rental car and stopped at a deli in Palm Springs to grab a sandwich to go, dictating the ingredients on a foot-long hero. Two layers of Black Forest ham, a layer of thin-sliced soft salami, two layers of provolone cheese, olive relish, green peppers, mayo, sliced tomatoes, and shredded lettuce.

I ate it in three delicious segments on the way to LAX, where I turned in the Hertz Lincoln, then hopped in a cab for the twenty-minute ride to the hotel in Redondo Beach. Which wasn't on the beach. The ocean and beach were across a busy thoroughfare from the hotel and beyond a row of restaurants, a string of condos, and a marina.

But from the balcony of my room I could see a body of water if I looked around the corner of the refinery.

Thurlene and Ginger weren't available for dinner. They did room service and worried about what Ginger should wear for the commercial. Besides, the call for the "shoot" was six-thirty a.m.

This left me to make my own fun in the lobby bar that night.

I listened to a guy who sold home furnishings tell me his problems with working for an asshole in Torrance. I listened to a man's problems selling medical supplies while working for an asshole in Long Beach.

At one point a hot-looking redhead sidled up to me at the bar. She couldn't have been more than twenty-two. She mentioned that she was in the "home entertainment" business and would come to my room and do anything I wanted for five hundred dollars, or a thousand for all night.

I thanked her for the offer and said I might ordinarily be interested but I was still trying to clear up this darn rash I'd picked up on my last trip to Bangkok.

That chased her, but I knew the incident could never compare with the Jim Pinch tale that had passed into journalistic legend.

It seems that back when Jim was still writing for the *Fort Worth Light & Shopper* he'd covered this Cotton Bowl game in Dallas between the Texas Longhorns and the Ole Miss Rebels. After the game, with time to spare before his deadline, Jim returned to the press hotel downtown to work in the quiet and comfort of his room.

But after he stepped into the elevator in the lobby with three other writers, an attractive whore lady slid into the elevator with them.

As the elevator went up, the whore lady looked around at the four gentlemen, and said, "I'll do anything any of you want for two hundred dollars."

History has it that only Jim Pinch spoke up. He said, "Can you write a lead, column, and sidebar?"

Everybody showed up for the six-thirty call except Garrett Hicks, PGA Tour idol to the retarded. But nothing happened for a while other than makeup, hairstyling, and wardrobe for the "principals," the performers. Ginger and the others. Nothing happened unless you wanted to count the sitting around and drinking coffee and eating sweet rolls and watching cameras and lights being moved around.

There was a greenroom for the performers and their guests. It was across the hall from the "set," the boardroom. It was where the performers could relax between takes. Crystal, the assistant director, had ordered a drone to make sure the greenroom was well stocked with coffee and tea and cookies and fruit and other snacks and bottles of water and soft drinks and functioning TV screens so the guests could watch and hear the "shoot" as it progressed, including the off-camera chitchat.

Crystal ordered the drone to see that this happened or she would grip a sand wedge and dig one of the drone's nuts out of a buried lie and feed it to the tilapia.

Words to that effect.

Thurlene and I sat in the greenroom and passed the time by reading the *L.A. Times* and *USA Today* and poking around at the delicacies and talking to members of the crew. Every now and then the mom would visit Ginger in the room where the kid was being fixed up and check on the progress.

"She's going to be a drop-dead knockout," Thurlene said, returning from a visit.

"She can't help it," I said. "Look who her mom is."

"Hit."

"A casual comment?" I said. "That's a hit?"

When Booty Grimmett emerged from makeup and walked over to select a sweet roll, I would have known it was a celeb for no other reason than the fact that he didn't immediately speak to anyone in the room.

Hefty, puffy-cheeked, and slit-eyed, Booty Grimmett was wearing a Hawaiian shirt and baggy shorts and sneakers. He was on his cell and laughing with someone on the other end of the conversation and sat down and turned away from the rest of us.

The comedian's TV series, *Booty's Gang*, was a show in which he plays a man who gives up a successful insurance business to join a black L.A. street gang. His problems with learning their slang and trying to become a white rapper was the basis for the weekly humor. The series was juvenile and hideously unfunny, which explained why it was a raging hit.

Happy Stoddard, a regular on the senior tour, was the next "principal" to turn up in the greenroom. The makeup person had done a good job of covering up the red splotches on his face, but there was little anyone could have done about his stringy hair—Oklahoma hair, as it's known to some of us—and his stoop-shouldered posture. I'd always thought Happy looked like a senior golfer before he was a senior golfer.

Happy's awestruck brother was with him. Happy introduced his brother, Harold. Happy shared with us that Harold was a decorated retired army colonel, 82nd Airborne—Grenada, Panama, Kosovo, Afghanistan, three tours in Iraq, and the greatest golf fan in the world.

When I thanked Harold for his service to our country, he said, "Aw, I'm nobody. Golf pros are the ones."

I said, "Anybody who wears an American military uniform . . . that's somebody to me, Harold."

"Aw, I'm not," he said.

"Yes, you are," I said.

"Naw, I'm not either."

"You certainly are."

"Naw, I'm really not."

"Indeed you are, Colonel. Afghanistan, Iraq . . ."

I paused to wonder why I was having this argument.

"I'll tell you who's somebody," Harold said. "Garrett Hicks."

"*What?*"

I didn't intend to say it so loud. Heads turned.

Harold went into this story about a wonderful thing that happened to him. Happy took him to a tournament shortly after he retired. He was privileged to see all of his golf heroes up close. People he'd only watched on TV and read about. One night during the tournament he and Happy went to dinner at a Red Lobster, and right across the room—right there, by golly, having dinner with business associates—was Garrett Hicks.

Col. Harold Stoddard teared up as he came to the next part. He said that Hicks, on his way out of the restaurant, stopped by their table and said hello to Happy and shook hands with lowly him, Harold Stoddard.

"He didn't have to take the time to do that," Harold said as a tear trickled down his cheek. "He didn't have to act like I was even in the room. But he did. Garrett Hicks shook my hand!"

I couldn't think of anything to say to that, so I went for more coffee.

It was around eight thirty when Crystal poked her head in the greenroom, poked it out again, and went up and down the halls, bellowing into her walkie-talkie, "Garrett Hicks is IN the building!"

With a glance at Thurlene, I said, "You're going to love this guy. You'll especially like his imitation of a human being."

Crystal made another sweep through the rooms on the mezzanine, announcing, "Garrett Hicks is IN the building! Garrett Hicks is IN the building. Hear me, people!"

"Roger that," I said, and picked up the L.A. Times again.

I wanted to reread the heartwarming piece about the Hollywood producer and his activist wife who were going to do their part to fight the catastrophic threat of global warming. For a whole year they weren't going to drive their Hummers anywhere but to their second home in Santa Barbara and the occasional premiere.

16

That old debonair matinee idol, Garrett Hicks, came barging into the greenroom reciting parts of the Spoiled Rotten, Accidentally Wealthy PGA Tour Player's Bill of Rights. He was leveling it at Larry Silverman, his agent, one of the most respected in the business, a partner in International Sports Corp., ISC, and a man who didn't need this shit but had learned to put up with it over the years from clients who could bring in wheelbarrows of coin.

"I ask for a limousine and what do you get me?" Garrett was saying. "A sedan. A fucking four-door with no TV! I want bananas in my room and what do I find? A basket of fag fruit! I ask for bottles of plain drinking water and all I find is some fizzy French crap, or it's that pelly-ginny greaseball shit. I want the TV in front of the bed, but no. It's over in a corner. Larry, what do you fucking DO? I know you're good at taking your cheating thirty percent out of my hard-earned money, but what else do you do? . . . I come on the tour, smart guys tell me I gotta have my own Jew. Okay, I get my own Jew. He's the best, they tell me, but what's the Jew good for? He can't hit a golf ball. He's not good for the limo. He can't handle the bananas. He can't arrange drinking water. What's he good for?"

Garrett saw the snack table and interrupted himself. "This shit for us?" Not waiting for an answer, he grabbed a banana and took a bite and chewed with his mouth open. I'd have won that one.

He said, "You sold me out too cheap on this fucking deal, Larry. If you can't bump these people up to three big ones, I'm walking. I'm outta here. You tell me two bills is twice as much as anybody else gets, but who the fuck is anybody else? I know who Garrett Hicks is.

Maybe you've forgotten who Garrett Hicks is. Maybe you've forgotten how much Garrett Hicks is worth to you."

I always enjoyed it when a sports star went third-person on himself.

Larry Silverman pretended to look interested and concerned, but I was sure he'd heard it all before, or something similar.

Four years ago Garrett was a big handsome guy who came on the tour fresh out of college with some big amateur titles in his satchel. He had all the shots and he could put a tee ball into the galaxy, but he didn't waste any time establishing himself as the most arrogant, ignorant, charmless crud who ever roamed a fairway.

Even the point-missers realized Garrett was a terminal shithead, although they continued to glorify him in print.

I, however, had taken a certain amount of pride in *not* glorifying him. Even when I'd covered tournaments he won, even the three majors. I'd skillfully found a way to write about who lost or who *should* have won instead of his sorry ass.

This might have annoyed Garrett if he'd ever read any of it, but it had long ago become clear that he never read anything above the intellectual level of a scorecard.

Garrett saw me in a chair against the wall. I was sitting next to Thurlene, but even though she was a looker she must not have resembled anyone famous, thus he ignored her.

"You look familiar," Garrett said to me.

"So do you," I said, "but I can't get the name."

Larry Silverman fought off a grin and said, "Hi, Jack."

"Hi, Larry," I said. "Say hello to Thurlene Clayton."

The agent came over and shook her hand. "We've spoken on the phone. You *do* have my proposal, right?"

She said, "I do. I'll let you know something soon."

Larry said to his client, "Garrett, you know Jack Brannon, I'm sure . . . with *SM* . . . the golf writer."

"*Golf writer,*" Garrett said with a smirk. "I knew you looked useless for some reason."

"Hold it," I said, faking surprise. "You've *read* something?"

Thurlene had been staring at Garrett. She looked as if she were sniffing spoiled meat.

She said to him, "Did I hear you say you're getting twice as much money as my daughter today?"

Garrett said, "Who's your daughter?"

"Ginger Clayton."

"Who's Ginger Clayton?"

"She happens to play on the LPGA Tour."

Garrett said, "Well, lady, I guess that's the difference between us and the bitches, ain't it?"

I edged over next to Garrett and said, "There you go, dude. Being yourself again."

He said, "Be what . . . ? What the hell you talking about?"

Larry Silverman led his client into a corner for a private conversation. During the lull, Happy and Harold Stoddard loaded up plates with snacks, and Booty Grimmett put away his cell phone and turned his chair around to face the room.

Then the next thing we knew, Booty Grimmett, celebrity comedian, toppled out of his chair and scrambled back up on his knees and spread out his arms in a come-to-Jesus fashion, yelling, "Sugar pie honey bunch! Hit me, beat me, hurt me!"

Ginger Clayton had appeared, is what had happened.

She stood in the doorway in spiked heels, hand on her hip, playfully striking a model's pose. Eyelashed up, with her blond hair flowing down to her shoulders, wearing a form-fitting pale yellow tank-top spandex minidress. Lot of curves, lot of skin. The franchise babe.

It was a spill-your-drink moment.

17

Everybody was in place for the shooting of "Gone With the Titleist." Or perhaps it was "The Maltese Callaway." Or it could have been "The Treasure of Sierra Graphite."

We could see and hear all of it on the TV monitors in the greenroom. The "we" consisted of myself, Thurlene, Larry Silverman, Col. Harold Stoddard, retired, and the occasional drone who came in to nab food and drink.

The director, Rick, placed the four of them in the boardroom—the set—the way he wanted them. Ginger and Garrett sat next to each other on one side of the table. Across from them were Happy and Booty. Notepads and pens and coffee mugs were in front of each of them. Set decoration.

There were guys with cameras on their shoulders in all four corners of the room, creeping, rising, kneeling, zooming, not zooming.

The director's voice could be heard off camera.

Rick said, "Booty will lead. He'll throw out the questions I tell him to ask. You talk, we shoot. That's the plan. We hope to lift out three-fifteens and three-thirties that'll run through the spring and summer. You're talking golf. All of you are experts. Prove it to me. But keep your answers short. One word will do. One sentence at the most. That's the ticket. We don't have any Hamlets in the crowd, do we? Show of hands? I thought not."

Crystal added a word.

"Relax, stay loose," she said. "You want to stretch, move around, grab something to drink, fine. Cough, sneeze, yawn, belch—it doesn't matter. You want to lift your butt and let one go, have at it. We're editing."

Garrett said, "What's this fifteen and thirty shit?"

"Commercials," said Booty. "They'll be editing commercials to run fifteen seconds and thirty seconds."

Happy said, "Is what we're doin' gonna be like those commercials where guys sit and talk about you-don't-know-what-the-product-is?"

"I hope not," said Rick.

Crystal turned up in a corner of the screen and said, "Booty, could you look a little less like you're in a produce market?"

Booty was having trouble keeping his eyes off Ginger's breasts, which were straining at the tank top of her spandex minidress.

He said, "It's not easy, darling. I'm torn between the honeydew and the cantaloupe."

"Try, please," Crystal said.

Ginger said, "I can change into something else."

"You're perfect," the director said.

"Boy, you got that right," Happy Stoddard said.

"Can we get started?" Garrett said, "I'm on a three o'clock flight this afternoon whether this shit's over or not."

Crystal yelled, "Okay, people! We're rolling."

"Wait!" Ginger blurted out. She was fanning her face with her hand. She turned to the director and assistant director, who were standing at the far end of the boardroom. "Can I change seats? Sit over there?"

"Why?" the director asked.

"Why do you *think*?" she said, still fanning the air.

Garrett said to Ginger, "You never smelled a fart before?"

Booty Grimmett jumped to his feet.

"Change with me, dear," Booty said. "I'll sit there."

He walked around the table and pulled the chair out for Ginger. As she gladly changed places with him, Booty said, "I love that smell in the morning. That smell . . . it smells like . . . *victory*."

And he howled with laughter.

When none of the others laughed, Booty said, "Nobody saw the movie? You're joking, right? Duvall? He's in 'Nam . . . ?"

"Uh, folks," the director said, coming into view, but in that instant all the screens went dark and the sound went off on our monitors.

Pacing in the greenroom, Thurlene said, "I'm sorry, but I have to have a cigarette. I'll go outside if anyone objects."

She was digging the pack and lighter out of her purse as Larry Silverman said, "Smoke in here. It won't bother me."

Col. Harold Stoddard said, "Me neither."

"Here's an ashtray," I said, handing her my coffee saucer.

After lighting up, she said, "Jack, be honest. Is Garrett Hicks not the most loathsome, insufferable, vomitous person you've ever been around in your whole life?"

"He's not contagious," I said. "That's the good news."

She turned to Larry Silverman. "How can you put up with him? Represent him? I don't care how much money he makes for you."

The agent shrugged. "If I may quote a movie line myself, 'It's the business we chose.' "

I said, "There's a line from an old movie I like to fall back on. 'Some of them will be dancing at the Savoy tonight and some of them will still be in Germany.' Clark Gable . . . *Command Decision* . . . war movie."

Thurlene stared at me.

I said, "He's counting B-17s coming back from a daylight bombing raid over Schweinfurt."

Thurlene was still staring at me, only more so.

I said, "I'll have to get back to you on what that has to do with anything we're talking about."

Larry smiled at Thurlene. "Feasting my eyes on your daughter today, I'd like to suggest something regarding the proposal I've sent you. Feel free to put a three in front of every number I've written down."

She said, "You're a nice man, Larry, but we're not going to make any decisions until after the Nabisco."

———

The first go-round of the shoot produced one or two moments you wanted to take home and tell your friends about, but I wasn't sure they could be used in a commercial.

It went like this:

BOOTY: Greatest golf course. Happy?

HAPPY: Augusta National.

GARRETT: Riviera.

BOOTY: Riviera? Surely you jest, my good fellow.

GARRETT: I won there, pal.

HAPPY: You really think Riviera is a great course?

GARRETT: Okay, Doral.

HAPPY: Doral? You must have won there too.

GARRETT: I did. What about it?

BOOTY: Ginger? Your favorite?

GINGER: Colonial.

GARRETT: Colonial? Geeah. What do women know?

BOOTY: Everything. They've got *all* the pussy.

GINGER: Tell me I didn't hear that.

DIRECTOR'S VOICE: Yo, gang. Can we stick to things we might be able to use? Appreciate it. Lead on, Booty.

BOOTY: Okay, here we go. What's your favorite golf club? I'll go first. Hooters. Sorry, Rick. Start again. Okay. Everybody say their favorite club in the bag. Mine's the sand wedge. It's the one I use the most.

HAPPY: I have to go with the driver. I'm a short hitter, but I can keep it in play with good old Bertha. If you don't keep it in play . . .

BOOTY: Garrett?

GARRETT: I don't have a favorite club.

BOOTY: *Pick* one.

GARRETT: Why?

BOOTY: Because . . . Rick . . . wants . . . you . . . to.

GARRETT: Shit, gimme a nine-iron.

BOOTY: Ginger?

GINGER: Seven-iron. My old reliable.

BOOTY: Okay, next question. You're playing golf naked and you

can put on only one thing. Do you choose shoes or glove?
Garrett Hicks? Shoes or glove?

GARRETT: Why would anybody play golf naked?

BOOTY: It's a hypothetical. Go with me on this.

GARRETT: Go where?

BOOTY: Make a choice. Shoes or glove?

GARRETT: It's a stupid question.

GINGER: I agree with Garrett for once.

HAPPY: I'll answer it. I say shoes. I have to make sure I can
stand up or I can't swing the club.

BOOTY: If I'm playing naked, I say glove . . . but I wouldn't
wear it on my hand.

GINGER shrieked—and couldn't stop laughing.

DIRECTOR'S VOICE: Seems like a good spot for a break.

18

Usually I have no thoughts to pass along on the subject of showbiz, because if I base my opinions on most of the movies I see today—Car Chase Meets Girl, Car Chase Loses Girl, Car Chase Finds Girl in Time for Sequel—I tend to wind up wishing the raghead terrorists would take out Hollywood. But I did have a suggestion or two for Ginger at the break.

We sat in a corner of the greenroom, Mom included, and spoke quietly while Ginger nibbled on an oatmeal cookie.

I said, "You have a chance to take over this deal, Ginger. You can use your looks and your golf knowledge to knock 'em dead. Happy is easygoing. Booty's strictly a comedian. And as he's proved, Garrett can't contribute an intelligent word about anything."

"I am so disappointed to meet him," Ginger said. "I thought he was a great player, but . . . yuck!"

Thurlene said, "He is a sickening excuse for a human being. He gives new meaning to 'trailer trash.' "

I said, "He's that lethal combination of loud *and* stupid. Garrett takes pride in the fact that he doesn't do anything in this life but eat, shit, sleep, and hit golf balls. Pardon the expression, but he's nine of the ten biggest assholes I've ever known."

"I don't feel like I have anything to say here," Ginger said.

I said, "You have plenty to say. Listen to me. No matter what the question is, throw in something about how you play golf. For instance . . . have you ever played a shot in a tournament you haven't practiced?"

"Maybe once or twice," she said. "But I try not to."

"Say that. When the opportunity presents itself, say something like, 'That's an interesting question, but I never play a shot in a tournament I haven't practiced.' Understand? The director will love it. He'll know you'll be giving the viewer a valuable golf tip, and he'll want to use it."

Thurlene said to her daughter, "You're getting this, right?"

Ginger nodded.

I said, "I guarantee you're going to be asked, 'What's the hardest shot to hit?' What do you say?"

"There's all kinds."

"That's not what you say. What you say is, get a long iron up out of a tight lie. Fairway wood out of a divot. The forty-yard bunker shot. Something like that. You with me?"

"It's hard for me to make myself swing easy in the wind. The stronger the wind, the easier you should swing."

"Say that. There must be other tips you learned at the academy or out on the tour by now."

"Yeah, there's stuff like 'Think about the target before you swing' . . . 'Take dead aim' . . . 'Take your driving range swing to the golf course' . . . 'Never give up on yourself after a bad shot' . . ."

I said, "Good. You and I know this stuff is bullshit—the game's ninety percent mental once you know how to grip the club—but America doesn't know this. America will lap it up."

"You *are* getting this?" Thurlene said.

"I've *got it*, Mom. Jesus."

In my judgment, the segment that came off the most interesting unfolded as follows:

DIRECTOR: I'm feeling good about it, gang. You're into the rhythm of things. Let's keep it going.

CRYSTAL: Okay, we're rolling! Quiet out in the hall, goddamn it! I'll eat my own people!

DIRECTOR: Go, Booty.

BOOTY: Okay, group. If you can play only one golf course the rest of your life, what would it be?

HAPPY: Easy question. St. Andrews.

GARRETT: St. Andrews? You just shit a trout, man.

HAPPY: St. Andrews is a shrine, Garrett!

GARRETT: I got your shrine right here.

BOOTY: I've never been there, but I hear Pine Valley is something else. I'll say Pine Valley.

GARRETT: Overrated. I thumped it around with my dick and shot sixty-seven.

GINGER: You're so descriptive, Garrett. For me, it's Augusta National. I haven't played it, but I can't imagine any course being more fun.

GARRETT: Augusta. Geeah. Another zoo.

GINGER: Why don't *you* name a course, Garrett?

GARRETT: I don't like any of 'em. Sumbitches stand between me and making a living. You'll learn that one of these days, missy.

GINGER: I hope not.

BOOTY: Moving right along. Toughest shot in golf? Happy?

HAPPY: Uh . . . tryin' to carve a three-wood out of a nasty lie.

BOOTY: Garrett?

GARRETT: There ain't none I can't hit.

GINGER: How did I know you were going to say that?

GARRETT: How'd you know what . . . ?

BOOTY: Toughest shot for you, Ginger?

GINGER: A six-foot putt on the last green for your own money. Lee Trevino said that in something I read one time.

DIRECTOR: I love that! Say it again, Ginger. But stand up and say it as you walk over to get a Coke. And leave out Trevino. Zoom in, Marty.

GINGER: A six-foot putt on the last green for your own money.

DIRECTOR: Great! Next question, Booty.

BOOTY: What's the main thing it takes to be a winner in tournament golf? I'll go first. Get born Jack Nicklaus.

GARRETT: Nicklaus didn't have a short game.

HAPPY: *Jack Nicklaus* didn't have a short game? He's the greatest putter who ever lived!

GARRETT: He was weak on pitches and chips. I seen tape.

HAPPY: I guess that's why Jack only won twenty majors, counting the two amateurs . . . and he was second in nineteen others.

GARRETT: Them amateurs don't count for shit.

HAPPY: You're an idiot, Garrett.

GARRETT: Yeah? How much money you won lately?

BOOTY: Can we move on here? What does it take to be a winner, Garrett?

GARRETT: You got to know how to play, is all.

DIRECTOR: Ask Ginger, Booty.

BOOTY: What about it, Ginger?

GINGER: Everybody wants to win. I know players on our tour who say they want to win, but they're happy to come away with a nice check when it's over. I believe all the great winners, past and present . . . they aren't necessarily the ones who try to win, or think they're trying to win, but the ones who really deep down *hate* the idea of losing. Despise it, absolutely can't *stand* the thought of losing. I mean, that's just what I think, you know?

DIRECTOR: Fantastico! Did we get that? Please, God, tell me we have that!

19

High on a plateau above the town of Ruidoso, and along the Billy the Kid Trail in the Sacramento Mountains, which are the southern Rockies if you want to be precise about it, I finally found the Mescalero Country Club & Casino Resort. There, the first people I met after turning over my rental car to the ski bum–slash–valet parking attendant were Sinking Canoe and Smokes Loco Weed.

The ski bum–slash–parking attendant told me their names and explained that they were the head Apache honchos for the casino, hotel, and country club. Sinking Canoe and Smokes Loco Weed were standing out in front of the lodge, smiling, acting as official greeters to the arriving visitors, one of whom was me.

Sinking Canoe looked like Geronimo would look if Geronimo had ever worn a gray pinstriped suit and a Schlitz cap. Smokes Loco Weed looked like Cochise would look if Cochise had ever worn a Dallas Cowboys jersey and a Texas A&M Corps of Cadets cavalry hat.

A large banner was draped from the roof gutter of the lodge. It said:

WELCOME TO THE SPEEDY ARROW
ENERGY BAR GOLF CLASSIC.

I shook hands first with Sinking Canoe, who said, "We have many squaws here to play golf. Good for our slots, you betcha."

"Welcome," said Smokes Loco Weed as I was shaking his hand. "I hope you like to gamble and donate much money to noble savage."

I confessed to being a golf writer who'd come for the tournament.

"You will write about our beautiful place?" Sinking Canoe said.

"And the golfing squaws," I said.

They looked pleased to find a consarned tarnation polecat varmint of a sportswriter in these parts. Probably hadn't been one around since Granny and Ring and the boys came through in '23, thinking they'd found a shortcut to Shelby, Montana, for the Dempsey-Gibbons fight.

The ranch-style lodge was three stories tall. It stretched as far I could see until it bumped into a mountain. I gathered the gambling casino was the enormous brown biscuit that was attached to the lodge by a glass-enclosed walkway. The biscuit looked big enough to cover all thirty-six holes at Winged Foot.

Part of the Mescalero Country Club golf course could be seen from the drive leading to the lodge. A green here, a tee there. Hanging on precarious ledges.

My two ladies were supposed to have been somewhere behind me. We had flown together from L.A. to El Paso, but Trey Bishop hadn't been there to meet them as he had promised.

Thurlene said, "The hotel in Taos says Trey checked out, but his cell isn't working, damn it."

I said, "I'll hang around for a while. If he doesn't show up, you can ride with me."

Ginger said, "He'd better not lose my golf clubs."

I said, "When was the last time you guys talked to Trey?"

"Two days ago," Thurlene answered.

"He could be having car trouble," I said.

Ginger said, "I don't care what kind of trouble he's having. He better not lose my golf clubs."

Thurlene said, "You go on, Jack. We'll wait here for an hour or so. If he doesn't show up, we'll rent a car."

"This is great," Ginger said. "I'm playing in a tournament with one day of practice, a pickup caddie, and a new set of clubs. Shit!"

Trey Bishop never turned up, but my ladies didn't rent a car. A shuttle bus for the Mescalero Country Club & Casino Resort happened to show up, and they climbed on board even though the driver's name was Soaring Foot.

By the time they reached the lodge they were exhausted from frustration, inconvenience, and worry. Thurlene let me know they'd arrived and would have room service for dinner and spend the rest of the night trying to find out where Trey was.

They'd still heard nothing from him by noon the next day, Wednesday. That's when Thurlene called the New Mexico state police to tell them a friend was missing and might have been in a traffic accident somewhere between Taos and El Paso.

Wednesday was also the day I went with a seething Ginger Clayton to the pro shop at Mescalero Country Club to watch her pick out a set of clubs she could use in the Speedy Arrow Energy Bar Classic.

Tyler Hughes, the head pro, introduced himself. Guy around thirty. He said he preferred to be known as the director of golf. This even though as far as I could tell his only assistant was a lazy-looking seventeen-year-old high school boy named Kenneth.

I didn't think we looked that inquisitive, but Tyler shared his personal history with us. His first job was assistant pro at Singing Winds muny in Amarillo. He moved from there to assistant pro at Howling Winds muny in Lubbock. His last stop before Mescalero was the head pro's job at Tornado Winds Country Club in Waco.

He filled us in on the history of the resort. It was developed in steps. The casino came first. The casino paid for the hotel. The casino and hotel paid for the golf course. The casino, hotel, and golf course were the lures for the home sites that were for sale surrounding the property. Private homes couldn't be built on Indian property itself.

Tyler said, "The course looks tricky, but it's not as tough as it looks. You stand on a tee like the seventeenth, a par-four, and you think

holy dang. The fairway's narrow and slopes to the left. You gotta
carry it about one seventy-five over this deep gully, but if you drive
it straight, you can reach the green."

Ginger said, "What if you don't drive it straight?"

"Don't miss it left. You might have to go down to Alto to find it, or
all the way to Ruidoso. Our members have learned to aim for the
trees on the right, hope for a good bounce."

"Who designed the course?" I asked.

"Afraid of Dogs," Tyler said.

"Excuse me?"

"Burch Webb did it. You know him, I'm sure. But Sinking Canoe
named him 'Afraid of Dogs' one day. Mr. Webb was standing out
there where the first tee is now, when the course was under con-
struction. These three little dogs got loose from the lady owner who
was staying in the hotel. Two little brown dogs, one little white dog.
They went yapping after Mr. Webb. I guess he didn't like dogs or
he'd never seen dogs that little and that loud. He started running.
Sinking Canoe watched the dogs chase him everywhere, all around,
and they didn't stop till the lady owner ran after them and yelled,
'Sit . . . sit!' She yelled it in a bloodcurdling voice. The little dogs
stopped right away and sat down and started to quiver . . . and so
did Mr. Webb. It was kind of funny."

Ginger began to rummage through the pro shop, looking for mallets
she liked. Tyler Hughes followed her, suggesting things.

Curious about Ginger's priorities, I said, "What are you worried
about the most, Trey Bishop or your golf clubs?"

She ignored the question and kept rummaging, slowly selecting
a blend of Callaway, TaylorMade, Ping, and Adams metal woods,
hybrids, irons, and wedges—and a Titleist Cameron putter.

Tyler said Ginger didn't have to pay for the golf clubs. He was
honored to let her use them, and she was welcome to keep them if
they helped her in the tournament.

Ginger thanked him and asked if the pro could find her a caddie.
"I'll pay twenty percent of what I win."

Tyler said, "First place is three hundred thousand this week. You're saying if you win you'll pay your caddie sixty thousand dollars?"

"He'll earn it."

"Damn, I'll carry your bag."

"You will? How can you leave the shop?"

"Nobody buys anything in here. Most of the members make their own clubs, and when they're not playing, they're wading in the creeks and crawling around in the rough looking for balls. Kenneth can sit here and stare out the window as easy as I can."

"If you're serious . . ."

"I'm serious. You intend to play a practice round today, don't you?"

"I would like to, yeah."

"I'll meet you on the first tee in an hour. Leave these clubs with me. I'll put 'em in a good bag. Couple dozen Titleists enough?"

"You da man, Tyler," Ginger said.

I asked Ginger the question again. What worried her the most? Her golf clubs or Trey Bishop's health?

"I'm not worried about Trey," she said.

"Why not?"

"Because I know where he is."

"You do?"

"I do."

"Care to share it with me?"

"He's found a honey in Taos with a hot bod and no morals. That's exactly where he is . . . and he's fired."

I started to say he'd found every man's dream, but I settled for "You're dumping Trey? Hasn't he been a good caddie for you? You've won with him."

She said, "Trey doesn't club me and he doesn't read greens for me. All I need is somebody to carry the bag, keep the clubs clean, and be on time. That's mainly what I ask."

"Maybe Trey's been in an accident," I said.

"What, he fell off the bed and broke his dick?"

20

The Trey Bishop mystery was solved when he phoned the ladies on Wednesday night before the tournament started. The details of their conversation were reported to me later when the three of us dined together in the Tomahawk Room in the lodge.

There were other restaurants in the lodge and casino, but the Tomahawk Room looked like the safest and quietest. Among the others to choose from in the lodge and casino were Dances with Jalapeños, Custer's Revenge, Soup R Bowl, and Fattest Woman.

Trey was in love and intended to change his life. That was the red meat of the phone call.

First, he apologized for having car trouble and not letting them hear from him. Second, he apologized for getting trapped in the sudden blizzard that gripped Taos for two days and rendered his leaving impossible.

Eventually he got around to saying they could ignore that—he lied—and he was sure Ginger and Thurlene would love Ashley if they ever came to Taos someday and met her.

"*Ashley*," Ginger said. "Jesus."

"It could be worse," I said.

"How?"

"It could be Amber."

Trey said he hadn't expected anything like this to happen to him, but Ashley had captured his heart the night he arrived—the moment she served him the bowl of chili at My Adobe Hacienda, the restaurant where she worked. They spent two days snowboarding, and were married last night.

They were married at the foot of Flame Out, the second toughest run in the Taos ski valley—next to Maxine's Miscarriage. The ceremony was performed by an old buddy of Trey's, Chigger Donnelly, who operated the snowboarding school. Chigger Donnelly had become an ordained minister on the Internet.

Trey had realized his body and mind were experiencing a change the moment he met Ashley. Now he intended to "take life to another level." Chigger had hired him as a snowboarding instructor.

Trey was sorry Ginger's clubs had been stolen out of the trunk of the car, but a golf club was only as good as the person swinging it. He asked that they send the money owed to him to his new address. He had moved in with Ashley at the Slalom Gates, Apartment 3, 2205 Edelweiss Circle, Taos.

I said, "Trey says he wants to take life to another level? Surely drugs don't have anything to do with it."

After dinner we cruised the casino. Long enough for me to drop two hundred at blackjack, for Thurlene to smoke Capris while dropping one hundred in the slots, and for the three of us to watch a poker game in which men in cowboy hats kept dealing a game called Little Tavarich. In the game your low red card in the hole, your little red, was wild in high only, and all like it in your hand and on the board were wild along with it. Four cards were dealt to each player and five were turned up on the table, one at a time, with betting on each.

A bystander in dark glasses and a Stetson explained to us that if you expected to win both ends of the pot in a high-low game like Little Tavarich, it was best to be holding "five tickets on American" for high—five aces—and "the course record" for low. Meaning a 64.

When we left the casino we went back to the lodge and wandered up and down the corridor where the shops and boutiques were to be found.

Ginger and Thurlene exchanged hellos and nods with other competitors who were browsing and shopping.

We looked at a lot of white beaded Apache dresses and assorted cowboy hats.

I expressed disappointment that I hadn't seen a bullfight poster or a painting on velvet of a pinto pony at sundown.

"Perhaps we can find you an art gallery in town," Thurlene said, with what I could have sworn was sarcasm.

I was fascinated with the shop that sold antique Apache weapons. I'd never known such a wide variety of tomahawks existed, or two-foot-long wooden-handled clubs with carved animal heads on the end.

I said to Thurlene, "I wonder if the Apaches turn these out as quick as the antique club makers in St. Andrews turn out their relics for the tourists. They've taken hickory and rust to a new artistic level over there."

She said, "Nobody's going to trick you, are they, Jack?"

"Not if I can help it," I said. "One day my mother tried to tell me that pickles were cucumbers, prunes were plums, and raisins were grapes. I said, 'Come on, Mom—what kind of fool do you take me for?' "

There was a surprise for the ladies before we left the corridor of shops and boutiques.

We ran into Debbie Wendell and Tang Chen.

Ginger and the mom had seen Tang Chen's name in the pairings for Thursday's first round, but they'd thought it must be a typo. Yet here she was, back in the States, back on the tour.

Debbie Wendell said, "Hi, Gin . . . Miz Clayton . . . Mr. Brannon."

Ginger smiled, looked friendly. Thurlene managed a nod before she tossed them in the refrigerator.

To me, Debbie said, "This is my friend Tang Chen. She's the best lady golfer in China."

Tang Chen said, "I am from Beijing. You have been?"

"I haven't had the pleasure," I said. "Are you a Communist?"

"No, no, no," Tang Chen said. "I am golfer. No Communist. Only government Communist. In China people different from government. People want to play golf, own McDonald's."

Debbie said, "Tang has fallen in love with American Indians. She bought a book so she can learn to speak Apache."

The Chinese girl said, "Ka-ya-ten-atee-nod!"

"Oh, for Christ sake," Thurlene said. "We should be going."

I said, "I know what that means if it's Mescalero dialect."

Thurlene looked at me.

"What does it mean?" Debbie asked eagerly.

I said, "It means, 'I want to shoot John Wayne and rape Natalie Wood.'"

Debbie blinked, thought it over, giggled. Ginger did the same thing. The Chinese girl looked puzzled.

"Hey!" said Debbie. "I got a tattoo Monday, in downtown Ruidoso."

"You did not!" Ginger said.

"It's only temporary. Want to see it?"

Debbie pulled up the slip-over golf shirt she was wearing and displayed her midsection. Below her navel with the rhinestone in it was the tattoo. An American flag postage stamp and three words:

Lick Me Here.

"I don't believe you!" Ginger said.

"Your mother must be very proud," Thurlene said coldly.

"Mom hasn't seen it yet," Debbie said. "I'm going to wait till I have a really good round before I show it to her. I think it's funny."

"I'm sure Ann will think it's hilarious," Thurlene said.

"Play good tomorrow," Debbie said to Ginger.

"You too," Ginger said back.

As we walked away we heard Tang Chen behind us, saying, "Is-zain-naad-zon-bahtee-eeche."

Thurlene glanced at me. "Which means . . . ?"

"One Big Mac, large Coke, fries."

———

21

Ginger Clayton's 66 in the first round, four under par, was carved out of the slopes with a new set of clubs, a new caddie, and only one practice round behind her. It was almost as remarkable as the way I handled the golf cart on the asphalt path that curved sharply around the death-defying turns on the mountainous layout.

Thurlene jumped out and opted to walk after three holes.

"I don't have enough Xanax with me to ride in this thing with you," she said.

The golf cart was provided for me by the genial tournament director of the Speedy Arrow Energy Bar Classic. His name was Hoyt Newkirk, a man in his seventies, paunchy, thick-lipped, wearing a white Stetson and a light blue Western-cut shirt with double breast pockets.

Hoyt was from Ruidoso by way of Abilene, Odessa, Midland, and Las Vegas, and he was the general manager of the casino, hotel, country club, and bordering real estate development.

I found Hoyt Newkirk likable right off. He rode in the cart with me over the last nine holes of Ginger's round, which at the end of Thursday gave her a two-stroke lead on the field.

"I knowed I had a lock on the deal when I scared up my first Indian," Hoyt said. "You get you a Indian to ask the federal gubmint for something, you can get anything you want. Indians make the gubmint feel guilty, don't you see? Ain't nothin' else to it."

"Your first Indian was Sinking Canoe or Smokes Loco Weed?"

"Canoe come first. He has a particle of sense. He brought in Loco, who thinks yesterday is next week. That Indian will smoke anything he can strike a match to. Smoke your pants leg if you stand still. Smokes gypsum weed, if you can 'magine that. It's where he got his name."

"What kind of business interest do you have in all this?"

"I got a taste of the casino, plus the real estate deal . . . Golf shot!"

Ginger had clubfaced a four-iron into the middle of the par-five thirteenth green in two.

"I believe that there's my head pro carryin' her golf bag."

"He volunteered. Ginger's regular caddie didn't show up."

"Some of these girlies can play good, can't they?"

"Yes, they can."

"They don't all dive for the frog hair, do they?"

"You mean are any of them straight?"

"What'd I say?"

"More are straight now than the old days. I'd say the majority."

"That there pretty little Ginger. She's straight, is she?"

"Uh-huh," I said. "All that and golf shots too."

"Son," he said, delighted to hear it. "She's stronger than laundry."

We rode along for three holes. We watched Ginger and Linda Merle Draper, the competitor Ginger was paired with. Debbie Wendell and a South Korean American were two holes ahead. Three holes back were Tang Chen and another South Korean American.

Going by the big scoreboard that hung on a ledge behind the fifteenth green, Debbie was two under par, having a good round, holding down second place behind Ginger.

It occurred to me that if Debbie could make it to the house with a 68 or 69, she would show her mother the tattoo.

"I enjoy a wager," Hoyt said nonchalantly.

"That's hard to believe, Hoyt," I said. "A man from Abilene . . . Odessa . . . Midland?"

"I'm seventy-six but I can shoot my age if you let me tee it up everywhere, even in the bunkers."

"I'll bet you can too, Hoyt."

"I like them dope dealers. They come out here with cigar boxes full of cash . . . nothin' else to do with it but give it to me on the golf course."

"Do the dope dealers let you tee it up everywhere?"

"I name the game. They spring for it."

"It doesn't sound like much of a wager."

"Best kind, is what it is."

"Do you ever go to the track in Ruidoso?"

"I can't beat animals. I can't beat the jockeys either. Them little warts can pull an elephant . . . they'll put you in the can like Maxwell House coffee. I stick with humans. I can beat humans. Lots of humans think they're smart. Hell, I used to win money on the Miss America pageant."

"You bet on the Miss America pageant?"

"I went up there for twenty-five years. A bunch of us would go together, stay at the Ambassador Hotel. Jimmy Choo Choo from Amarillo, Eddie Wing Tips from Dallas, Both Hands Billy Bridges from Houston, Green Sheet Garvey from Tulsa, Circus Face Jordan from Fort Worth."

I said, "You must have had a nickname."

He said, "Aw, some folks called me 'Halftime Hoyt' in those days. Biggest lock I ever had in the Miss America was Phyllis Ann George from Denton, Texas. She won it in 'seventy-one. Actually, she was my *second* biggest lock that year. My mortal lock was Nebraska over Alabama in the Orange Bowl."

"Did you ever have another lock in the Miss America?"

"Tara Dawn Holland in 'ninety-seven. She come from Kansas. There was something about the name. I had her all the way. I quit goin' when they moved the pageant out of Atlantic City. I don't pay much attention to it anymore. You married, Jack?"

"What . . . ?"

I was watching Ginger drain a ten-foot birdie putt.

"I was askin' if you're married."

"Not now. I'm a two-time loser."

"Ain't nothin' to be embarrassed about—or take pride in either, for that matter. I'm on number four. We're close to the same thing as happy."

"Congratulations."

"She's a Jap, is why."

"Oh . . . ?"

"Name's Miyuki. If you go at it again, Jack, you ought to get you a Jap. You don't have to go over to Hawaii. I found Miyuki in L.A. Japs is good-natured. They're hard workers. They're real clean. They don't know shit to talk about. Most of your Japs come a little light on the tits, but you can have that taken care of."

"Thank you, Hoyt. I'll keep that in mind."

"What done it for me, the first time I seen Miyuki, she reminded me of that woman in *Love Is a Many-Splendored Thing*. The old movie? I love that old movie, but they shouldn't have killed William Holden. He had the good sport coats."

"Are you talking about Jennifer Jones? She played Han Suyin."

"That who it was?"

"I'm pretty sure her character in the movie is supposed to be Chinese or Eurasian. She wasn't Japanese."

"She wasn't? I should have scared me up one of them Hand Sueys instead of a Miyuki. They're clean too, I reckon."

We were behind the eighteenth green. I'd driven the cart up on the rise so we could sit and watch Ginger finish her round. She was down the hill, back on the tee. The scoreboard on the veranda revealed that Debbie Wendell had come in with a 68. Debbie was the leader in the clubhouse, to coin a phrase.

There wasn't much gallery on the course. It was therefore easy to spot Thurlene trudging up the left side of the fairway toward the green. Despite the fact that she'd been up and down the hills today, she looked plenty good in her khaki skirt that hit her about four inches above the knee and her snug white knit top that was starting to make her look like she was entered in a wet golf shirt contest.

I'd pointed out Ginger's mother to Hoyt Newkirk earlier on the back nine. He'd said they were a jam-up mother-daughter combo, the kind that would entice a man to buy them automobiles in assorted colors. Good-looking women like slick automobiles, he said. It had been his experience that new cars made women horny.

"You sure you ain't been there with the mama?" he said.

"Not even close, but that doesn't mean it hasn't crossed my mind. She's something, isn't she?"

"Make a mummy over there in Egypt hammer on his box, is all."

"We've become friends," I said. "I like the kid too."

Hoyt said it had been his experience as he traveled the road of life that friendship tended to get in the way of cooze.

"*Cooze*," I said. "I haven't heard that word since high school."

"You got a word you like better? Some folks prefer *juicy*."

I was thinking about it when Hoyt's cell phone beeped.

Answering, he said, "It's me. Go ahead on."

"Uh-huh," he said. A pause. "Uh-huh . . . that's a pile of it . . . uh-huh."

Hoyt looked at me. "It's Canoe. You ain't gonna believe this."

Back on the phone, he said, "Uh-huh. Limping Turkey said that? . . . Uh-huh." Another pause. "Smells a Possum is part of it too, is he? . . . Here's what you do. You tell them two drop cases if they put my golf tournament in a jackpot, they're gonna think the whole damn United States cavalry is after their war-paint asses."

He hung up.

"Ain't no end to trouble in this world," he said. "Two local piss-ants, Limping Turkey and Smells a Possum, they're talking about organizing a protest out here Saturday. They're threatening to bring a thousand 'social conscious' residents to dance around and holler and disrupt things. They say they've discovered that Burch Webb, the architect we give a million-five to design the golf course . . . they say he 'knowingly' and 'with careless disregard' designed and built this eighteenth green on top of a sacred Apache burial ground."

"Is it possible?" I asked innocently.

Hoyt said, "Who gives a shit? It's not like I went and throwed a bunch of bent grass on top of live Indians."

"What are you going to do?"

I could have sworn he grinned.

He said, "Aw, I been in worse traps than this, don't you see?"

22

The commissioner of the LPGA, Marsha Wilson, arrived at the Mescalero Country Club & Casino Resort on Thursday afternoon and left notes for Thurlene and me, insisting that we join her and a group of other "important people" for dinner that evening. Cocktails at seven thirty. She had arranged for a private dining room in the lodge that would be easy to find. It was directly across the hall from Dances with Jalapeños.

Ginger Clayton, the tournament leader, was taken to dinner that night by her new caddie, Tyler Hughes. He wanted to show her that there was a "gourmet" restaurant in downtown Ruidoso.

I told Thurlene that the last time I was in downtown Ruidoso a restaurant qualified as "gourmet" if it didn't have ketchup.

We went to the commissioner's dinner together, and you would be guessing correctly if you said I was startled by the sight of Marsha Wilson. She was in a buckskin skirt and jacket with fringe hanging off it, and animal-skin boots, and she wore a beaded Apache headband with a feather sticking up in the back.

Other than that, the commissioner looked like everybody's aunt who'd always worked in ready-to-wear and dyed her hair shoe-polish black.

"Jack Brannon, Jack Brannon!" the commissioner squealed as she pumped my hand. "I am so thoroughly, genuinely delighted to hear you have discovered our wonderful world of women's golf! I have heard nothing but good reviews about your visit to Toppy and Connie's. Aren't they the cutest couple in the world? And generous!

May I say bravo for our sport? May I say *grrreat* for our sport? May I gush?"

"May she?" I said to Thurlene.

"She may."

Undaunted, the commissioner said, "Jack Brannon, Jack Brannon, I am *so* happy you are here. I must tell you how much I love—love, love, love—*SM* magazine! Dare I say it is my sports bible?"

"Dare she?" Again to Thurlene.

Thurlene nodded her approval.

Still undaunted, the commissioner said, "The major reason—major, major, major reason—I am thrilled you are here with us is because this little raffle—the Speedy Arrow Energy Bar Classic—is my very own brainstorm. How did it come to me, you ask?"

"I did?"

"It came to me when I was eating—yes, yes, yes—a Speedy Arrow Energy Bar. It was on the corner of Sixty-third and Madison Avenue. So full of nutrition. The brown rice, the oats, the barley malt, the roasted soybeans, the palm kernel oil, the rice crisps . . . the sugar cane drippings."

"That's it?" I said. "No amphetamines?"

The commissioner pressed onward. "To myself, I said, I must have Speedy Arrow for a title sponsor. That's when I called Rusty Morrison, Speedy's vice president in charge of marketing. You'll meet Rusty. He'll be along. Rusty and I go way back. But that's another interesting story. Rusty came on board *el pronto*. Now I needed a venue. Somewhere out West. I thought of Ruidoso. I'd heard of Mescalero. New. Needs exposure. The old marketing mind ticking away. What did I do? I called Hoyt Newkirk and asked him if he liked to sell dirt. That's real estate talk. He said, 'Does a brown bear . . . ?' Well, I won't repeat it, but it was a yes. So here we are!"

There are times—and this was one of them—when a man wished he had gotten himself boxed before he arrived at the dinner party.

The slouchy teenage girl in the dirty jeans who was taking drink orders didn't look like she could handle a Bombay Sapphire gin martini with four olives. She wasn't an Apache American or a Mexican American. She was more on the order of a High School Dropout

American. I made it easy for her. I asked her to bring me a Budweiser. Thurlene asked for a glass of white wine.

Hoyt Newkirk wasn't free to join us, the commissioner said. A problem concerning the golf course would be keeping him busy for the next two days. "I understand it's nothing strenuously important," Marsha said.

Thurlene said, "That would be the worst kind, wouldn't it?"

Two of the commissioner's underlings were in attendance. Monique, I knew. The snooty interview lady. Monique Hopkins. The other one introduced herself. She was Claudia Bradley, a businesslike woman in her forties who could slide by as attractive if you like bangs.

Claudia proudly told us that she was the LPGA's new deputy commissioner, and she was excited about the "challenge." She had "come over" from the U.S. Golf Association, where she had been an expert on rules. She could still play to a four, she said.

When Rusty Morrison arrived I watched Marsha and Claudia engage in something of a footrace to see who could reach him first. Claudia let Marsha win.

They led the Speedy Arrow VP of marketing over to me as soon as they finished hugging on him, or as soon as he could struggle free. Rusty was a smooth guy who may not have undergone more than one dewrinkle job. He wore creased jeans, Guccis, and no socks, and his sweatshirt might have distracted anyone who read "Eat Me" on the front and didn't bother to notice the likeness of a Speedy Arrow Energy Bar under the words.

By way of introducing him to anyone, the commissioner said, "Here he is—the man, the man, the man! Would we be here without him? No! Do we love him? Yes!"

"Exactly!" the deputy commissioner said.

Looking more or less unimpressed to meet either Thurlene or the writer from New York, Rusty Morrison said, "I have been in telephone *purgatory* since I arrived. Voices, voices! Life is a torture. An absolute torture. Why did Herman Einstein invent the telephone? Weren't we happier with our carrier pigeons, our parchment, our quills? Time didn't fly by, leave us so out of breath, my God! There was no twenty-four-hour news cycle where we can watch the world crumble away in ruins, hourly. People used to sail away on ships and stayed gone *forever*, didn't they? And when they returned nothing had really changed, had it? I mean, people who stayed home were still wearing the same clothes! You see it in films."

"To be continued," I said to Rusty, and pulled Thurlene away.

It was surprising to find that two of the older golfers had been invited. Jan Dunn and Linda Merle Draper. They were standing in a corner talking with a short, slender gentleman in a dark blue pinstriped suit, dark glasses, and slicked-down black hair. He looked about half foreign.

Thurlene whispered that Jan and Linda Merle had obviously been invited because they were the two current player reps on the LPGA's board of directors. They'd been elected by a vote of the competitors.

She explained that there were six other members of the board, none of whom were present. They were captains of commerce whose names wouldn't mean anything to me. But I could be assured that they had been handpicked by Marsha Wilson and were safely in the commissioner's pocket on every issue.

I asked what a member of the board received in return for loyalty to the commissioner.

"Free trips."

"What kind?"

"Oh, golfing weekends to Pine Valley, Augusta National, Pebble Beach, St. Andrews. Take the whole family to Paris for a week. Or take them to London, Venice, Zurich, Hamburg, Athens. Travel on a corporate jet. Nothing but the best hotels. Mostly a variety of things the average person would kill for."

"Sounds like my life."

"Is that a fact?"

"Except for the private jet—and I don't have to go to meetings."

"Or run a corporation."

"That's no trouble. Corporations are run by middle-age executive secretary ladies who wear black and drink lattes. They make one twenty-five a year but work seven days a week running the corporation so the CEO can make seventy-nine million a year and go to

Pebble Beach and St. Andrews. Let's go say hello to Jan and Linda Merle."

"Let's."

Though I hadn't formally met Jan and Linda Merle, they pretended to know me and said they were aware I'd been at the Firm Chick last week, and they understood I was working on a story about Ginger Clayton.

Linda Merle's hair was down, she wore a dress and heels, and she could have passed for a PTA mother. Jan was in slacks, shirt, blazer, and her hair was cut short, the kind of style that makes women look like they go to my barbershop.

"Ginger is the next great player," Jan Dunn said. "I don't say this because Thurlene is standing here. Ginger has it all."

Linda Merle Draper said, "She can't be anything but good for our tour . . . with her combination of looks and talent."

Jan Dunn said, "What do you know about our tour, Mr. Brannon, if anything? Aside from the fact that Ginger Clayton is a dish?"

"I'm no big authority on it," I said, "but I covered Annika at Colonial and found myself rooting for her to do good. I know something about your history . . . who your immortals are. I know Patty Berg won fifteen majors . . . Mickey Wright won thirteen including four U.S. Opens . . . Babe Zaharias and Louise Suggs both won ten majors . . . so has Annika. Betsy Rawls won eight, and she's the only other player with four U.S. Opens. Juli Inkster and Karrie Webb have seven . . . Kathy Whitworth has six. You two have four each. Jan, you've won two Dinah Shores, or I should say Nabiscos, and two LPGAs. Linda Merle, if I'm not mistaken, you have an Open, a Dinah-Nabisco, and two LPGA championships."

Jan smiled. "You can stay in the room, Jack."

I said, "I think you people ought to right the wrongs of history . . . give Mickey Wright fourteen and Kathy Whitworth seven. They both won the Dinah before it was a major, but it soon was."

"I'll go with that," Jan said.

"Oh, my goodness!" Linda Merle said. "You people haven't met

Francois! Thurlene Clayton, Jack Brannon . . . this is our distinguished visitor—Francois D'Auby La Foo."

That's what I thought I heard. His actual name was Francois D'Aubigne Lagoutte.

He didn't offer a handshake.

Jan Dunn said, "Francois is from Paris."

"Bordeaux," he said.

"That's right, Bordeaux," Jan said. "Which part?"

"All," he said.

Linda Merle said, "I hope Francois doesn't mind me saying that *Forbes* magazine lists him as one of the ten richest men in the world."

"*Cinq,*" Francois said flatly. Another correction.

"Boy, top five now!" Linda Merle said. "We're moving up. How about that, folks?"

Thurlene smiled. I tried.

Jan said, "Francois came here in his private plane from his home in France."

"Many homes," Francois said.

I wondered if he was making a joke.

Jan said, "He has many homes in France. You have a Citation jet, don't you?"

"The Citation *Deece.*"

Linda Merle said, "Francois came all the way here for the bombshell Marsha is going to drop tonight—and tomorrow at her press conference."

"Bombshell?" I said. "I'm into bombshells."

"You're getting a sneak preview tonight after dinner."

"But it's a bombshell? You promise?"

"I'll say!"

23

Over the years I've lived in trembling horror of dinner parties where the host might announce, "I hope you don't mind, but I've taken the liberty to order for all of us."

At one time or another in my troubled dinner-party past, this has resulted in . . .

Tripe and onions.
Haggis.
Prairie oysters.
Gator tail.
Fried liver.

So it was that when Marsha Wilson said she had taken the liberty to order for all of us after we were seated at the table in the private room, I was prepared for the worst—and she didn't disappoint me.

Sushi tacos.

By way of preparing for the worst, I had slyly taken the precaution of slipping the waitress, the High School Dropout American, a hundred-dollar bill and kindly asking her to run over to Fattest Woman on the second floor of the casino and bring me back a bean and cheese burrito.

"Do whut . . . ?" the waitress had said, gawking at the hundred.

I repeated the request, slowly, clearly, and told her she could keep the change, and stressed that I hoped and prayed she would make it back to me in less than an hour.

She did. No more than fifteen minutes passed before my bean and cheese burrito from Fattest Woman turned up.

Headline: Man Avoids Idiotic Tacos.

I was pleased to find that my burrito was only slightly larger than Arnold Schwarzenegger's forearm.

The waitress said, "This didn't cost me nuthin'. Kin I still keep the hunnert you give me?"

"You can," I said.

She said, "Dang, I'm quittin' this stinkin' job right now."

And she was outta there.

Sitting between Thurlene and Jan Dunn, I took pleasure in watching them push aside their beet and okra salad with chipotle sauce, and then push aside their untouched sushi tacos, hence to accept the offer I made of part of my burrito.

Most of us had passed on the banana daiquiri yogurt sundae for dessert by the time the commissioner stood up and rang on a glass.

"Friends and loved ones," she said. "The things I am privileged to tell you tonight are undoubtedly the most important words I will speak in my lifetime. In fact, I believe I will go so far as to say these words will be remembered as the most important words anyone connected with the game of golf will ever have spoken. When I say this news is enormously big, I stress big, big, big."

"Exactly," said Claudia Bradley, sitting on the commissioner's right.

"Tomorrow morning," the commissioner said, "a simple Friday in March, the world will awaken to the news on network TV, in the *Wall Street Journal,* and, well, heaven knows where else, that Le Compagnie Lagoutte has purchased Kraft Foods, the world's largest manufacturer of food products, a division of Altria. Kraft Foods has been bought by Le Compagnie Lagoutte. Needless to say, the financial terms are known only to Altria and our special guest this evening, my dear friend Francois D'Aubigne Lagoutte. That's right—I see you people nodding! Francois is an owner of Le Compagnie Lagoutte!"

"*The,*" Francois said. "The only."

"*Excusez-moi* and correctomento!" Marsha said. "Francois is *the* owner of Le Compagnie Lagoutte!"

Francois shook his head approvingly.

The commissioner continued. "This news will be addressed in my press conference tomorrow morning here at the lodge, and so will the things I shall now share with you. By the by, Monique has arranged for a rather impressive list of media to be present . . . aside from our new good friend Jack Brannon with *SM* magazine. I believe we will have the *Albuquerque Journal*, the *Roswell Record*, the *Clovis Daily*, the *Santa Fe New Mexican*, the *Los Alamos Exploder*, the *Ruidoso Bugle* . . . the AP . . . and our capable Monique Hopkins will be filing for *USA Today*."

"Exactly," Claudia Bradley said.

"Where shall I begin?" the commissioner said.

Rusty Morrison, who'd had more than one vod, interrupted to say, "I'm often tempted to begin by saying I come from humble orgins, but of course I don't."

"Darling Rusty," said Marsha. "Clever as always."

"Can we get to it?" Francois said in perfect English.

Marsha did precisely that. The bombshells the commissioner dropped on her listeners were these:

Le Compagnie Lagoutte, as we may or may not realize, was the world's largest maker and distributor of horse meat and dog food, a fact that Francois was very proud of. Francois had many other "holdings," but horse meat and dog food were his "storefronts."

In buying Kraft Foods, Francois acquired the Kraft Nabisco golf tournament and was increasing the prize money by $1 million. This meant $500,000 for the winner. The biggest first-place check of any of the four major championships.

The LPGA's board of directors had voted unanimously to allow Francois to change the name of the tournament to something that he, himself, came up with—Le Grand Cheval et Petit Chien Classique.

Indeed, that was how next week's first major of the season was going to be known, now and in the future. A hasty change, to be sure, but the pieces had been put in place behind the scenes. No doubt the press would shorten the name.

Incidentally, the winner's trophy would have a new name—the Lagoutte-Dinah Cup. Keeping Dinah Shore's name involved was, of course, a way of paying respect to the past. This was something Francois generously gave in on during the discussions, after arguing, rather convincingly, that Dinah, after all, had been dead twenty years.

The tour would be sad to leave Mission Hills in Rancho Mirage—where the championship had been played since 1972—but Francois had purchased Hollywood Dunes Country Club in Palm Springs, an old course that had been redone by Burch Webb. It would be a marvelous venue.

Francois had played Hollywood Dunes and was particularly fond of the fourteenth hole, the ninety-nine-yard downhill par-three with no bunkers and no water.

The commissioner concluded by saying, "Am I bothered by the fact that our tour now has a French sponsor that sells horse meat for human consumption? Not in the least. Francois hopes to popularize horse meat in this country, as his family has for years and years overseas. As Francois and I both say, if it's good enough for France, Belgium, and Italy, it should be good enough for the United States. And by the way, isn't the world becoming a more richly diversified place by the day? Well, there you have it. The whole ball of wax."

I raised a hand to ask a question.

"Yes, Jack," Marsha said.

"My French is a little slipshod," I said. "Does the new name of the tournament translate into the Dog Horse Classic or the Horse Dog Classic?"

"Oh, Jack," she said. "You are such a devil."

24

S plashed across the front of the *Ruidoso Bugle* Friday morning was the wire story concerning women's golf, Palm Springs, Dinah Shore, the wealthy Frenchman, and horse meat for humans. But the piece I found more intriguing was spread along the bottom of the front page. It dealt with the discovery of a historical event that occurred locally on August 23, 1881, and involved a fierce battle between a band of courageous Apache warriors and three dozen troopers from the U.S. Seventh Cavalry Regiment.

The headline said:

SCORE ONE FOR THE HOME TEAM!

The byline read:

By P. W. (Pecan Waffle) Spurlock

The writer opened up by saying that the battle took place on the very site of the Mescalero Country Club golf course. In fact, the thirty-seven doomed troopers that engaged in hand-to-hand combat with the Apaches, including the commanding officer, Col. Bright Finnegan, were buried where they fell, which was underneath the eighteenth green, a par-four.

The battle was known to most historians of the Indian Wars, according to P. W. (Pecan Waffle) Spurlock, as "Finnegan's Folly."

There ought to be a monument near the eighteenth green at Mescalero, the writer suggested. Not a monument to honor the soldiers who paid the price for attempting to seek revenge for Gen. George Armstrong Custer and the Battle of Little Bighorn, which had occurred five years earlier, but for the gallant Apaches "who won a big one for Native Americans of yesteryear and today as well."

The writer said the people of Ruidoso and the surrounding territory should be proud to learn that two local residents were related to the biggest Apache heroes in the engagement.

One was Limping Turkey, the great-great-grandson of Chief Sitting Turkey, who is credited with planning and leading the surprise attack on the arrogant troopers of the U.S. Seventh Cavalry. Limping Turkey was best known today as the pleasant fellow who retrieves your grocery carts in the parking lot at Wal-Mart.

Smells a Possum, the other local, was the great-great-grandson of Tall Possum, the Apache brave who disarmed Col. Bright Finnegan and clubbed him to death with the colonel's own fifty-two-caliber short-barreled carbine. Smells a Possum, the writer said, would be familiar to all those who have bought one of his wood carvings of a possum at Stuff & Things on Sudderth Drive, the main street in downtown Ruidoso.

I was reading the paper over breakfast in the coffee shop. My breakfast consisted of three fried eggs over medium that had been served with the yolks already broken and seeping under the three strips of raw bacon while the cold, stringy hash browns had been plopped down on top of two slices of unripe cantaloupe.

Hoyt Newkirk came in with a mug of coffee and sat across the table from me. He looked at ease with himself.

"What's the name of your chef here?" I said. "Hates Breakfast?"

Hoyt said the chef, David, wasn't no Indian.

I said, "David must be a terrorist, then."

"Naw, he's just one of them hippies from bygone days who liked to shut down college campuses. Life ain't been fun for him since."

"I wish he hadn't thought of my breakfast this morning as the administration building."

Nodding at the newspaper, Hoyt said, "You read all of it yet?"

I said, "I'm reading it again, trying to decide which parts I like best. It's a work of art."

"I like them diaries," Hoyt said. "I had some input."

I laughed.

"You think them diaries is funny?"

"I do."

The diaries were to support the story in the *Ruidoso Bugle*. What made them even funnier to me was that P. W. (Pecan Waffle) Spurlock, who claimed he had obtained the diaries from an "undisclosed source," wrote that the diaries had been kept by Maj. Marcus Reno and Capt. Frederick Benteen, two members of the Seventh Cavalry who had escaped the slaughter of "Finnegan's Folly." And what made *this* funny was that, if my memory of history was correct, Major Reno and Captain Benteen were the same two famous officers who'd survived the Battle of Little Bighorn.

I said, "Hoyt, don't you find it, well, ironic as well as a miracle that Major Reno and Captain Benteen survived both massacres, Little Bighorn and here?"

"Yeah, ain't that somethin'?" he said.

I laughed again.

Hoyt said, "Son, you don't want to miss the big picture here."

I said, "You can show me the big picture after you tell me what your writer is getting out of it . . . Mr. P. W. Spurlock. Sorry, but it's hard for me to refer to a fellow writer as Pecan Waffle."

"This ain't for your magazine, is it?"

"It's too good for a magazine. I'll save it for the memoir."

"Now you're talkin'," he said. "Mr. P. W. Spurlock has been made a full-fledged member of Mescalero Country Club, only he won't pay monthly dues. Aside from that, he'll be receiving a five-thousand-dollar line of credit at the casino."

"Nice. I'm glad *somebody's* making money out of journalism."

Hoyt said, "The story in today's newspaper saved my golf course and this golf tournament. That's your big picture, Jack. Sinking Canoe spoke to Limping Turkey and Smells a Possum this morning. He called up to make sure they'd seen the paper. They had. Canoe informed me an hour ago that Limp and Possum ain't gonna organize a protest Saturday 'cause there ain't anything to protest no longer, don't you see? What they're gonna do instead is organize a celebration around the eighteenth green. It'll take place when the tournament's over. They'll be celebratin' the fact that there's cavalry soldiers buried down there underneath the bent grass green—no dead Apaches whatsoever."

I said, "Hoyt, do you realize you're telling me all this news with a straight face?"

"Straight as a Indian goes to shit," he said.

25

S how me somebody who never has a problem with a computer and I'll show you a ten-year-old on a skateboard.

After breakfast there wasn't much to do but skip the commissioner's press conference, have lunch, and wait around for the tournament leaders, Ginger Clayton and Debbie Wendell, to tee off in the last group at one thirty. So I went to my room and opened up my trusty laptop. Thought I'd make some notes and go online to see what catastrophes had occurred in the world overnight.

But when I opened the laptop, it greeted me with something I'd never seen before—a blue screen with peculiar words and numbers on it.

The worst thing was, I couldn't get rid of it, no matter what. The mouse was useless and the machine wouldn't even let me turn it off. I unplugged it and plugged it back in. The screen was still blue.

I petted it and stroked it and promised it a trip to Europe. I begged it to talk to me. I punched around on the toolbar. I held down keys and clicked on others. I picked it up and shook it.

Finally, I thought of one last thing to do before I threw it against the wall and called it a motherfucking piece of worthless cocksucking shit.

I called Thurlene's room and asked if she or Ginger knew anything about computers.

Thurlene said, "I know very little, but Ginger knows everything. We travel with her laptop."

I said, "Mine's been invaded by evil little people who want to chase me to a rubber room. I hate to bother Ginger on a game day, but do you think she'd mind taking a look at it? Maybe she knows the secret words to whisper to it."

"She'll be happy to look at it. She's selecting her outfit for the day. I'll send her around as soon as she's dressed. Please don't keep her long. She needs to hit balls and putt for an hour before she plays."

"I won't waste her time," I said. "If she thinks the disease is irreversible, that's good enough for me. I'll fire a jump shot at the recycle bin and head for Office Depot."

Ginger brought her own laptop to my room. She was dressed for what she expected to be a chilly day in the mountains. She nicely filled out a pair of tan corduroy pants and wore a gray V-neck cashmere sweater over a red cotton turtleneck.

"I appreciate you coming," I said. "It's either something simple or it's going to die screaming. All I know about computers is I can turn it on and off . . . I can e-mail . . . I can attach . . . I can go to Drudge and read stuff. I've recently mastered the art of cut and paste, and I can Google."

She said, "Good, Jack. You're way ahead of most grown-ups."

She placed her laptop on a table beside mine and did numerous things with plugs in the two machines and in the wall.

When she sat down and opened up my laptop and saw the screen, she actually laughed.

"Ah-ha!" she said. "The blue screen of death!"

The Blue Screen of Death? Harry Potter and the Blue Screen of Death? Indiana Jones and the Blue Screen of Death?

"You're familiar with the problem?" I said. "This blue screen of death thing?"

"Yep," she said.

Her fingers danced over the keys, her machine and my machine. "Can you fix it?"

"Yep."

"That's great. That's beyond great."

"Want me to tell it not to do this again?"

"By all means—if it wants to live."

Her fingers danced again. One minute. Two minutes.

"Done!" she said. "You're all set."

I had rarely been as impressed with anything, and told her so.

She closed her own laptop and said, "I don't have to rush off. You got a Coke in the minibar, Jack?"

"I'm sure I do," I said. I got the minibar open after putting the key in the wrong way twice, threatening it, and kicking it. Gave her the Coke.

Ginger said, "My mom likes you a lot, Jack. A *lot* . . . if you know what I mean."

I said, "Your mom is a dynamite lady. I like her a lot too. But how do you know she likes me a lot—if you know what I mean?"

"I can tell."

"How can you tell?"

"Lots of ways."

"Give me one."

"She's smoking more."

"Give me another one."

"She won't talk about you."

I said, "Boy, I can see where that would be a dead giveaway. She won't talk about me."

"It is! I say, 'How's Jack?' She says 'Fine.' I say, 'He's a neat guy.' She says, 'I suppose.' I say, 'He's a good-looking guy.' She hums and says, 'Do you think so?' I say, 'What do you two talk about when you're together?' She says, 'Nothing.' I say, 'That's all?' She says, 'Whatever.' I ask if she's not interested in you, why does it take her so long to pick out something to wear before she goes to meet you? She says, 'Don't be silly.' "

"Has she gone out with many guys since the divorce?"

"Losers."

"Losers?"

"She comes home and says now she knows everything there is to know about building strip malls."

I smiled. "Tell me about your dad."

She gave me a long look.

I said, "You don't have to if you don't want to."

"Is this for your story?"

"Nope, Just for me. The guy your mom likes a lot."

"My dad is a loser jerk."

I only looked at her.

"He's a liar and a thief too," she said.

I said, "It sounds like he's moving up on the grand slam. Is this you talking or with your mother's input?"

"It's me."

"Your mom told me about him taking the money that was supposed to belong to you."

"He was a loser jerk before that. I hate to say it since he's, like, my own father, but I think there are people in the world who are just no damn good. He's one of them. My mom is gorgeous, intelligent, witty . . . like, really quick, energetic, a hard worker . . . Well, you know . . . And he let her get away. How smart is that?"

"Your mom is blessed, Ginger. It's against the rules for teenage girls to like their mothers. You're a refreshing exception."

"They don't have a mom like mine. My dad never appeciated her. He always put her down . . . always acted like she was lucky to be married to *him*. For as long as I can remember. I'm sure he hit her sometimes. I know he batted her around. She'll never admit it. She should have dumped him a long time ago. Jesus."

"But he got you interested in golf, didn't he?"

"That's a myth."

"It is?"

"My mom did it. When I was like eight or nine. She saw me out in the backyard swinging her seven-iron. I'd watched golf tournaments on TV. I had a natural swing, Mom said. So she started working with me. We'd play together on this public course. Mom has a good swing too. She can still break eighty. She'd read instruction books and articles and give me swing tips. She always encouraged anything I was interested in. I know she would rather have had me on the golf course than sticking pins in my body and experimenting with drugs . . . which I really can't understand anybody doing. We played so much golf together. I loved it."

"What did your dad think about it?"

"He was embarrassed. He'd rather have had a cheerleader in the family. *He* was the golfer. Yeah, sure. Like he ever beat anybody. But when I started to win juniors, he took credit for it."

"Do you talk to him much?"

"Now and then. He calls. He says, 'Way to go.' He says I should have laid up instead of going for it. Stuff like that. I don't really hate him. I just . . . feel sorry for him. He's not a bad person or anything. He's just kind of, you know, good for nothing."

I glanced at my watch. "You still have time to practice. I want to ask you about something else."

"The Debbie thing, right?"

"You're as quick as your mom. Yeah, the Debbie thing. I'm intrigued. I'm curious."

She sighed. "I don't know what to think about it, honestly."

"What do you *think* you think?"

"It's hard for me to believe Debbie wants to hurt me. We've known each other forever. We're friends, you know? The only reason it might be true—the poison thing—is my mom believes it."

"And your mom is usually right about things, huh?"

"She is. Definitely."

"What about the Chinese girl?"

"I don't know anything about Tang. She's from, like, *China*, right? She's a terrible player. She can't keep it on the world. I don't know why she keeps trying. Man, if she's the best they've got in China . . . I guess I have to say she's a little flip-o too. She wants to learn how to speak *Apache*? Where do you go with *that*?"

"Debbie's mother," I said. "How do you feel about Ann Wendell?"

Ginger shrugged. "She acts nice and friendly, but . . . look out, man. She's Cruella de Vil."

"You should get going," I said.

"Yeah, I should."

We high-fived.

"Play good," I said. "Make us proud."

"You got it!"

26

Although Debbie Wendell shot a 68 in the first round of the Speedy Arrow Energy Bar Classic, her lowest LPGA score to date, it was a given that she'd pay dearly for the tattoo on her tummy. Friday morning, looking at her face you'd think she'd wised off to Joan Crawford.

The dark glasses didn't completely cover up the purple around her left eye, and her swollen jaw was turning the color of red beans and rice.

Her golf swing looked slightly restricted as well. Probably the result of three or four body blows.

Thurlene had agreed to ride in the cart with me if she could drive, and we caught up with Ann Wendell walking in the Ginger-Debbie gallery on the front nine. We both were eager to hear the mother's version of what happened to her daughter's face.

She pulled up next to Ann Wendell along the gallery ropes and asked the question.

Ann Wendell said, "The poor child. There are times when she simply seems to be unlucky. Last night she came out of the bathroom and tripped over the coffee table in our living room and fell down hard on the entrance hall tile. I almost had a heart attack."

"I can imagine," Thurlene said.

"What a lousy thing to happen," I said, going for sincerity.

Ann Wendell said, "It didn't appear that we needed to bring in a doctor. I treated her with ice packs . . . and of course we always travel with painkillers. It's not as bad as it looks."

We let it go at that.

Steering us back onto the cart path, Thurlene said, "Ann Wendell needs to be *confined*."

"How does her husband put up with her?"

"Ed, the hardware king? He'd *better*."

"Or else?"

"Start with whip dog."

"That would be a beginning."

Giggling at a thought, she said, "Ginger calls her the Thermostat Queen. Not to her face. It's our own little joke."

"The Thermostat Queen?"

"Gin noticed it first . . . and imitates her, Ann never lets Ed be comfortable. At home or anywhere else. We would visit them in their cabin at the golf academy. If Ann saw Ed relaxing in a chair with a book or a newspaper, she would say, 'Ed, turn the thermostat up a little.' Fifteen minutes later, when he'd look comfortable again, she would say, 'Ed, go turn the thermostat down a little.' Ed would shuffle back to the wall. I'm sure she does it in private too. We started watching for it. If it wasn't the thermostat, it was 'Ed, empty the wastebasket,' or 'Ed, move that chair over here,' or 'Ed, close those blinds,' or 'Ed, open those blinds,' or 'Ed, sit here, don't sit over there,' or 'Ed, go see what that noise is in the bathroom.' Then it would be back to the thermostat again."

"The Thermostat Queen," I said. "I can't believe I was never married to Ann Wendell."

"But you had the elegant Renata Schielder."

Debbie was a gamer, you had to admit. Bruises and all. Through the first nine holes she was even par for the round and only four strokes behind Ginger, who turned two under. Debbie was still in second place in the tournament.

Further back were Linda Merle Draper and Jan Dunn and one or two South Korean Americans. They were the only other serious challengers to Ginger. Everybody was battling the gusty winds and cold weather that made Mescalero a tougher golf course. The Lorenas and Paulas hated the place, one heard.

On the back nine we noticed Tang Chen strolling along in the Ginger-Debbie gallery. She had shot an 82 in the first round and had struggled so much on the front nine Friday, she had WD'd.

Tang Chen saw us in the cart and came over.

"You quit?" Thurlene said to her. "What happened?"

"I have injury," Tang said. "I shoot forty-three on first nine."

"Those forty-threes will give your scorecard a bruise," I said.

Tang Chen looked like she was trying to get her mind around my comment.

"I go follow friends now," Tang said. "Hana ogi, ha-na-ta okee!"

Thurlene muttered something obscene as she sped the cart up a hill.

Ginger threw down a 69, the only subpar round on Friday, and it put her five under for the tournament. It gave her a four-stroke lead over Debbie Wendell going into Saturday's final eighteen. Debbie had dug out a 71 in Friday's tough conditions. Ran the table on the greens.

We were parked in the cart behind the eighteenth green to watch Ginger and Debbie finish their rounds. As Ginger tapped in for a par, another cart pulled up next to us. It was Hoyt Newkirk and a lady.

Hoyt was wearing a large black Stetson today and a Western-cut suit and string tie. He introduced the lady by saying, "This here's Fay."

I said, "Hi, This Here's Fay. I'm Jack. This here's Thurlene."

The lady said, "Hoyt says you're a good sport, Jack . . . and honey, he's moved you ahead of Babe Ruth on the all-time homer list."

"Why, thank you, Hoyt," Thurlene said.

Fay said, "Don't wet your panties. He's still got Sophia Loren ahead of everybody."

Hoyt said, "Fay runs my bidness. She's been with me for twenty years."

"Longer than any of his wives. You can book *that*."

"I saved her life," Hoyt said. "I pulled her out of a piano bar on Clark Street in Chicago. I don't rightly remember what I was doin' in Chicago at the time."

"I know what I was doing," Fay said. "I was singing 'On a Clear Day' and fightin' off them Notre Dame drunks."

Fay was a thin lady in slacks and a sweater. Her big hair had yet to escape the Sixties. It was dark blond and plastered with so much hairspray, the brisk wind was no match for it.

Hoyt reported that the Frenchman and the LPGA commissioner had left town together. They'd gone to Palm Springs in the Frenchman's airplane. Hoyt said he wished the Frenchman had stayed around longer.

"I like to stand next to rich people. See if anything falls off."

"It don't usually," Fay said.

Hoyt said, "Good thing my older brother wasn't here. Hank is eighty-three and he still remembers how much he don't like the French. I was too young for the war, but Hank volunteered when his time come. He was in the Fifth Infantry Division, the Red Diamonds . . . part of General Patton's army. Got his butt shot a time or two in France. I'm kind of proud of him."

I said, "He wasn't injured seriously, I hope."

"Aw, he got him some Silver Stars and Purple Hearts. But when Hank come home all he talked about was how much he hated the French Underground. He'd go to a movie and couldn't understand why Hollywood liked to glorify them phony assholes. Hank said the only thing the French Underground did for him was point him toward the gray suits."

Hoyt said his wife, Miyuki, would be back from shopping in time for dinner. He invited us to join them.

"They serve a good chateau briggan in the Tomahawk Room," he said. "Bring Sweet Baby Doll along if you want to."

Thurlene said, "Thank you, Hoyt, but 'Sweet Baby Doll' likes to have room service the night before the last round. I'll dine with her."

I said, "A chateau briggan sounds good, Hoyt, but I have work to do. The computer beckons."

"Y'all take care then," Hoyt said. "Tell Sweet Baby Doll hidy."

"Chateau briggan," I said as Thurlene drove us away. "I like that."

"You'd never guess Hoyt was from Texas."

"I like 'Sweet Baby Doll' too. That may stick."

"Well, you can *un-stick* it," she said.

There was a message in my room to call Gary Crane.

It was six forty-five in New York, but I knew he'd be in the office at *SM*. On the average of two Friday nights a month he liked to pretend he was compelled to work late. This was to keep him from having to go home and take his wife, Alicia, to a dinner party in Old Gun Barrel, Connecticut.

He would spend the night in the apartment the company kept at the Lowell Hotel, and take a researcher to dinner. One of the newest young ones who might have already reached the conclusion that her best career path was giving upper echelon blowjobs.

"Jackie-boy!" Gary said on the phone. "How's the weather in Aspen?"

"I can call and ask. I'm in Ruidoso."

"Ruidoso," he said. "Ruidoso . . . Sounds like a dance craze. Everybody do the Ruidoso."

"What's on your mind, Gary?"

"One of my legionnaires passed along the news about this French character. The chap who bought the Nabisco thing."

"Uh-huh."

"We should get it in the book. Could you give us sixty lines by tomorrow? We'll slip it into 'Hots and Nots.' "

Gary Crane and all of my recent managing editors had spoken the same language. A legionnaire is an editor. As opposed to one of the shock troops, who are the writers. But an editor can also be a reader, as in first reader, second reader, last reader. One of the guys who pulls up your story on his screen and tries to ruin it before it goes to print. Two or three years ago our baseball writer leaned on the old cliché and wrote, "Derek Jeter is a legend in his spare time." But a bow-tie editor named Hodges Colby changed it to read, "Derek Jeter is a legend when he's not busy."

Researchers like to be known as reporters, but mostly they're checkers. Checkers of facts. Photographers are still shooters. The book is the magazine. But if you're on the publishing side of the book—like if you sell ads—you look upon everything the editorial side does as "fill." Something between the ads. A bridge from one ad to another. I was therefore a shock trooper who provided fill.

"I can do the sixty," I said. "I met the guy."

Sixty lines was roughly a page and a half of copy, which was words.

"You met him?" said Gary. "What do you think?"

"Another guy in a five-and-a-half shoe."

"Maybe we can leave that out. How's it going with the babe yarn?"

"The babe yarn?" I said. "It's spinning right along. It looks like she may win her second tournament in a row tomorrow."

"Heather, isn't it?"

"Ginger."

"Right, Ginger. Rhymes with *danger.*"

"If you insist."

27

The chanting that came from the crowd around the eighteenth green didn't sound much different to me from a rapper spewing out his uplifting message to society, but I doubted the Apache phrases could be translated into "rape your girl, shoot heroin, kill a cop, steal a car, rob a store, your mama's a ho."

Not everyone in the crowd was an Apache, but it was hard to miss Limping Turkey and Smells a Possum. They were the fellows in the feathered headdresses.

Sinking Canoe and Smokes Loco Weed were also easy to spot as they stood among the fans, many of which were golf fans.

Sinking Canoe wore a purple pinstriped suit and a shirt and tie and a Mescalero Country Club golf cap. If he'd been wearing an NFL football helmet instead of a golf cap with his suit and tie, he would have looked like a congressman in a photo op.

Smokes Loco Weed was the guy in the Dallas Mavericks warm-up jacket, a pair of Bermuda shorts, black socks, high-top tennis shoes, dark glasses, and a Humphrey Bogart hat. A man's hat.

The chanters were only warming up. It was early. No group had come to the last hole yet.

Thurlene and I were in our cart on the veranda near the eighteenth green, waiting for Ginger and Debbie Wendell to tee off on number one.

We heard another low chant.

"Ah na, oh na ah, nindy otay yooma tak."

Sounded like.

Thurlene said, "What do you suppose they were saying that time?"

"Unless my Apache fails me," I said, "it's something on the order of 'O Great Father of the Wind and Sun, we are grateful you gave us so many soldiers' butts to kick."

"I thought that's what it might be."

The mom was worried about the day. Ginger was cocky. The kid was thinking all she had to do was put it on cruise control. Debbie would do her predictable fainting spell somewhere during the round.

"A four-stroke lead is nothing," the mom said. "One bad shot followed by a bad decision and it's a new ball game. Was it last year when Sheila Dozier blew a five-shot lead on the last three holes? How 'bout when Marian Hornbuckle had a three-shot lead with one hole to play? She hits a bad drive, has to take a penalty, flubs a pitch, scoops a chip, then three-putts, and someone nobody's ever heard of wins. It happens."

I said, "You have to help it along. Like Snead helped everybody with the eight at Spring Mill . . . like Palmer helped Casper at Olympic . . . like Norman helped Faldo at Augusta. If she doesn't play good, she won't deserve it."

"I'm sorry I brought it up."

The weather was no problem. It was a sunny, calm, shirtsleeve day. Ginger was decked out in short, low-riding yellow shorts, a white shirt with blue stripes, and yellow cap. Debbie wore white slacks, a red shirt, and a white visor.

On the first nine holes the pins looked a little severe to me, and four of the tees were set back to make it a longer course.

Ginger didn't help her case by three-putting twice for bogeys while Debbie scratched out par after par. When they turned the front nine, Ginger's lead had dwindled to two strokes.

"This is exactly what I was afraid of," Thurlene said.

"She swinging good," I said. "She's playing the best golf."

"It doesn't seem to be helping her much . . . and what kind of a head pro is it who can't read his own greens?"

I said, "Tyler Hughes isn't the person with the putter in his hands."

She said, "Thanks for the reminder. At what point are you going to tell me it's only a game?"

"Soon, probably."

While we stayed out of Ginger's eyesight as much as possible, we couldn't help noticing Ann Wendell in the gallery. She was as close to Debbie as she could manage from behind the ropes, staring at her with a murderous look, practically daring her daughter to hit a bad shot.

Hit one bad shot, her look said, and I will personally peel that tattoo off your belly with a butcher knife.

The crowd following the leaders numbered about five hundred and was scattered along the fairways and up ahead around the greens as Ginger and Debbie went to the back nine.

Thurlene commented that we hadn't seen Tang Chen anywhere in the gallery. I said she was more than likely on the practice range, hoping to perfect her duck-slice-top-scrape shot.

Extremely visible was Claudia Bradley, the deputy commissioner. She had designated herself the official referee for the final twosome. She was the lady in the blue blazer, khaki pants, and white bucket hat. The person weighted down with walkie-talkies, cell phones, badges, credentials, and armbands. The only thing missing from her blazer was the braid.

A golf cart moved along slowly behind her. The driver was Rusty Morrison, the always-clever Speedy Arrow VP. He was talking on his cell. Each time the cart stopped, Rusty would climb out and walk around in a harried circle and keep talking on his cell. Life was a torture.

Ginger and Debbie both parred the first five holes on the back nine, the tenth through the fourteenth. Ginger was still two strokes ahead of Debbie, and when the kid drove it in the fairway on the long, narrow fifteenth hole, a difficult par-four, Thurlene sighed with relief.

The mom said, "Gin needs to play one shot at a time, one hole at a time . . . take care of business. I can't believe the way Debbie is hanging in. She's never done this before. She would be perfectly happy with second or third. Why doesn't she go ahead and make her double or triple and get out of our way?"

I said, "Sometimes golfers try to find a way to lose without looking like they're choking. Make it look like rotten luck. If I were Debbie, I wouldn't want to humiliate my mother again."

"I wish she'd hurry up and think of something."

Here was where Ginger walked hurriedly off the other side of the fairway from us, ducked under the gallery ropes, and disappeared in the trees. We assumed she was heading for a Port-O-Let.

Nothing unusual about it. There's never been a professional golfer, woman or man, who hasn't found an occasion to use a Port-O-Let during a competitive round.

However, when Ginger didn't reappear after five or six minutes, we left the cart path and drove down a slope and stopped next to the deputy commissioner in the fairway.

"Does the LPGA have a Port-O-Let rule?" I asked.

"What do you mean?" Claudia Bradley said.

"A time limit?" I said.

"I'm not sure," she said. "I'll have to consult the rule book. I believe the USGA has it under delay of play. I would think it's something like ten or twelve minutes."

I said, "Unless it's Hogan, Nicklaus, or Tiger. Then it would be indefinite, wouldn't it?"

"Is that an insinuation of something?" the deputy commissioner said.

"More like a statement of fact. You've never heard of a big-name player receiving special treatment under the rules?"

"Not on my watch," Claudia Bradley said.

Thurlene said, "I want to go check on Ginger."

She drove us over to the edge of the trees. We left the cart and walked up an incline toward the Port-O-Let, part of which we could see through the limbs and leaves.

We found Ginger a few feet from the front of the Port-O-Let, sitting in a pile of dirt and rocks, rubbing on her left knee and the back of her neck and cussing.

"What in the world happened?" said Thurlene, kneeling beside her.

"Somebody knocked me down," Ginger said.

"*Who* knocked you down? What are you talking about?"

"I didn't see who it was. They hit me in the back of the head and I fell on these damn rocks."

Mom: "Where did this somebody come from?"

Daughter: "I don't know. I never saw anybody. I did hear a yell from up in the trees. It sounded like an Indian. Yelling something like 'Tinde tomma naka yacky' . . . some shit like that."

I said, "If an Indian ambushed you, he was either drunk or betting on somebody else."

Thurlene said, "It wasn't an Indian. It was that Chinese girl!"

"Are you serious?" I said.

"It's obvious."

"You don't know that."

"The hell I don't!"

Ginger said, "I have to stand up."

I helped her to her feet.

"We have to take you to a doctor," Thurlene said.

"I'm not quitting," Ginger said.

"Your knee is going to swell up by the minute."

"I'm not quitting, Mom! I can play. I'm okay."

Claudia Bradley, the deputy commissioner, came up the path.

"Had a little mishap here, have we?" she said.

"I fell down," Ginger said.

"That's not exactly what happened," Thurlene said, "but this isn't the time to discuss it. I'll be taking it up with Marsha, you can be sure."

"What are we talking about?" the deputy said.

Thurlene said, "I will *discuss* it with the commissioner."

"As you wish," Claudia said, and turned to the kid. "Are you able to continue play, Ginger?"

"Yes," Ginger said.

"No!" said Thurlene.

Ginger pulled her arm away from her mom and said, "I'm *playing*, Mom. Jesus!"

28

Where would I rank Ginger Clayton's performance over the last four holes of the Speedy Arrow Energy Bar Classic?

Would I put it up there with three other amazing golf moments I'd seen with my own eyes and written about with my own fingers? Would I put it up there with Jack Nicklaus winning his sixth Masters in '86 when he overtook Greg Norman, Seve Ballesteros, and Tom Kite in the final round? Would I put it up there with Ben Crenshaw's tearful victory at Augusta in '95 only a few days after the death of Harvey Penick, his close friend and mentor? Would I put it up there with Tiger Woods having his way with Pebble Beach when he lapped the field and won the U.S. Open of 2000? I couldn't compare it with anything Ben Hogan did, seeing as how I'd made the mistake of not being born yet.

I might, however, compare it with a scene from that old black-and-white movie about Ben Hogan, *Follow the Sun,* where Glenn Ford is cast as Hogan. Although I never saw Hogan play, I know he didn't have a swing like Glenn Ford's, and I was reasonably sure he never wore a golf cap that was too big for him.

But there's this scene near the end in which Hogan is making his comeback from the car crash and Glenn Ford trudges up a steep fairway at Riviera. Limping, hurting, but hanging on gamely. It's the Bataan Death March of golf. Mood music by some death march composer guy.

I couldn't help thinking of that scene as I watched Ginger hit courageous golf shots despite her swollen knee and the scratches and scrapes on her arms, and the lingering trauma of having been bushwhacked.

Ginger's first gimp shot was her 180-yard approach to the fifteenth green. She went with a five-iron, but her knee wouldn't let her put as much strength into the swing as she needed.

The shot wound up ten yards short of the green. But that didn't seem to matter, because Debbie's second left her off the green and facing a difficult chip to a pin that was all the way across the green.

When Ginger pitched up to a foot of the pin for a gimme par, Thurlene whooped, clapped, rocked the cart.

The mom's jubilation was short-lived, however. Although Debbie chipped her ball too strongly and it was heading over the green and even down a slope and out of sight, it struck the flagstick, bobbed straight up in the air, and plunked down into the cup for a birdie three.

"That's outrageous!" Thurlene yelped. "Destiny sucks!"

In the crowd on the other side of the green, Ann Wendell could be seen punching the air with her fist. Once, twice, three times. Her daughter was now only one shot behind Ginger with three holes to go.

"Debbie Wendell is going to win this tournament. I know it! You don't hole out a shot like that without Destiny sticking a nose in things. It's tragic, is what it is."

"It's not over," I said. "Do you see a fat lady anywhere?"

"Do I see what?"

"The fat lady hasn't sung yet," I said. "Find me a fat lady in the crowd, I'll throw a body block on her before she can sing."

"Cute."

She drove us across a bridge that was built to accommodate fans and carts to a spot behind the sixteenth green, which was a dangerous par-three hole requiring a long carry over a deep, you-don't-want-to-know-what's-down-there canyon, gorge, barranca thing.

I had this crazy idea that when Burch Webb—or Afraid of Dogs, as he was known locally—designed the hole he may have been a big fan of the fifth at Pine Valley, the sixteenth at Cypress Point, the tenth at Bel-Air, the thirteenth at Black Diamond, or the ninth at Jupiter Hills.

Having the honor, Debbie prepared to hit first.

Thurlene, in a low voice, said, "I don't suppose she could top this one, could she?"

"It's too early to start begging," I said.

I didn't know whether or not Thurlene was buying my nonchalant act. The truth of the matter was, I had this lab rat running back and forth in my stomach, and Ginger wasn't even my kid.

Debbie was forced to go with a three-wood off the tee. It didn't sound like she got all of it when she took the swing, but the ball cleared the canyon and found the green. It came to rest about forty feet from the flag.

"I hate this hole," Thurlene said. "A wood is too much and an iron may not be enough if she doesn't nail it."

"She's going with a four-iron."

"I can't look."

The mom didn't see Ginger rip it, swollen knee and all. The shot soared high and straight. "Be the stick!" Ginger yelled.

The ball found the center of the green—and bit, stayed.

"This kid of yours," I said. "That was one hell of a shot. She *is* stronger than laundry."

Ginger and Debbie both two-putted and came away from the sinister sixteenth with pars, but then the mom found something else to worry about.

"I hate seventeen worse than sixteen," she said.

Mescalero's seventeenth was the hole where the tee shot could wind up in downtown Ruidoso if it was hooked or pulled too far left.

Debbie did her best to take her tee shot to downtown Ruidoso, but a long, thin bunker had been strategically placed on the left edge of the fairway for the explicit purpose of catching drives that weren't hooked or pulled too severely. A safety net for high-handicap members.

Debbie's ball bounced like it wanted to go downtown, which would have ended her challenge to Ginger, but the bunker saved her. She could rescue a par-four from there, or escape with no worse than a five.

"Destiny is still sucking," I observed.

"I know," said Thurlene. "It's disgusting."

Ginger's drive was a rocket. She aimed a little left of the tree line on the right and let the tilt of the fairway take the ball down toward the green after it landed. Even with a weakened knee, it was a 290-yard lick, mountain air assisting. Her second shot would amount to no more than a dainty chip.

We were feeling good about the prospects here, but Destiny wasn't through with us.

Debbie's bunker shot was a pull-lunge that tried again to go out of bounds, but the ball hit the trunk of the only tree on the left side of the green and it bounced thirty yards to the right and onto the green, and somewhat astoundingly gave her a twenty-foot birdie putt.

"That's ridiculous," Thurlene said. "I mean, it just *is*."

When Ginger ran her chip shot up to within four feet of the cup, she was still the favorite to gain a stroke on the hole. I was thinking of this, and I knew the mom was.

But there are times when competitive golf is the cruelest of games. It's the only sport where luck can trump talent. This was one of those times. If talent gets trumped in any other sport it's because a zebra, an official in a striped shirt, who is either a fool or a criminal, interferes.

First, Debbie staggered in her twenty-footer for a birdie. The ball hung on the lip for a second before it fell. Then Ginger missed the short one.

Ginger's putt was stroked on the correct line and with the right speed, and the ball rolled directly into the center of the cup—it hit nothing but air—and yet it refused to drop.

Ginger shook her head angrily. She glared at the world. Her caddie looked stunned, baffled. She mouthed something that might have been, "Can you fucking believe this shit?" Then she listlessly raked the ball into the cup.

Bizarre birdie for Debbie. Unlucky par for Ginger.

Now the girls were tied with one hole to play.

On the other side of the green, Ann Wendell was punching the air again with her fist.

Back in our cart, Thurlene was beyond cussing. In a calm, re-signed voice she said, "I hate this game. I hate Scotland for inventing it. I hate New Mexico. I hate this day . . . I hate this golf course . . . I hate this tournament."

She drove the cart halfway up the left side of the eighteenth fairway and stopped parallel to where the tee shots should land.

"Hate is good," I said. "It's the reason I read about politicians in the papers every morning. I like to start off the day with a lot of healthy hate."

She changed her tone. "I don't actually hate anything, if you want the truth. This game just frustrates me so damn much. I don't even hate Debbie Wendell and Ann Wendell."

"I'm going to remember you said that."

"You want to know why?"

"I would love to know why."

"I don't hate them, because no matter what they do—today or any other time—they'll still be Debbie Wendell and Ann Wendell."

As cutting remarks go, I rated that one fairly high.

The par-four eighteenth hole presented the golfer with a wide-open fairway. You could drive the ball practically anywhere and be safe. The second shot was a slightly uphill midiron to a huge, sprawling green that wasn't even protected by bunkers. It was a nothing hole. The only thing you could say in defense of Burch Webb is that sometimes a golf course designer is restricted by a developer who wants to reserve certain acreage for home sites.

We happened to be looking back at the tee in time to see Debbie Wendell almost whiff her tee shot. She did top it, get a piece of it, but the ball only scooted seventy or eighty yards along the ground.

It was an embarrassing example of an athlete having a train wreck.

"Oh . . . my . . . God," Thurlene said slowly.

With no show of emotion, Ginger pounded her own drive about 275 yards into the heart of the fairway, accepted a high five from Tyler Hughes, and walked ahead in a businesslike manner.

Poor Debbie. She topped her second shot with a three-wood. It traveled about forty more yards. Then she topped her third shot with the three-wood. By then she knew the tournament was lost, over, and so did everyone else.

After Ginger smoothly put a five-iron in the middle of the green, the only thing left for Debbie to do was complete her collapse. In order, she shanked a three-iron into the right rough, slashed out of the rough with a sand wedge, smothered a six-iron into the left rough, slashed out of there with the sand wedge again, and finally put her eighth shot on the green. There, she dejectedly three-putted for the eleven that would find her finishing in a tie for twenty-third in the tournament.

As Debbie struggled through her calamity, shot by shot, Thurlene was saying, "This is painful to watch, isn't it? It's very sad. It's awful. It's really pathetic. It's just so humiliating . . . so embarrassing for her . . . and I can't begin to tell you how much I'm enjoying it."

We were out of the cart and standing by then, and in Thurlene's excitement, she suddenly gave me a kiss. On the mouth. It was a happy kiss, a friendly kiss, but at the same time it was more than that. It lasted just long enough, and was just intense enough, for me to read something else into it. You could call it the kind of kiss a guy wouldn't forget for a while.

A big moment for me, but maybe a bigger moment for the kid's career. It would be a big story in the golf world. Two wins in a row on the LPGA Tour. Good-looking teenage babe plays hurt and still does it. Does it on the eve of the year's first major coming up the next week in Palm Springs. Ginger Clayton was a hotter property than ever.

When the kid holed out her final putt in the Speedy Arrow Energy Bar Classic and high-fived her caddie and raised a victorious fist at her mom, Thurlene raised her own fist back and hollered:

"Yeah, baby!"

Ginger then hobbled over on her sore knee to shake hands with Debbie. Do the public-display-of-sportsmanship thing. But Debbie was rushing off the green to escape the wrath of her infuriated mother, who was coming after her—and closing fast.

29

On a previous occasion there'd been this heated discussion between Hoyt Newkirk and Rusty Morrison about the design of the trophy the winner would receive. I learned from Hoyt that he'd argued for a tomahawk mounted on a plaque, while Rusty wanted a replica of his nutritious candy bar mounted on a plaque. Hoyt won out in the end when he told Rusty that he was losing his patience and on the verge of calling Eddie Wing Tips in Dallas, an associate who could arrange for Rusty to walk with a limp the rest of his life.

It wasn't too long ago that golf trophies were tasteful and sparkling. They were made of real silver and consisted of claret jugs, water pitchers, plates, bowls to put fruit in, and tall vases to put flowers in, and the lettering on them was artistic and engraved by old men in eyeshades who lived in broom closets in Inverness, Scotland.

Not anymore. Every tournament sponsor in the world now—for men, women, or kids—strives to come up with something unique, original. Whether the striving sponsor's trophy succeeds in achieving this goal generally depends on the observer's sense of humor or complete lack of a sense of humor.

I'd discussed the subject in the past with colleagues and we'd settled on a list of modern golf's most unique trophies. They are:

The shining conquistador's helmet.
The heavy pewter alligator on a wood base.
The bronze sculpture of a golfer swinging a club that looks nothing like the Arnold Palmer it's intended to be.

The golden pineapple on a wooden base.

The curious object on a small wooden pedestal that could well be a Buick hood ornament.

The plastic toy Goofy lining up a putt for the plastic toy Mickey on a base of artificial turf.

The red plaid blazer that even the Salvation Army won't accept.

The wood carving of a lady golfer with mysterious wings on her back as she hunches over a putt.

The tall round clear glass sculpture carved into a knob at the top that no golfer will dare kiss in a photo op out of fear that the photo's nationwide circulation will ruin his or her sex life forever.

The ancient Apache tomahawk mounted on a polished wood plaque that Ginger received was to be admired even if the tomahawk might only date back to 2008 and wasn't the exact weapon used by the great brave Tall Possum in 1881 when he outfought Col. Bright Finnegan of the U.S. Seventh Cavalry on the patch of ground that was now the eighteenth green at Mescalero Country Club.

The presentation ceremony for the winner of the tournament took place on that very spot.

Golf fans and Apaches surrounded it. Thurlene and I were given folding chairs inside the ropes, in the front row. We were in the same row as This Here's Fay and Miyuki and other distinguished guests, such as Sinking Canoe and Smokes Loco Weed.

Had Debbie Wendell even made a double bogey six on the last hole, she would have been invited to the front row and introduced as the proud runner-up. As it was, Linda Merle Draper was enjoying that role, having finished five strokes behind Ginger.

We could only imagine where Debbie and her mother were at the moment, and what sort of medieval punishment the daughter was absorbing.

The deputy commissioner acted as the MC.

The first thing Claudia Bradley did was apologize for Marsha Wilson's absence. The LPGA's "fantastic" commissioner was unable to return from Palm Springs and attend the ceremony. She was simply too busy getting "all the ducks in a row" for next week's first major of the year, Le Grand Cheval et Petit Chien Classique.

I nudged Thurlene. "They seriously think that sounds like a major?"

She said, "Jack, you of all people should know that golf tournaments today are named whatever the money wants them named."

"You're right. I forgot who I am for a minute."

Claudia Bradley introduced everybody she deemed important. We didn't make the cut.

Rusty Morrison, the always clever VP of marketing for Speedy Arrow, presented Ginger with a foot-long replica of the $300,000 winner's check. The real money would travel from the sponsor to the LPGA office and on into Ginger's bank account. That's how it works.

Handing Ginger the replica, Rusty Morrison said, "Congratulations, darling. This should keep you in mascara and lip gloss for a while. I know it would be enough to keep *me* in stock. Heh, heh."

Ginger thanked everyone involved with the tournament. She especially wanted to thank Tyler Hughes, Mescalero's head pro, who came to her rescue as a caddie and saw her through a tough week.

This was as good a time as any, she said, to announce that Tyler was resigning as the head pro and coming on the LPGA Tour as her regular caddie. She pointed to Tyler in the crowd. He waved at everyone.

The deputy commissioner introduced Sinking Canoe, explaining to the audience that he was one of the "big chiefs" of the hotel, casino, and country club.

At the mike, Sinking Canoe said, "May the warm winds of the Heavenly Father blow upon your putts and chip shots . . . May the same winds jack up your ball in the rough."

Next, Smokes Loco Weed insisted on going to the microphone although he wasn't introduced.

He said, "May the Great Spirit give us plenty herbs to heal our brains, you betcha . . . May the rainbow always touch the shoulders of the paleface girls in the short pants who come here to show us their bodies. May their moccasins make happy tracks to my teepee. May their—"

Hoyt Newkirk was there to snatch the mike from him, cut him off, and tell him to go sit down and stare at something.

Hoyt announced that he was always easy to find if anybody was interested in buying a home site. And he took a moment to recount the battle of "Finnegan's Folly," and mentioned that Limping Turkey and Smells a Possum, descendants of the heroes of the battle, had organized a little surprise for everyone.

He motioned for Limp and Possum to step out of the crowd and lead the other Apaches who'd gathered there in the song they'd rehearsed for the occasion.

They came to the mike. Limp wore his red Wal-Mart vest and Possum was in a yellow and blue softball uniform with a patch on the back of the shirt that said, "Teddy Crow's Auto Repair and Service Center."

Limp said into the mike, "This is in honor of the soldiers our people fought and killed that are buried here right now under this bent grass green."

With that, he raised his arms like a musical conductor and the band of Apaches joined Limp and Smells in song. We heard:

"Around their necks they wear the yellow ribbons,
Ladies wear 'em in the springtime
And anytime we say.
And if you ask us why they wear 'em,
It's for the ones we killed that day."

There was more to the song, but Thurlene and I caught up with Ginger and the three of us filed out, along with most everyone else.

Thurlene said, "Next stop, Palm Springs."

"Right," I said. "Onward to La Vie En Horse."

PART THREE

TOO MUCH
WOMAN

30

I t only took two cups of coffee, a cinnamon roll, and one conversation to go from Ruidoso's Sierra Blanca Regional Airport to Palm Springs International, but this was in the private jet Thurlene chartered on Sunday.

The Falcon 20 was out of El Paso. It would accommodate nine passengers comfortably, but there were just six of us. The other three were Tyler Hughes, Jan Dunn, and Linda Merle Draper. Giving the two LPGA board members and competitors a lift was good politics on Thurlene and Ginger's part.

The jet was designed with six plush seats and one couch. Thurlene and I sat across from each other in the front row. I complimented her on her low threshold for inconvenience.

She confessed it was the first time she'd chartered a plane, but Ginger needed to get to Palm Springs as quickly as possible and rest her knee. Why should they waste a day driving to El Paso and then flying commercial to Palm Springs with a stop in L.A.?

I said, "Don't apologize. Tiger Woods doesn't . . . and he charters a jet just to go to dinner."

Nobody said anything for a while. Eventually I leaned over and said, "I've known you for two weeks now, right?"

"Yes."

"Which means you've known me for two weeks."

"Uh-huh. So . . . ?"

"Don't you think it's time I ask you out on a real date?"

"A real date?"

"Yeah. Like I open doors for you. We dine. I stare into your eyes

when I light your cigarette, except you can't smoke indoors anywhere. That kind of date."

"This is a serious hit. There's no getting around it."

"What do you think?"

"It sounds okay."

"*Okay?*"

"It sounds fine."

"*Fine?*"

"What do you want me to say—it's about time?"

"That would do it for me."

"It sounds wonderful, Jack. How's that?"

"Great. This will happen in Palm Springs, then."

I sat back in my seat. She glanced over at me. Grinning.

Good sign.

We were staying at the Desert Mystique Hotel & Spa. It was tournament headquarters and five minutes from downtown Palm Springs.

My room was in the main building. So was Tyler's. So were most
of the competitors' and LPGA officials'. Ginger and her mom were
in one of the sumptuous two-bedroom cabanas facing the Olympic-
size swimming pool.

A press packet for the Grand Cheval et Petit Chien Classique—
"The First Ladies Major Championship of the Season"—was waiting
for me at the front desk when I checked in.

Directions from the hotel to the golf course were provided in
case I was driving a car and not taking the shuttle bus that would run
every thirty minutes. The directions were tantalizing. They read:

"From the Desert Mystique Hotel on Frank Sinatra Drive go 4
miles east to Barbara Stanwyck Avenue.

Turn left on Barbara Stanwyck Avenue. Go two miles to Fred
MacMurray Highway.

Go 5.4 miles on Fred MacMurray Highway. Turn right on Gloria
Swanson Parkway.

Take Gloria Swanson Parkway 1.8 miles to Zachary Scott Road.
Take Zachary Scott Road 2.3 miles to Gail Patrick Loop.

Stay on Gail Patrick Loop until it becomes Ralph Bellamy Street. Ralph Bellamy Street leads to Carole Lombard Boulevard.

Carole Lombard Boulevard is the main entry to Hollywood Dunes Country Club. But before you reach the clubhouse you will be directed to Parking Lot A on the south side of the club. This space is strictly reserved for Contestants, Officials, Celebrities, and Working Press."

There was another fascinating document, the tournament program. It was filled with photos and brief descriptions of the golf holes at Hollywood Dunes. Burch Webb's creative do-over was said to have retained the unique character of the layout that was originally designed in 1936 by W. C. Fields and Adolphe Menjou, two of Hollywood's most ardent golfers.

Clubs were known to name golf holes long before Bobby Jones did it with blossoms at the Augusta National, which is where you find the famed Amen Corner—the eleventh, twelfth, and thirteenth holes—known as "White Dogwood," "Golden Bell," and "Azalea."

The other Augusta National holes have names too, but some don't stir the heart as much as others. "Tea Olive," for instance, which is number one, doesn't have the lyrical charm of "Yellow Jasmine," which is number eight. Most of us who cover the Masters every year agree on this.

Names for holes on courses in Scotland, where the game was born, go back at least as far as Old Tom Morris and Willie Park.

To pin it down, you'd have to dig up Old Tom or Willie or any of those guys who played golf in heavy tweed coats, knickers, and neckties, and who smoked pipes on their backswings.

You could probably find out who named the eighth at Royal Troon the "Postage Stamp," who named the fifth at Prestwick "Himalayas," or who named the sixteenth on the Old Course at St. Andrews "Corner of the Dyke."

However, what knowledge I had of golf history couldn't have prepared me for the names of the holes at Hollywood Dunes, which was going to play at 6,528 yards and a par of 70 for the championship.

Digging into the tournament program, I learned that W. C. Fields had named the holes himself and had furnished the comments on each:

No. 1. **Ann Sheridan**—356 yards/Par-4—*"It takes some oomph to clear the bunkers."*

No. 3. **Howard Hughes**—353 yards/Par-4—*"Howard lost a stunt flyer near here when he was shooting* Hell's Angels.*"*

No. 8. **Cecil B. DeMille**—520 yards/Par-5—*"Very long, like most of his films."*

No. 16. **Mae West**—174 yards/Par-3—*"Aim between the mounds."*

No. 17. **Sam Goldwyn**—400 yards/Par-4—*"But Mr. Goldwyn, every director has to start somewhere."*
"Don't you believe it!"

I was familiar with Palm Springs. They could call the neighboring areas Palm Desert, Rancho Mirage, Indian Wells, La Quinta, or Bob Hope City, but it was all Palm Springs to me.

When I'd been there four times to cover the Hope, what it meant was a six-pack of golf courses scattered everywhere, a pressroom, a hotel, and a few bars and restaurants.

But I'd never been in Palm Springs for this particular week. A festive week that was now known as "the Dinah Shore Weekend" or "Lesbian Spring Break," take your pick.

The tournament had become an excuse for ladies on the Other Team to bust out and entertain one another while inadvertently or maybe intentionally tormenting straight folks.

I'd read enough about it to know what to expect and what to avoid.

For instance, I knew not to go looking for a cocktail in a joint called Big Girl's Saloon, or wander into a "dance club" called Don't Even Try.

In recent years, the week had turned into more of an occasion for successful professional women—brokers, hedge fund managers, credit card execs, doctors, and so forth—to rent a condo or a house and impress people by throwing a party that said, "Yo, hey, I make big bucks and wear Meryl Streep Prada, and I can afford to have this catered even though I'm gay."

I assumed that out on the golf course I'd find some of those groups that gave the tournament a considerable amount of notoriety in the first place—the ladies who'd have inspirational tattoos on their upper arms. I'd heard **Golf Bitch** was popular and **Sex Tramp** was a big seller.

I did hope none of those people would feast their eyes on the swimming pool at our hotel on Sunday afternoon. This was after we'd settled in. They'd see Thurlene and Ginger in their small bikinis, stretched out on reclining chairs in the sunshine.

That sight wasn't for the fainthearted of any sexual persuasion.

31

My game plan was to stay in the room for two days and fondle the laptop. Start to work on the piece about the kid. First, as was my custom, I went prowling around the net Monday morning to see how the death of Western civilization was coming along, and that's how I stumbled onto the news about Toppy Pemberton.

The headline was a grabber.

"DINOSAUR MAN" SHOT ON LA JOLLA STREET

Even before I read the story I knew it couldn't be anyone else.

Toppy had been taking his annual stroll in his dinosaur suit, costume, whatever it is. He was out on the downtown streets of La Jolla, celebrating his Sinclair wealth, when a "crazed gunman" shot him twice in the chest, or rather the dinosaur's chest, with a .22 handgun.

Toppy was rushed to Scripps Memorial Hospital in La Jolla, where he was said to be in stable condition. The bullets had struck nothing vital, but bullets inside a person were not good things, I'd wager.

The gunman was identified as Carlos Menchaca, a twenty-six-year-old unemployed illegal immigrant. Some people would say that was a redundancy, not to linger on the subject.

Menchaca surrendered soon after the incident. Actually, it was as soon as he discovered that the dinosaur wasn't a real dinosaur but a man wearing a dinosaur costume.

Menchaca argued that the unfortunate accident wasn't altogether his fault. He blamed it on the high quality of the weed he'd been smoking and the fact that only the night before he'd watched *Jurassic Park* on TV in his oceanfront condo.

When the police wanted to know how he happened to be living in an oceanfront condo, Menchaca said, "Ask the gringo in the United States government. He give it to me for free."

A lady answered the phone when I called Toppy in his room at the hospital.

I said, "Hi, it's Jack Brannon calling. I just found out about Toppy Pemberton, and I'm calling to see how he—"

But the lady cut me off. Singing.

"Who's stupid now?" I heard. "Whose head is breaking for sinking that bow?"

I said, "Connie?"

"Right to the bend . . . FedEx will send,
I tried to corn him somehow . . ."

"Connie?" I said again.

"But he went away . . . now I can play,
I'm glad that he's home no doubt."

I said, "Connie, it's Jack Brannon. I'm calling to see how Toppy's doing. I'm sorry to hear about what happened. I read about it on—"

"He's right here," she said.

Toppy came on. "Hello, scribe. Good of you to call."

"You sound okay for a wounded trouper," I said.

"Well, it was only a shitty little twenty-two," he said. "Can you imagine somebody thinking I was a real dinosaur? It says something about our educational system, if you ask me. How long would you say they've been extinct, scribe?"

"The dinosaurs or our educational system?"

Toppy wheezed.

I said, "I can't resist asking, Toppy. What is your dinosaur suit made out of?"

"Remember oilcloth?"

"No. I was raised on linen and candelabra."

"You too?"

"Of course I know what oilcloth is. It was on our kitchen table."

"My suit is made out of oilcloth and quilting and I don't know what else. One of our housekeepers made it for me a long time ago. She copied the Sinclair logo, as you might guess."

"I like to think I would have."

"It's sturdy, but not thick enough to stop a bullet."

Toppy wheezed again, then said:

"Where are you calling from, Jack?"

"I'm in Palm Springs . . . for what used to be the Dinah."

"I read about the Frenchman. It's too bad. But a Frenchman is better than an Arab. You ever dealt with Arabs, Jack?"

"No, I can't say I have."

"It's like trying to talk to a flock of low-flying ducks."

"How long will you be laid up, Toppy?"

"Oh, I should be out of here in a week or two. Back out on the golf course in no time . . . hitting every club the same distance."

"I just called to see how you're doing."

"Good talking to you, Jack. You know what some folks will say about what happened to me, don't you?"

"What's that?"

"Guns don't kill dinosaurs, people kill dinosaurs."

He was wheezing again as I hung up.

———————

32

Tuesday was date night. I'd suggested Tuesday evening and Thurlene said fine. Or okay. One of the two. I was picking her up at seven. My ankles would be taped by six.

But first I was privileged to be entertained that afternoon by a crowd of demonstrators down on the street in front of the hotel. I wouldn't have known they were there if I hadn't taken a break from writing—or not writing—and gone out for a stroll.

The demonstrators had assembled to let the LPGA know what they thought about France in general and the idea of horse meat for American dining tables in particular.

There were handmade signs being pumped up and down and waved around by the "activists."

GIVE US BACK THE BISCUITS!

———

YO, FRANCE! WE DON'T EAT OUR DERBY WINNERS!

———

TRY THIS ON GERMANY AND SEE WHAT HAPPENS!

I spoke to one of the Charles Mansons as he paraded with two Frau Bluchers, three turbans, a Keith Richards, and a Woody Guthrie. He said he had no thoughts on the subject. He had only joined the crowd because a "human rights" protest excused him from his job at Kinko's.

"I misunderstood," I said.

I approached one of the Frau Bluchers. She was in pedal pushers and a sweater and wasn't carrying a sign.

"I gather you feel strongly about this?" I said.

"About what?" Frau Blucher said.

"France."

"I love France."

"You do? What are you doing in this picket line, if I may ask?"

"I hate golf."

"You hate golf? Why?"

"*Why?* It's all my husband does, for God's sake!"

As any of my friends can tell you, I've never been a big fan of protests. Take a good look at your average group of demonstrators and you realize they're a mixture of out-of-work slugs and welfare units who've been hired by some far-left organization headed up by Joseph Stalin's great-nephew to stir up shit for the TV cameras.

I often wonder if the sport known as "civil disobedience" couldn't have been stopped in the Sixties before it became a fad. Maybe if just one university president had grown a spine. He could have confronted the protestors on the ad. building steps and said, "Guess what? You assholes don't go to school here anymore. Now get the fuck off this campus."

If you've ever been a college student, you have a good idea that the "revolutionaries" in the Sixties weren't really protesting the Vietnam War anyhow. And it wasn't about "free speech" either. They were using those issues as an excuse to not get drafted in order to stay home and partake of getting stoned and falling into piles of naked strangers.

Old film clips and TV footage of those overly romanticized days are falling-down hilarious. Here are these swarms of unbathed hippie scum waving their "Make Love, Not War" signs, and the whole scene looks like *The Last of the Mohicans* meets mud wrestling.

I confess that in the early Eighties at the University of Texas we looked for excuses to do our share of getting stoned and laid, but we thought of it as a weekend reward from studies, not an occupation.

I had friends back then, however, who held that if everybody would make it a full-time occupation to stay stoned and wallow in piles of naked strangers, the world would be a better place.

My argument against this was that the hard-ons would wear out soon enough, and one day there wouldn't be anything left but the getting-stoned part, and then there wouldn't be anybody around to invent the telephone, the steamboat, the reaper, the wireless, and radioactivity.

For certain individuals, though, protests hold a special appeal. Protests are usually held outdoors, and nearly always in good weather, which means you can catch a little sun while you're yelling at Republicans.

The restaurant I selected for the evening was Guido & Luigi. It was on Palm Canyon, the main drag, at the corner of Rhonda Fleming Lane, not far from the hotel.

I'd dined there twice in the past. I tried it in the first place because somebody told me it had been one of Frank Sinatra's hangouts. I'd found it to be quiet, cozy, dark wood and brass—and the meat sauce didn't come out redder than a University of Oklahoma football jersey.

I gambled on it being the same as it was, hoping a new age quality-control nitwit menace hadn't changed it. There's an army of them out there, the new age quality-control nitwit menaces. They ruin everything they touch in the name of "improving life" or "seeking a broader audience."

They try to put avocado and quail eggs on cheeseburgers.

They hide the gas tank release button on rental cars.

They keep moving things around in grocery stores so that finding the bread that was on a particular shelf last week is a scavenger hunt now.

They make it impossible to open a package of anything, large or small, without a chain saw.

They've put cell phones in the ears of SUV drivers, thus making them more dangerous than Islamic jihadists, or people who own red cars.

They make you press one for English even though you're a law-abiding citizen of the United States, and what's the point anyway if you're going to be speaking to somebody in Calcutta?

If you have a dish or you're on cable, they've worked it out so that every TV screen in the eastern half of the United States will suddenly go dark at a single drop of rain in Anchorage, Alaska.

They've made the paper jam a part of day-to-day living.

They've changed the look of newspapers and magazines so that newspapers now look more like magazines and magazines look more like supermarket tabloids.

But they never do anything worthwhile. Like, for example, invent a simple key on the computer that says, "Put All My Stuff Back Where It Was Before I Accidentally Hit a Key That Made It Disappear Forever."

Ginger greeted me in golf togs when I knocked on the cabana door to pick up my date. She'd returned only moments earlier from playing eighteen and practicing at Hollywood Dunes.

"Whoa, it's Mom's date!" she said. "He's suited up . . . ready to roll."

I was in my one and only black double-breasted blazer, gray slacks, a light blue open-collar button-down shirt, and cordovan loafers polished to a blinding luster.

Ginger motioned me inside as she called out to Thurlene.

"He's here, Mom! Mr. Right . . . is . . . IN . . . the building!"

"That makes it easier," I said.

"Don't sweat it, Jack."

"What do you think of the golf course?"

"It's sporty. Kind of tight. Looks like par's a good score. We'll see. I'll have a better idea after I play it again tomorrow."

"How's the knee?"

"Knee's good."

"What are you doing tonight?"

"I'll be dipping into room service and TV."

Thurlene appeared. She came out of a hallway and into the living room, fiddling with an earring.

If I hadn't been a strong-willed person, the sight of her would have caused me to stagger and grab on to something.

Her hair was down below her shoulders, straight and smooth, like that of the shampoo models on TV—and she could give any of those chicks two up a side for my money.

She was wearing spike heels and black silk pants and a white silk halter top with what you call your plunging neckline.

Going for wise-mouth to cover up my basic awe, I said, "Would you stand here and keep looking like this till I get back from the jewelry store?"

"Does that often work for you?" she said.

"Hardly ever. It usually takes explaining. How about . . . you've never seen Venice till you see it with me?"

"What are y'all talking about?" Ginger asked.

"This is grown-up stuff," I said.

Thurlene said, "What else have you got?"

I looked at her seriously and said, "Damn, you look terrific to-night."

"That's the one," she said. "Shall we go?"

33

The hundred-dollar bill did its time-honored magic. As soon as the bill reached the palm of the maître d' in Guido & Luigi, a gentleman who looked like Tony Bennett's long-lost twin brother, it upgraded us from a squalid table by the kitchen door to a quiet booth in an intimate corner that even came with a waiter.

Word circulated fast about the hundred-dollar bill, because our waiter, Rossana Brazzi, brought our cocktails instantly. The Bombay Sapphire gin martini for me, rocks, four olives, and a bottle of Frascati for Thurlene.

I hoped the waiter might say, "This was Frank's booth," but he only poured Thurlene a glass of the white wine and disappeared.

I raised my martini to her. She raised her glass.

She said, "I know how expensive this wine is. I would have been happy with a glass of chardonnay."

I said, "It's not as expensive as the Tignanello we'll have with dinner. Drink what you want and we'll donate the rest to a Presbyterian night shelter and all the old golf instructors who live there. Here's to dating."

The glasses clinked.

On the limo ride to the restaurant I'd started telling her about the demonstrators I mingled with that afternoon. She hadn't heard any of the commotion while she was reclining by the pool, but the poolside waiter who brought her lunch had told her there were some "whack-o-damia" nuts out in front of the hotel, but he said they were peaceful and harmless and only wanted to take out France.

Protests dominated our conversation over cocktails and dinner.

I was relieved to hear her say she'd never protested against anything, although she said she might protest against standing in lines—if it didn't require standing in lines.

She said, "I was born in 1968 but I was in college before I found out it was the 'Summer of Love.' "

I said, "I was eight years old then. It was the year of the Chicago Seven and the hippie protests at the Democratic Convention. But since none of the Chicago Seven played football for the University of Texas at the time, their names weren't worth knowing. Now I can name them . . . in a bar, for money. Bobby Seale, Abbie Hoff—"

Thurlene said, "I'll take your word for it. My parents were as far removed from hippies as you could be. Hippies didn't sell insurance, like my dad. My Aunt Sylvia married well and still lives in Highland Park, and I know for a fact that in the Sixties she would have floored her Cadillac Coupe de Ville and run over any hippie who sat down in the street and tried to keep her from going to Neiman Marcus."

"I suppose we have to credit the American Revolution for giving us protests," I said.

"I suppose we do," she said, "unless something happened in Rome or Greece that SMU kept from me."

I said, "If I recall my high school teachers accurately, we were evenly split on declaring our independence. On one side were the shit disturbers, the revolutionaries, who would become patriots. They marched and held up signs saying, 'The King Sits Down to Pee.' On the other side were the stoned pacifists. They marched and held up signs saying, 'Make Turkey Dressing, Not War.' "

"I remember studying that," she said.

I said, "I often think about Paul Revere on his horse, galloping through the streets of Boston, hollering, 'The British are coming, the British are coming—don't let them have my table at Locke-Ober!' "

"I've been to Locke-Ober," she said. "I was in Boston for a banking seminar. A group of us went there for dinner one night. It was great."

I said, "You can't discuss the Revolutionary War without talking about Ticonderoga. That was the battle where Ethan Allen realized he had two first names."

"It's all coming back to me."

"Ticonderoga is often confused today with the language spoken by basketball players in the Southeastern Conference."

"I've been aware of that for some time."

We got around to dinner.

Thurlene was pleased with her half of a Caesar salad appetizer and the six-ounce filet of beef with asparagus for the main course. I went with the pasta fagioli as a starter, and the soup was followed by the veal piccata with a side of spaghetti and butter sauce.

A bottle of Tignanello for the lady, and two more martinis for the gentleman.

As we dined, I told her about the silliest protest I'd ever seen. It occurred five years ago. A whole pack of Writers Guild members in our SDC building organized a protest against management.

"They wanted a four-day week," I said, "but as far as I could tell, they were already off seven days a week. None of them did anything at work but send jokes back and forth on their computers and go to lunch. Naturally, they chose two mild spring days to carry their signs up and down Forty-eighth Street in front of the main entrance of our building."

"And you, of course," she said, "were the first person to break the picket line."

"Maybe not the first, but certainly the first to congratulate them on looking so downtrodden in their cashmere and Guccis."

Caught her grinning.

I said, "One time when I crossed the picket line a guy said, 'You should be with us, Jack.' I said, 'I would, but I'm late for lunch at 21.' Another time when I was sliding through the picket line I asked if anybody had seen my limo. It was supposed to meet me there and take me out to the Hamptons for the weekend to play National, Maidstone, and Shinnecock."

"Ginger would love to play those courses someday."

"I can get her on. I have friends in high places. But if she keeps on winning she may not need anybody's help . . . Aren't we sorry we missed the Sixties, you and me?"

"Why would we be sorry?"

"You could have dressed like Hiawatha. I could have dressed like Gandhi. We wouldn't have had to do anything but roll joints and talk about ice cream flavors and watch horror movies."

She said, "One of my bosses at the bank was an older guy who moved to Texas from Chicago. He said the best time of his life was when he was in school at Northwestern and was part of the mob that shut down the campus for two days."

I said, "There's a reformed hippie lady at *SM*—she's in charge of the library. She says the greatest thing about the Sixties was you didn't have to go to Woodstock to get laid."

Thurlene smiled, took a sip of wine, snuggled up to me in the booth, and said, "What's your position on getting laid in Palm Springs?"

It was hard to swallow. The look on her face told me this was no joke—this was a direct hit. I held it together and managed to say absolutely nothing. No attempt at humor that would spoil the moment.

Headline: Man Urgently Motions for Dinner Check.

34

Thurlene didn't leave my room until three in the morning, but she was back in my room by nine in the morning. Which was shortly after Ginger left for the golf course. We didn't have breakfast, we didn't have lunch, and it was sometime in the middle of the afternoon before we noticed from my crumpled bed that the TV had accidentally been on the Spanish channel for what must have been hours.

If that wasn't love, what was it, I ask you?

Wednesday night we donned our nonchalant poses and went to dinner with Ginger in the hotel dining room.

We believed we looked like the same people. The magazine writer and the golf mom.

Thurlene hoped she didn't have that telltale glow that says "I'm getting laid and the world is a wonderful place." I hoped I didn't have that look that says "This man is in bad need of rest or may have to be taken to the hospital soon."

Ginger wasn't fooled.

It was moments after the drinks came before dinner that Ginger grinned at Thurlene and said, "So, Mom . . . you got lucky last night, huh?"

"Christ," Thurlene said, her head dropping.

I almost choked on the celery stalk I'd taken a bite out of from the Bloody Mary I didn't even want.

Ginger smiled at both of us. "It's okay, guys. It's cool."

"Cool," I said. "I've always wanted to be cool."

"We're not cool," Thurlene said harshly.

"We're not?"

"No, we're not."

"What are we?"

"We're all grown-ups here, including this kid, and I'm changing the subject."

The kid said, "You don't have to get mad."

"I'm not mad," Thurlene said. "I'm embarrassed."

"Jesus, Mom," said Ginger. "Chill. Take your meds."

Thurlene said, "We'll discuss it *later*. I want to talk about the *major championship* that's starting tomorrow—if nobody minds."

"Are we still at Defcon four?" Ginger said.

Mom glared and said, "What about the golf course, Gin? Any low scores out there in practice? What are the other players saying?"

"We're talking golf now, is that it?" the kid said.

"We most certainly are!"

What Ginger allowed:

Most of the players were trying not to laugh too hard about the differences between the Kraft Nabisco when it was played at Mission Hills and this year's deal at Hollywood Dunes.

"The Horse Dog," they were calling it.

Everybody was happy the pro-ams were dumped. The players and press always thought the tournament's reputation suffered by having a pro-am. A major with a pro-am? The Dinah had started with one pro-am and wound up with two. A two pro-am major. Wow.

Ginger had played in one of the pro-ams last year—her first time in a major—and she remembered her amateur partners being four fat men who never spoke to her the whole eighteen.

Everybody was talking about the things that were missing at Hollywood Dunes.

One was the Oscar Mayer Wienermobile. It had become a fixture behind the first tee at Mission Hills.

The Oscar Mayer Wienermobile was being replaced with something tomorrow that was a surprise. Something Marsha Wilson was excited about, and the rumor in the locker room was that the surprise was the commissioner's idea and it was expressly designed to impress the generous French guy, Francois D'Aubigne Lagoutte.

Another thing missing was the statue of Dinah Shore. It was still on the golf course at Mission Hills. The members at Mission Hills wouldn't let the LPGA move it, even temporarily.

Worst of all, the eighteenth hole at Hollywood Dunes didn't have water around the green, so another tradition would be lost. The winner on Sunday wouldn't be able to celebrate by jumping into the pond as the winners did at Mission Hills. The winner would have to jump into a bunker or something.

Oh, there was one other thing. Tang Chen was in the field. Ginger had seen her playing a practice round with Debbie Wendell on Wednesday.

That news made Thurlene want to drop-kick an inanimate object. She said only a "foreigner" could receive a special invitation at the last minute to a major championship in the United States. It was ridiculous.

The field for the Dinah Shore, Thurlene pointed out, was always limited to one hundred players: ninety-four pros taken from the money list—tour winners, former champions, and world rankings—plus six amateurs. A qualification system similar to the Masters. Well, copied from the Masters.

She said, "You can be sure a high-minded busybody in our State Department used his influence on the LPGA to see that Tang was invited."

Ginger said, "She's not worth thinking about, Mom. She'll shoot straight up and boogie on out with a WD."

Skillfully changing the subject, I said to Ginger, "You finished tied for thirty-third in this championship last year. I looked it up. Not bad for your first time in a major."

"My game sucked last year," the kid said.

Thurlene said, "She was better in the LPGA and the Open. She was top fifteen in both."

"I still sucked," she said.

I said, "You didn't go to the Women's British Open last year, the other major. How come?"

Thurlene said, "It was held at this course way up north in Scotland that wasn't even Dornoch. We decided it wasn't worth the trouble. But we're going this summer. It's at Royal Woodhills Foxheath. It's close to London so we can stay in the city, which will be fun."

I said, "I know Royal Woodhills Foxheath. It's near Swinley Forest, the most exclusive club in England. You can't join Swinley Forest if you've ever had a job."

Later on. Coffee for Thurlene and me. No dessert for anyone.

I asked Ginger, "What's it going to take to win this thing?"

She said, "There are only two par-fives, the fifth and the thirteenth, and you can't reach either one. Tyler is saying even par-two-eighty is the number. I'm thinking lower if I can keep the bomb squad in the fairway and get the harpoon going."

"It's all up to you, huh?" I said. "Nobody else has anything to say about it?"

"Yep, just me," she said with a grin. "Why not?"

I said, "I like your attitude. The game *is* ninety percent mental."

"Z time," Ginger said, rising. "You guys have fun. See you at breakfast, Mom."

Thurlene reacted to her daughter's remark by doing the old reliable frustration thing. She propped her elbow on the table, put her thumb and forefinger on the bridge of her nose, rested her head, and closed her eyes.

35

Was it possible I spotted the LPGA commissioner mingling with the demonstrators outside the gates of Hollywood Dunes? It was, and I did. Which was why I asked the driver of the press shuttle to drop me off there at midmorning on Thursday, the day of the first round of the Horse Dog.

Thurlene and Ginger had gone to the course earlier in a courtesy car so Ginger could warm up for her noon tee time in a pairing with Suzy Scott and Mandy Park.

Thurlene didn't say how she felt that morning on two hours' sleep, but I was wide awake. It's a medical fact that when all you want to do every moment of the day or night is put your mouth, your hands, and your body on someone you're insanely in love with, you don't require much rest.

The crowd of protestors numbered in the dozens, and the commissioner was chatting with a girl in granny glasses and a prairie-woman dress who held a sign that said: HONK IF YOU HATE FRANCE.

"Marsha Wilson," I said. "What a coincidence . . . finding you here . . . in Africa . . . fighting Zulus."

"*What?*" she said.

"Don't mind me," I said. "I heard that in a dumb movie one time. I've always wanted to say it to somebody."

"What in the world are you talking about, Jack Brannon?"

"What are you doing with these people, Commissioner?"

"I'm trying to talk sense to them. Women's golf does not need this distraction. And poor Francois. What must he think?"

The demonstrators were circled around us, staring. I counted two caftans, a Pancho Villa, a Pocahontas, two Che Guevaras, and two—no, make that three—Buffy Sainte-Maries.

"You are going to see hundreds of us on the weekend," the girl in the granny glasses and prairie-woman dress said.

"Why do you want to disrupt the golf tournament?" I said to her. "It's a big deal for the city."

She said, "Golf is a pagan sport. It occupies land in this country that should be used for affordable housing."

Marsha Wilson said, "You would demolish all of the golf courses that beautify America's landscape?"

"I would torch them first," said Granny Glasses.

"You are an unintelligent and unreasonable person," Marsha said, "and I suspect the only reason you are out here is to be on TV."

Pocahontas stepped in to say, "Yes. That *is* the best way to reach the most people. 'The French Are Irrelevant.' That's a song I've been working on. I may perform it later."

"Not a bad thought," I said, "except it's hard to go up against their omelets."

Pocahontas said, "I'll ask you a question . . . whoever you are. Do you eat horse meat?"

"Not that I'm aware of," I said.

"Do you think dogs should eat horse meat?"

"I can only speak for the Lab I had for twelve years. Maggie preferred veal marsala and chicken Kiev."

Marsha Wilson said, "You people are trying to keep a wonderful group of American ladies from making a living in their chosen profession. You might consider that."

Pocahontas said, "Games are for children. Pain is for adults. Pain and suffering. We protest against France and golf in the name of peace, love, and understanding."

"I don't see Cindy Sheehan anywhere," I said, looking around.

A Buffy Sainte-Marie gave me the finger.

Marsha Wilson said, "What do you think the new sponsor should do? Our generous Frenchman? Is there anything he can do to win you over?"

Pocahontas said, "He could crash and burn to death in his private jet. That would be accommodating."

There were other surprises Thursday.

One was the statue that mysteriously had risen behind the first tee—Commissioner Marsha Wilson's surprise replacement for the popular but now missing Oscar Mayer Wienermobile.

It was the towering statue of Francois D'Aubigne Lagoutte.

He would rise over Ludwig Beethoven in Central Park, or any of the Yankee and Confederate generals scattered around Gettysburg. He was in a business suit, one hand in his pocket, the other hand reaching out at something. Perhaps at "Darryl Zanuck," the sixth hole.

The statue was made of wood and plaster—there hadn't been time for granite, marble, or bronze—and it was painted. The statue of the Frenchman was painted in a blue pinstriped suit, orange shirt, and green necktie, and his sunglasses were a mirrored purple.

He stood on a pedestal in the center of a flower bed.

Thurlene and I were staring at it when we were joined by Marsha Wilson and a white-haired, deeply tanned gentleman in a cream blazer.

"What do you think, Jack Brannon?" the commissioner asked.

I said, "I'm not sure. I'd like to have seen the Wienermobile in person. What does the French guy think about it?"

"He approves of it, although he says the artist has parted his hair on the wrong side."

"Darn," I said. "You work hard, you make plans, but something always falls through the cracks."

"Joke if you must, Jack Brannon, but Francois is touched, and the artist—the sculptor—says it will be no trouble to fix the part in the hair before next year's tournament. Francois was quite moved at the unveiling ceremony this morning before the first group went off."

I stuck out my hand to the guy with the tan in the blazer. "We haven't met. I'm Jack Brannon."

"Indeed you are," the guy said, shaking my hand.

"I am *so* sorry," Marsha Wilson said. "Jack . . . Thurlene Clayton . . . this is Norris Mason. Norris is president of Hollywood Dunes Country Club and the tournament chairman for our wonderful event."

"It's *Mason Norris*," the man said.

"Well, of course it is!" Marsha said. "This week has me coming and going. I do apologize, Mason. What must I have been thinking?"

"You look familiar," I said to Mason Norris.

"Oh, you're catching that, are you?" he said with a smile. "I was in films for years. One of those chaps you know the face, but the name escapes you. I was sometimes Best Friend, but most often I was Casual Acquaintance of Best Friend. I was known in the industry as 'the poor man's Cesar Romero,' which I found rather flattering."

I asked, "Have you always been a golfer?"

"Goodness, I don't play golf," he said. "I wouldn't go near it, but I do like the real estate end of it. By the way, you must come to my hospitality tent. It's the big one on the right side of the eighteenth fairway. The food and drink will meet with your approval, and you'll see a lot of old familiar faces."

I said, "Most of the old familiar faces will be alive, will they?"

"Oh, that is funny," Mason said. "I must pass it on."

Marsha Wilson gazed at the statue and said, "My first thought was to have a horse on one side of Francois and a dog on the other, but my deputy said it would be over the top. Claudia also brought up the point that no matter which breed of dog the sculptor might choose, the owners of that breed would be offended."

"Excellent point," Thurlene said.

I said, "I can only speak for myself, but I would have hated to walk in here today and see Maggie sitting next to Francois."

Mason Norris said, "I agree wholeheartedly with your deputy. I have two Yorkies—Hedda and Louella—and the thought of them being minced and sitting in a can on a shelf is unbearable."

I said we had to be going. Time to watch a little golf.

———

The biggest surprise of the day was Ginger Clayton shooting a miserable 76. Thurlene took every bogey personally.

It was a six-over-par round that left Ginger in a three-way tie for twentieth place, nineteen players and six strokes behind Lorena Ochoa's even-par 70, which led the Horse Dog.

There was no big mishap for Ginger in the round. More a day of slow bleeding. A missed putt here, a bad bounce there, a questionable club selection somewhere else.

We talked to Tyler Hughes while Ginger was in the scorer's tent.

The caddie said, "When she three-putted the first two greens, it put her in a bad frame of mind. She never got out of it. It didn't help that Suzy Scott got off to a great start and shot seventy-one. When Suzy birdied two of the first three holes, Ginger spent the rest of the round trying to catch Suzy instead of playing her own game. She forced things, and the golf course bit her back."

Thurlene said, "She's not blaming you, is she?"

Tyler said, "No, she's just hot at herself. It was one of those days. We'll get it together. She hasn't lost her swing."

Ginger was still furious when she came out of the scorer's tent.

"I made six mistakes today and paid for every damn one," she said. "I even bogeyed the lollipop."

A reference to the fourteenth hole, "Shirley Temple," the ninety-nine-yard par-three with no water and no sand. Ginger had three-putted it.

"How can I three-rake that hole?" she said. "The green is totally flat, it's slow as mud, but I miss it from two feet. Two feet! Jesus. Talk about a sanitarium case. Lock me up, man."

We tried to console her.

Thurlene said, "It's only the first round, Gin. There's a long way to go. Lot of golf to be played."

I said, "Your bad round is behind you, Ginger. The course is playing tough. Every player's gonna take some lumps."

Ginger shook her head. "I don't make a single birdie all day. Is that lame or what? How 'bout my first putt at the seventh? I'm looking at a fifteen-footer for birdie and all of a sudden I'm looking at a ten-footer for par! What was *that* all about?"

"It was about chasing Suzy Scott," I said.

"I know," she said, "but I couldn't stop myself. Idiot. Jesus! I'm gonna go putt. I gotta work on the harpoon. You guys go on back . . . and don't wait on me to eat. I may be here till dark."

She stalked off.

Thurlene relaxed at a table under an umbrella on the veranda and smoked while I went in the pressroom to grab a score sheet. This being a major, it was more crowded than most LPGA pressrooms. There must have been twenty writers on hand. Three times as many as there were at the Firm Chick or the Speedy Arrow.

I visited with a couple of pals from the lodge. Cy Ronack with *Golf World* and Smokey Barwood, who was once a sports agent and was now an editor at First Glimpse Publications.

The three of us were among the scant few golf writers today who don't wear short pants. We discussed that issue. We also discussed the fact that we were rooting for a heterosexual to win the Horse Dog.

Burch Webb, the famous architect, was in the interview area. By way of explaining the improvements he'd done to Hollywood Dunes, he was taking his listeners on a journey through the history of golf course design.

He was dressed in a heavy jacket, vest, necktie, knickers, and a wool golf cap, doing what he could to look like Alister MacKenzie in 1927.

I listened to Burch say that the biggest change in course design— until *his* work—occurred when the gutty airmailed the featherie. The improved golf ball. Which hastened the widening of fairways in the middle 1800s.

I left when Burch went into the old lie of how golf courses began to consist of eighteen holes instead of three, six, twelve. It was when someone realized that a bottle of Scotch contained eighteen jiggers, therefore . . .

The score sheet wasn't a pretty sight if you were a Ginger Clayton rooter. The top twenty after one round read like this:

1.	Lorena Ochoa	70
2.	Suzy Scott	71
T3.	Annika Sorenstam	72
T3.	Jan Dunn	72
T3.	Morgan Pressel	72
6.	Penny Cooper	73
T6.	Linda Merle Draper	73
T6.	Paula Creamer	73
9.	Tricia Hurt	74
T9.	Sophie Gustafson	74
T9.	Marian Hornbuckle	74
T9.	Angela Stanford	74
T9.	Peaches Crowder	74
T9.	Juli Inkster	74
15.	Suzann Petterson	75
T15.	Natalie Gulbis	75
T15.	Nu Sung Kim	75
T15.	Brittany Lincicome	75
T15.	Mandy Park	75
20.	Ginger Clayton	76
T20.	Cristie Kerr	76
T20.	Michelle Wie	76

"It's not the six strokes," Thurlene said. "There are too many good players ahead of her. How in the world is she going to jump nineteen good players?"

"Shoot lower," I said.

"Terrific idea. I'll tell her that."

I said, "There was some good news today. Debbie Wendell shot seventy-nine . . . Tang Chen shot eighty-six."

"Two short of wonderful," Thurlene said.

"What do you mean?"

"If Tang had shot eighty-eight, she would be off this tour for a year—and out of our lives. It's an LPGA rule. It was put in place to eliminate players who don't deserve to be out here. Shoot an eighty-eight or worse and you're history."

"I've never heard of the rule, but I like it. The golf course is playing hard. Maybe Tang Chen can shoot an eighty-eight tomorrow."

"Maybe I can help her."

36

W̲e took the night off. Well, more or less. There was grop-
ing and kissing and tangling and untangling, but sheer
exhaustion kicked in and we were better off for laps-
ing into seven hours' sleep, both of us drifting off in the middle of
the same sentence about life, health, divorce, romance, marriage,
daughters—or it could have been golf.

Thurlene dashed to her cabana Friday morning to be doing one
thing or another when Ginger woke up. I met them for breakfast in
the hotel coffee shop. We read newspapers as we ate.

Ginger said something that sounded like "Ug" when she read the
short piece about herself in *USA Today*, a story saying the Hollywood Dunes course gave the "child star" and "one of the championship favorites" her comeuppance in the first round.

"This track owes me one, I'll tell you that," Ginger said.

The three of us rode out to the club in a courtesy car driven by
a volunteer lady in her seventies. She wasn't wearing a volunteer's
polka-dot blouse and skirt, but she *was* wearing what Thurlene esti-
mated as $150,000 worth of jewelry. She was bronze as a casket, and
she took the liberty of telling us that she was a member of both El-
dorado and Thunderbird country clubs and had no idea Hollywood
Dunes existed until this week.

"I'm sure Ike or Jerry never played here," she said as we neared
the front gates and the same dozens of demonstrators from the day
before.

As the courtesy car glided slowly through a path of demonstrators
that was cleared by the police, our lady driver wearily said, "Isn't

this a shame? There's never a suicide bomber around when you need one."

"I like this woman," I whispered to Thurlene.

"What a surprise," she whispered back.

The first thing we did was survey the big scoreboard on the clubhouse veranda near the statue of the Frenchman. We were curious to see if the golf course was giving up any low rounds among the early starters. It wasn't. Everybody was over par.

Ginger went off to practice. She wouldn't be playing for three hours.

The thing that delighted Thurlene the most on the scoreboard was Tang Chen's first nine holes. She was out in 45, ten over.

"Let's go," she said, giving me a tug. "We have nothing to do for a while. We can catch up with Tang on the back."

"Why?"

"Maybe I'll get a chance to step on her ball in the rough."

"You wouldn't do that."

We were already walking toward the back nine.

"I wouldn't, huh? She poisons my daughter and nobody does anything about it. She physically attacks my daughter and nobody does anything about it. You don't know how many letters I've written to Marsha Wilson. All I get back is 'It's something we're tracking,' 'It's on our agenda,' 'Perhaps an overhaul of our invitation system should be examined more thoroughly,' 'It's not a *branding* issue' . . . What a commissioner."

I said, "I wonder if Ginger has talked to any of the other players about Tang and Debbie. Do you know?"

"I know she hasn't . . . and I know she wouldn't. She wouldn't want to stir up a shitstorm. She thinks winning is the best revenge. That's what she's about, and I'm proud of her for thinking it."

"But you're the mom and you have an obligation to protect her—in whatever way you can."

"Damn right I do. So if the little chink gets close to an eighty-eight out here, and I'm standing near her golf ball . . . turn your head."

———

We found Tang Chen on the fifteenth hole, "Ginger Rogers."

"Her real name was Virginia Katherine McMath," I said.

"Whose real name?"

"Ginger Rogers's, for whom this hole is named."

"You know this how?"

"I know it because she was raised in Fort Worth. We take pride in these things . . . Ginger Rogers, Ben Hogan, and yours truly all went to the same high school . . . but not at the same time, of course. Dear old Paschal High . . . purple and white, fight, fight."

"You and Ben and Ginger, huh? That must explain your occasional arrogance."

"I'm only arrogant when I'm around arrogant people. I can tell you something about your old high school you can be proud of: Woodrow Wilson in Dallas is the only public school in America that's turned out two Heisman Trophy winners. Davey O'Brien in thirty-eight . . . Tim Brown in eighty-seven."

"I know that. Everybody who went to Woodrow knows that."

"A lot of sportswriters don't know it, but they know not to jack around with me on that kind of stuff."

Tang Chen was in a twosome with Fujita Izama of Japan, who spoke no English and was almost as bad a golfer as the Chinese girl. It was what the pressroom wits call a "U.N. pairing."

Tang was now fourteen over par and had driven into the rough at fifteen.

I was relieved that her golf ball was on the opposite side of the fairway from us, mainly from Thurlene.

I enjoyed watching Thurlene delight in the sight of Tang chopping around in the rough and taking a double bogey on the hole. Which put her sixteen over with three holes to play.

Tang could afford one bogey. One bogey and two pars and she could make it to the house with an 87—and escape banishment from the tour.

Good thing there was no gallery. Thurlene let out a groan when Tang sank a thirty-foot putt for a par at "Mae West," the sixteenth hole. She had put her tee shot in the bunker and played a poor sand shot, but the putter saved her.

One hole later, at "Sam Goldwyn," the par-four seventeenth, Thurlene let out a louder groan when Tang sank a twenty-foot putt for a bogey five when it looked certain she'd make another double bogey after hacking around in the rough again.

"I'm announcing this is no longer fun," Thurlene said.

Now the Chinese girl was at "Tinsel Town" the eighteenth hole, an easy par-four if the golfer could keep it in the fairway off the tee. There were trees on the left and out of bounds on the right, due to the row of hospitality tents.

A par was a must for her.

"I promise you she doesn't know what's riding on this," Thurlene said. "She has no idea the eighty-eight rule exists. None of us knew it until the Tricia Hurt thing last fall."

"What Tricia Hurt thing?"

"Something else our earnest commissioner covered up. Last October at the Hootinannie Classic in Nashville, Tricia withdrew in the second round with a sudden 'wrist injury' when she was two holes away from shooting an eighty-eight or worse. We weren't there. Gin was still recovering from being poisoned, but Linda Merle Draper filled us in. Linda Merle, as a matter of fact, was paired with Tricia when it happened."

It was Tricia's agent at ISC, a man named Bloody Tillis, who saved her butt. Bloody Tillis jumped in a golf cart and rushed out to the sixteenth hole and told Tricia to WD *right now*. If she didn't, the eighty-eight rule would kick her off the tour for a year, and this would cost her—and the agency—a great deal of endorsement money. Tricia withdrew on the spot, claiming an injured wrist. What made the incident more scandalous was that two hours later Tricia was seen hitting balls on the range. Most of the players went nuts, but Marsha Wilson convinced them that keeping the incident "in house" was for the good of the tour. Tricia Hurt was a lovely young girl and a stellar gate attraction. The commissioner thought they should keep those things in mind.

"You people sure have a lot of things out here nobody can write about," I said.

That statement had barely come off my lips when Tang took a swing at her drive on eighteen and sent a wild slice into the sky that appeared to be heading over the boundary fence toward Mason Norris's hospitality tent.

As the ball curved through the air, Thurlene said, "Aw, gee . . . heck . . . darn . . . she's going out of bounds."

Then when the ball landed on the patio and bounced around looking for a plate of smoked salmon to settle on, Thurlene yelled, "Yes . . . yes!"

I said, "I'm very pleased she did it without your help."

"Come on," she said excitedly. Another tug. "Maybe I can be the first person to tell her she's pork-fried rice."

37

M uch to Thurlene's pleasure the Chinese girl struggled to a quad on the hole, a pitiful eight, which gave her a round of 91 for the day. Three over the rules limit.

It was hard for Thurlene to hide her glee.

I said, "I can't help noticing. You haven't had this much fun since, when? Two nights ago?"

She may not have heard every word of that. Tang Chen was coming out of the scorer's tent and walking over to us.

"I play so bad," Tang said. "I miss cut."

"It's a little worse than that," Thurlene said.

"What worse for me?" Tang said.

Thurlene said, "A little thing about the rules. The LPGA rules state that if a player shoots eighty-eight or higher, that player is barred from our tour for one year and must go through the qualifying process to return. I'm sure you will be informed of this officially."

"Oh, no! No more play golf in States?"

"You . . . are . . . out . . . of . . . here, my dear. History. Beijing bound. And I can't say I'm sorry. Not after what you and Debbie did to my daughter in Oklahoma and New Mexico!"

"I do nothing. Debbie do nothing."

"You know damn well what you did."

"No, no, please. I do nothing. I make joke is all. Play tricks."

Tears came to Tang's eyes. I almost felt sorry for her, but of course she was a Chinaman.

Thurlene said, "You make *joke*? You put rat poison on Ginger's popcorn in Oklahoma City . . . in Ruidoso, you sneak up on her and knock her down in the trees, try to cripple her so Debbie Wendell can win the golf tournament! Those were fucking *jokes*?"

"How you know this?"

"How I know this? I know this because I'm not *stupid*, Tang. Now I want the truth out of you and maybe there's something we can do about it."

"You can help me?" Tang sniffled. "No go back China?"

"Maybe," Thurlene said.

That drew an inquisitive look from me. What did Thurlene have in mind?

Tang said, "I tell truth, you can fix?"

"If I hear the whole truth, I might try."

"No Debbie. She do nothing."

"You acted alone? No Debbie?"

"No Debbie."

"I don't believe you."

"I do myself. But I never want to hurt Ginger. Just scare."

"You could have *killed* Ginger with the rat poison, goddamn it!"

"No, no. Never. I only use tiny bit. Make sick."

"How would you know how much to use?"

"Everybody in China have do-shoo-chang . . . know how to use. I get do-shoo-chang from father. China have many rats. I only want to scare. Bad joke. Very bad joke. I do it for money."

"You tried to harm my daughter for *money*?"

"I poor China girl. I make mistake."

"You sure as hell did! Who paid you? Debbie?"

"No Debbie. Debbie my friend. Miz Wendell pay. I so sorry now."

"*Mrs. Wendell?*"

"Miz Wendell pay me to scare Ginger . . . make her no win, maybe."

Thurlene was too stunned to speak for a moment. She looked at me with what I would describe as fire in her eyes, if that description hadn't already been used somewhere.

"Can you *believe* this?" Thurlene said to me.

I shrugged my shoulders and raised my eyebrows. Which generally translates into "Stuff happens."

Thurlene looked back at Tang. "How much did she pay you?"

Tang Chen said, "She pay two thousand dollar."

"Ann Wendell paid you two thousand dollars? That's what I'm hearing?"

"I poor Chinese girl . . . have nothing. I buy good jeans. Government buy golf clubs, no buy clothes."

"Come with me," Thurlene said.

"Come where?"

"We're going to the LPGA office. It's in the clubhouse. You're going to tell them exactly what you told me. In fact, you're going to put it in writing. You come along too, Jack. Having the press there will guarantee their full attention."

"Pleased to be invited," I said.

Tang Chen said, "Why I go with you? Why I do this?"

Thurlene said, "Why you do this? I'll tell you why you do this. You do this because your fucking life depends on it!"

And Thurlene dragged Tang Chen away by her shirt collar.

38

We barged into the LPGA office unannounced. I took a seat in a corner as Thurlene slammed Tang Chen into a chair across from Claudia Bradley, the deputy commissioner, and told the Chinese girl to start talking.

Everything was news to Claudia.

The deputy had not heard a word about the poison incident six months ago. Claudia was appalled to learn that Tang Chen was responsible for Ginger being bushwhacked last week in Ruidoso, and only moments before the deputy had found us in the trees outside the Port-O-Let.

When Thurlene mentioned that Ann Wendell had slapped her own daughter around at the Estee Lauder Classic, it was news to Claudia.

Claudia paused between the revelations to stare out a window, and it crossed my mind that the deputy was wondering if all this could add up to Marsha Wilson losing her job and Claudia taking over as commissioner.

Claudia called out to someone, "Go find Ann Wendell for me . . . and bring her in here at once. The last time I saw her she was in Norris Mason's hospitality tent."

"It's Mason Norris," Thurlene said politely.

Claudia said, "Of course it is. Thank you."

Then she yelled at the doorway, "And find Marsha somewhere!"

While we waited for Ann Wendell, Claudia asked Thurlene what she would like to see done about all this. Did she wish to press charges against Tang Chen?

Thurlene said, "No, not now. For months I've been thinking Tang and Debbie were the culprits. Now I know the real culprit is Ann Wendell. Debbie had nothing to do with any of it, and poor Tang here . . . she knows not that she knows not. I do have an idea Marsha may go along with, knowing how much she dislikes scandals involving the tour."

Claudia said, "You're referring to the Tricia Hurt affair. I wasn't on board then, but I do believe the commissioner was acting in the best interest of the tour. What are you suggesting?"

Thurlene said, "Tang Chen will put a confession in writing, right here, right now, in English . . . explaining what she did and who paid her to do it. In exchange for this, she never turned in a scorecard today with the ninety-one on it. She withdrew. Her scorecard has been corrected by an LPGA official. You, perhaps. Tang meant to withdraw, but she wasn't sure how to do it, being unfamiliar with the language. So she actually hasn't broken the eighty-eight rule. Therefore, she's not barred from competition in the United States."

Claudia stared at Thurlene. "And what do we do about the player Tang was paired with, hypothetically?"

Thurlene said, "She was paired with Fujita Izama of Japan. Fujita speaks no English. She was shooting an eighty-five herself and paying no attention to what Tang was shooting. She signed the card without looking at it . . . and I'm sure she has no earthly idea the eighty-eight rule exists."

Claudia studied Thurlene again for a moment, then said, "I'll take a wild guess at something. If we don't go along with this charade, is it likely that everything I've heard here will appear in *SM* magazine? Is that a possibility?"

"A very real one," Thurlene said.

Claudia fixed a look at me. "And what is going to keep you from writing this anyway, Jack Brannon? You *are* a journalist, are you not?"

Thurlene answered for me with a smile. "I will ask him not to."

Claudia Bradley gave Tang Chen four sheets of blank stationery and a pen and told her to sit over to the side and start writing. Next, she asked an office worker to go to the scorer's tent and bring her the scorecards for the last twenty players who had completed their rounds—there were things she needed to take a look at. Nothing important. Just checking figures on various holes.

While we waited, the deputy asked if any of us wanted something to drink. Tang shook her head no. I passed. Thurlene said she'd take a Coke but what she really wanted was a cigarette.

"Have one of mine," Claudia said, and offered her a Merit Ultra Light.

Thurlene was shocked to learn the deputy smoked, but recovered hastily and took the Merit. Claudia lit it for her, and one for herself.

"I knew there was something I liked about you," Thurlene said to Claudia Bradley.

"I'm gradually quitting," Claudia said.

Thurlene replied with a grin, "Yeah, me too."

Tang Chen coughed and waved her hands.

"No smoke 'em. Smoke 'em very bad."

"*You*," Thurlene snapped at Tang. "Shut the fuck up."

Taking an ashtray out of a desk drawer and pushing it toward Thurlene to share, the deputy said, "I assume you have an idea about what should be done with Ann Wendell."

Thurlene said, "She ought to go to jail, but I'll settle for her being barred from the tour for as long as possible. I'll help make the case in front of the board, if that's necessary."

Claudia Bradley said, "It's frustrating that Marsha kept me out of the loop on all this."

"Yes, it is," Thurlene said. "Not very commissioner-like, if you ask me . . . if you want of the opinion of *Ginger Clayton*'s mother."

Claudia said, "You don't need to turn up the heat, Thurlene. I get it."

The office worker, a young woman, brought the stack of score-cards into the room and put them on Claudia's desk. At the same time she looked horrified to find Claudia and Thurlene smoking cigarettes.

"We're not smoking," Claudia said, glancing at her.

"No. Of course not," the young woman said, and fled.

Claudia thumbed through the scorecards until she found Tang Chen's and pulled it out of the stack. Then she reached for a pencil.

"It seems a little artwork is required here," she said, scratching out the 91 on the card and drawing lines all over it and marking a big "WD" on it.

"I'm not seeing this," I said. "I'm not here, I wasn't in the room, I don't understand the question—and nobody is smoking."

Tang Chen finished the confession, then sat quietly with her hands folded in her lap, staring at the floor. Claudia made copies of the confession on a machine behind her. Thurlene stuck a copy in her shoulder bag.

About then, Ann Wendell entered the office, jerking her arm away from a security guard.

"What am I doing here?" she snarled.

Claudia Bradley handed Ann Wendell a copy of Tang's confession.

"Read this and we'll talk," the deputy said.

Ann Wendell momentarily looked alarmed as she began to read the document but swiftly managed to cover it up with a chuckle.

She sneered at the paper.

She tossed it on Claudia's desk.

"Anything in there look familiar to you?" Thurlene said.

Ann Wendell glared at Thurlene with a world of hate. "Did you put her up to this, Thurlene? What is she getting out of it? How much money?"

"Good act, Ann," Thurlene said. "It's not working."

Ann Wendell squinted at Claudia Bradley. "Are you prepared to take the word of this lying little Chinese slut over mine?"

Claudia said she was bringing the matter before the LPGA's board of directors in an emergency session as soon as this championship was over.

The deputy added, "You will be asked to appear, and you are welcome to bring an attorney. We understand and accept that your daughter is in no way involved in any of this. As for Mrs. Clayton, she's not interested in filing criminal charges against you, provided our board of directors bars you from our tour, but she may ask for a restraining order."

"A restraining order for *what*?" Ann Wendell said.

Thurlene said, "To keep you a hundred miles away from my daughter, you sick piece of shit!"

Thurlene told me later that she'd been torn between "low-rent cunt" and "sick piece of shit" and settled on the latter. It was more ladylike.

Ann Wendell gasped. Then gruffly said, "I don't have to listen to any more of this!" And she marched out of the office, holding her head high, doing her best to look offended.

Moments later Monique Hopkins, the assistant who handles player interviews, stuck her head in the door.

"I hear you're looking for Marsha," she said to the deputy.

Claudia said, "Do you know where she is?"

Monique said, "Marsha's in Denmark."

"She's *where*?" Claudia almost shouted.

"She flew to Copenhagen last night. She's attending a world seminar on marketing and branding."

Claudia said, "Are you standing here telling me that Marsha Wilson, the commissioner of the Ladies Professional Golf Association—in the middle of our first major championship of the year—has gone to *Denmark*?"

"I thought you knew." Monique shrugged and left the room.

Thurlene and Claudia stared at each other and began to laugh. After they had gotten back under control, Thurlene said, "This looks like something else to bring up before the board."

Claudia said, "I won't rule it out."

Out on the course, where Ginger was working on a 73, Thurlene kept saying the same thing over and over and laughing at herself after she'd say it. I would hear:

" 'Excuse me. I'm here for the first major of the year. I would like to see the LPGA commissioner, please.' . . . 'Oh, I'm sorry. She's in Denmark.' "

"You like that, don't you?" I said.

"It will stay with me for years . . . 'May I speak to Commissioner Wilson, please?' . . . 'I'm sorry. She's in Denmark.' "

I was happy to see Thurlene in a good mood. It kept her from moaning about Ginger spoiling her two birdies on the back nine with four bogeys, all of which resulted from tee shots that rolled into the rough.

At the end of the second round, the score sheet looked like this:

1.	Penny Cooper	73–71—144
2.	Natalie Gulbis	75–70—145
3.	Mandy Park	75–71—146
4.	Paula Creamer	73–74—147
T4.	Linda Merle Draper	73–74—147
T4.	Cristie Kerr	76–71—147
T4.	Jan Dunn	72–75—147
8.	Annika Sorenstam	72–76—148
T8.	Sophie Gustafson	74–74—148
T8.	Angela Stanford	74–74—148
T8.	Marian Hornbuckle	74–74—148
9.	Ginger Clayton	76–73—149
T9.	Suzy Scott	71–78—149
T9.	Suzann Petterson.	75–74—149
T9.	Morgan Pressel	72–77—149
T9.	Lorena Ochoa	70–79—149
T9.	Tricia Hurt	74–75—149
T9.	Hee Bee Kim	78–71—149

Thurlene studied the sheet and sighed. "My God, she's in a seven-way tie for ninth . . . and still five strokes and eleven players behind. Penny Cooper's going to be tough to catch. She's a good front-runner."

"Penny Cooper was one of the first Lolitas, wasn't she?"

"Yes. Penny was part of the first group of good young ones . . . Penny, Tricia, Paula, Michelle, Natalie, Morgan . . ."

"The new wave of cupcakes."

"The cupcake Lolitas, that was them."

I said, "It's good for Ginger the course is playing tough. She shoots three over par today and still moves up from twentieth to ninth."

"Her bad start isn't helping your story, is it?"

"The story's not riding on whether Ginger wins here or not."

"Do you think she'll still make the cover if she finishes sort of okay? Like, I don't know . . . top ten or whatever?"

"There's no way to outguess my boss. I don't know what else could be competing for the cover this week. Middle of March? Probably a college basketball player somewhere . . . maybe an NBA guy. We've had hoops on the cover three weeks in a row, but that doesn't bother Gary Crane. He likes armpits."

39

Ginger Clayton wasn't surprised by the news regarding the Thermostat Queen. Ann Wendell had long ago retired the trophy for Mom from Hell. Ginger said she must have had a best-buy thing goin'. She only paid the lettuce wrap two large to do the deed. Jesus.

This was Friday evening before dinner. I was with Thurlene and Ginger in the living room of their cabana. We were filling Ginger in on everything that had taken place that afternoon.

Well, nearly everything. We skipped the scorecard artwork. Maybe when the statute of limitations was over—around 2019.

Thurlene informed Ginger that the kid wasn't to discuss *any* of the rest of it with *anybody*, not even Tyler, her caddie.

Ginger said, "I'm happy Debbie skated. I've never been able to get my head around Deb wanting to hurt me."

Thurlene said, "I owe Debbie a big apology."

We started out as a table for four in the hotel dining room. Thurlene and myself with Ginger and Tyler. But soon we made room for a fifth person at our table—Debbie Wendell. We noticed her sitting alone across the room. Ginger waved her over, and she eagerly joined us.

It was quite a contrast to me, seeing Ginger and Debbie together. Debbie was a year older, but she seemed much younger, not to mention naive and sort of clueless.

Her mom, Debbie said, was suffering from a bad headache and staying in the room. And her friend Tang Chen, in case we didn't know it, had withdrawn with a wrist injury. Tang was in her room tonight, not feeling well either.

Debbie had barely made the cut with rounds of 77 and 79, but she was was hoping to play better over the last thirty-six holes and pick up a good check.

"You're still in it, Gin," Debbie said.

"Maybe, but I gotta lay down a good one tomorrow," Ginger said. "I couldn't stay out of the damn rough on the back side. If you go one yard off-line, you're scrambled eggs. That stuff is so grabby. And these fairways are like cement. The ball keeps rolling. Man, my tee ball got broke today."

"Your tee ball 'got broke'?" Thurlene said. "I knew you should have gone to college."

Tyler Hughes said, "We're fixing her tee ball tomorrow morning. I know what's wrong. She started to stand too far away from the ball—and spread her feet too wide. Players do this without realizing it. It makes them feel strong. Ginger was going for distance instead of accuracy."

At the risk of finding myself trapped in a *Golf Digest* instruction article and thereby falling into a coma, I said, "What's the remedy?"

Ginger said, "I stand up taller and relax my upper body."

"Set your feet the same width as your shoulders," Tyler said.

"You don't want your body tense," Thurlene said.

"No, you want to be able to give yourself time to wind up, and you want to keep your left shoulder behind the ball," said Tyler.

Ginger said, "Swing inside out."

"Right. That way, your weight will move in the same direction as the club. When the club goes back, your weight goes back. Same thing when you come forward. We'll work on it."

By then, I was pretending to doze off, leaning sideways, looking as if I was in danger of falling out of my chair.

Nobody laughed.

———

Saturday brought out bigger crowds—it didn't hurt that network TV was on hand—and prominent among the galleries were the roving bands of postgraduate female drunks in shorts, tank tops, and flip-flops, most of them dangling beer cups at ten in the morning

Right. Those people. The ones who made "the Dinah" famous in the first place.

Along with them, predictably, came the Unsightly, the Demented, the Get-in-the-Holes, and the You-Da-Mans. The sophisticates who always come out of nowhere when there are TV cameras on the premises.

As for the demonstrators outside the front gates, they hadn't grown much in number by Saturday. Say a half dozen.

Among the additions I believe I observed a Morticia Addams, an Alexander the Great, a Joan Baez, two more Che Guevaras, and what looked like three more Buffy Sainte-Maries.

All of the instruction stuff must have worked. Ginger played jam-up, threw down a 71. Marian Hornbuckle, who was paired with Ginger, shot the same score. That 71 was nearly the best round of the day, but Sophie Gustafson came in with an even par 70, which moved her into a tie for first.

At the end of the day the scoreboard showed an unusual number of accomplished players in contention going into Sunday. The top ten:

1.	Penny Cooper	73–71–74—218
T1.	Sophie Gustafson	74–74–70—218
3.	Paula Creamer	73–74–72—219
T3.	Marian Hornbuckle	74–74–71—219
5.	Ginger Clayton	76–73–71—220
T5.	Jan Dunn	72–75–73—220
T5.	Natalie Gulbis	75–70–75—220
8.	Morgan Pressel	72–77–72—221
T8.	Suzy Scott	71–78–72—221
T8.	Hee Bee Kim	78–71–72—221

Before I joined Thurlene and Ginger in their cabana for a room service dinner, I received a long-distance call from Hoyt Newkirk in Ruidoso.

He said, "Son, I got Jimmy Choo Choo and Eddie Wing Tips out here playin' a little golf and they want me to give 'em some action on the girlie tournament you're at. How's that there Ginger playin'?"

"She's in contention," I said.

"Hell, that don't tell me nothin'. I know she's in contention. I ain't brain dead even though I live in New Mexico. She's two shots and four girlies behind, tied with two of them others, and one shot ahead of three more. Is she gonna win it, is what I'm asking."

"She thinks she is," I said.

"That's all I need to know. Choo Choo and Wing Tips want to give me Ginger at twenty to one against the field," Hoyt said. "I gotta go for it. Man's got to make a bet every day, don't you see? He might be walkin' around lucky and not know it."

Not much was said at dinner. Ginger ate soup and salad and was quiet, although not in her mind. I knew she was already focusing on tomorrow's round. The hardest thing for a golfer to do in competition is keep concentrating, stay in the present, not be bothered by outside influences, take the course one shot at a time, one hole at a time. But I didn't say any of that to Ginger. She knew it, and I wasn't in the guru business anyhow.

Ginger retired to her own room after dinner to let a TV movie put her to sleep. Thurlene and I went to the hotel bar for a while. I had a beer and she had a white wine. We took our drinks to an outdoor terrace off the bar so she could smoke.

I said, "You can be proud of that kid of yours . . . playing herself back into this championship the way she has. The leaderboard is something else. This is some kind of tournament. It's certainly more fun for me than watching Tiger Woods play blindfolded and beat up on the slugs."

"It *is* a golf tournament," Thurlene said. "I wish I could enjoy it."

Nothing was said for a moment, and for whatever reason I found myself laughing quietly about something. Thurlene looked at me with what you call your curiosity.

"What?" she said.

"It's not important."

"It must have been. What?"

I said, "Aw, I was just thinking how there are those in the world who might question my scrupulous journalistic objectivity these days."

"Because of what's going on with us, I take it?"

Forcing a smile, I said, "To be honest about it, yeah. Here I am bedding down the mother of a cover subject, giving her career advice, and rooting myself silly for her. You probably can't find that in the *Columbia Journalism Review* handbook."

"No, I suppose not. What shall we do about it?"

"I hope we don't do anything," I said. "Love trumps journalism every time. Anybody with sense knows that."

40

In my day I've run into my share of professional disaster-dodgers. The people who tell you, "I was supposed to be on that plane," or, "We had left the island only an hour before the tidal wave hit," or "The molten lava came within fifty yards of our cabin."

I never expected to become a professional disaster-dodger myself, but Sunday morning changed that. Now it was possible for me to say to somebody in the future, "I could have been standing there when the statue toppled over."

The fact is, the statue didn't topple over. It was pushed over by a turban, a caftan, a Charles Manson, and two Buffy Sainte-Maries. They had bought tickets to the tournament for the express purpose of doing it, and they had proudly surrendered to a TV news crew.

Thurlene and I arrived a half hour after it happened. We found Claudia Bradley supervising the workers who had lifted the statue back up on its pedestal and were securing it with two-by-fours and wires attached to the clubhouse roof.

The statue hadn't been drastically damaged. Claudia was holding one of the statue's arms in her hand, the arm that had reached out toward the sixth hole, "Darryl Zanuck." It was hoped the arm could be glued back onto the body of Francois D'Aubigne Lagoutte.

Claudia was a professional disaster-dodger herself.

"I was standing right there," she said, pointing. "But I saw it coming quicker than Ann Wendell and Francois did. Ann had the audacity to be out here acting like nothing happened yesterday. Nothing that involved her in the least. They were standing together. She was saying something to him, but Francois wasn't listening. He was admiring himself."

It seemed to happen in slow motion, Claudia said.

"It was like watching on TV when the statue of Saddam came down in Baghdad. I remember thinking that very thing. I was thinking, 'God in Heaven . . . here comes Saddam. Saddam is coming down on top of me.' But I jumped out of the way in the nick of time."

Ann Wendell and Francois weren't so nimble. They were struck and pinned under the statue. Both were rushed to a hospital, Ann with a broken arm and broken leg, Francois with cracked ribs.

Claudia said, "Ann was in a daze on the stretcher when she was carried to the ambulance. She kept mumbling cuss words . . . and saying things to somebody named Ed. She was saying something about a thermostat. I have no idea what she was talking about."

Thurlene said, "I do. I'll tell you about it someday over cocktails and cigarettes."

When Francois was carted to the ambulance on a stretcher, according to Claudia, the Frenchman was mumbling that he might have to rethink his involvement with the sport of golf and the United States along with it.

I said, "That should be welcome news to everybody, except Marsha Wilson."

Thurlene smiled. Claudia smiled.

Claudia had raced out to the practice range in a golf cart to catch Debbie Wendell before her tee time, to tell her what had happened to her mother. Claudia offered to send her to the hospital in a courtesy car immediately, but Debbie said if her mother's injuries weren't life-threatening, she wouldn't withdraw. Her mother would want her to play. She would visit her mother in the hospital after the round.

Debbie asked, "Is it her right arm that's broken?"

Claudia nodded, wondering if it was the right hand Ann Wendell used when she'd punch her daughter around.

Disguising a grin as best she could, Debbie said, "Gee, I hope it's not too painful."

And went back to hitting practice balls.

———

The golf bitches were out in force Sunday. They made themselves known in the grandstands behind the ninth and eighteenth greens, rooting for their favorites.

As the players came onto the greens, one group after another, it was impossible not to hear:

"Squat on it, baby!"

"Tongue it, sweetie!"

"Line me up next, honey!"

Thurlene was worried about Ginger being distracted in the pairing with Jan Dunn in the last round, Jan a big favorite with the hand-holding-shorts-tank-tops-hiking-boots-tattoo people.

This being California, play started early in the day, so the Horse Dog would be concluded before the network news came on in the Eastern time zone. West Coast sports events are always a problem for TV and the daily print swine from the East and Midwest who have deadlines to meet.

I was not on such a deadline. My piece on the franchise babe was a feature story, one that would have a "slow closing" and would be known around *SM* world as "rather a long takeout on this teenage whapper."

Pairings sheets were passed out freely to fans as they entered the grounds, and even a loon-dancing professor might figure out that the winner was likely to come out of the last five twosomes.

Which were as follows:

12:04	Suzy Scott & Hee Bee Kim
12:13	Natalie Gulbis & Morgan Pressel
12:22	Ginger Clayton & Jan Dunn
12:31	Paula Creamer & Marian Hornbuckle
12:40	Penny Cooper & Sophie Gustafson

Thurlene and I walked down to a spot behind the first green to watch those five groups come through.

Behind the first green was where the *SM* photographer found me.

He was a muscular, blond, blue-eyed guy about my age with six or eight cameras draped over him and around him.

In a German accent, he said, "Your papers, please!"

"*Mein Fuhrer*, I can walk!" I replied.

We shook warmly.

He was Manfred Gunther, one of our ace shooters. Once with *Stern*, once with *Der Spiegel*, and with *SM* the past five years. One of the shooters I didn't mind socializing with. He rarely talked about lenses.

I said, "I knew we had a photographer here somewhere. This is Ginger Clayton's mother. You'll want to shoot her too . . . looking concerned . . . but attractively."

Thurlene took out a mirror.

Manfred Gunther said, "I came in last night from L.A. I was shooting Lakers. They weren't too cooperative. But no athlete in team sports is cooperative today . . . unless you have drugs to share."

"I've heard the rumor," I said.

Manfred creeped around Thurlene, firing away with one of his cameras, shooting from different angles. She frowned at him, raised her eyebrows at him, laughed at him, and eventually pretended to gaze down the fairway for him, looking concerned.

"Where's the babe?" Manfred said. "I only have an hour to shoot her. Gary wants me in Dallas tonight for the Mavs and Spurs."

I said, "The babe is in the short navy blue shorts, wheels you'll dream about, white shirt, white visor, blond ponytail. You can't miss her unless you're more interested in her caddie . . . which I know better than."

"Ya vol," Manfred said, and ducked under the gallery ropes and walked over to join the pack of other shooters.

All of the serious contenders parred the first two holes. Ginger greased the lip on birdie putts of twenty feet and fifteen feet on both greens, twice almost causing Thurlene to risk straining a muscle in her back as she tried to body-English the golf ball into the cup.

Then everybody but Ginger parred the third hole, "Howard Hughes." Ginger's approach shot left her a twenty-five-foot birdie putt, but she three-putted for a bogey five, missing her second putt from three feet. She mouthed an obscenity at the face of her putter.

The bogey put her three strokes behind the leaders, Penny Cooper and Sophie Gustafson, and two behind Jan Dunn and Marian Hornbuckle.

"I can't believe she three-putted from there," Thurlene said with a heavy sigh. "It's crazy."

I said, "Lot of holes left to play."

"Gosh, I hadn't thought of that," she said. "I feel better now."

41

The charming yells for Jan Dunn, reminiscent as they were of high school cheerleader squads, came from her rabid support group—the beer-swilling-shorts-tank-tops-hiking-boots-tattoo people:

"Jan, Jan . . . she's our man . . .
If she can't do it, nobody can!"

She was their *man*?

The chant was heard on several occasions as Ginger and Jan walked from green and tee, or tee to green, throughout the front nine.

Another of their faves:

"Let's go, Jan!
You're the babe!
Win it for us, honey.
We'll get you laid!"

Not exactly what cheerleaders had once yelled to encourage the Paschal Panthers or the Woodrow Wilson Wildcats.

Ginger said afterward that when she and Jan were standing on a tee, waiting for the group ahead to move on, Jan repeatedly apologized for the behavior of "those people." Jan swore she didn't know any of them and she didn't *want* to know any of them.

Ginger confessed that they bothered her now and then but overall she was proud of herself for keeping her head on and shutting out everything but her own golf game.

Thurlene, of course, wanted to pour Drano down their throats, or set fire to them, or both.

The mom was all set to break out a Xanax only a moment before Ginger ran in a putt for a birdie at the seventh hole, "Yvonne de Carlo." It pulled her back to even par on the round, tied with Jan Dunn and within one stroke of the leaders, who were now Penny Cooper and Marian Hornbuckle.

Sophie Gustafson, the coleader after fifty-four holes, and Paula Creamer had gradually fallen out of contention with a string of three-putt bogeys.

"My kid is going to win this golf tournament," Thurlene said. "She believes it too. I can tell by the way she looks, the way she walks, the way she acts. I don't know how she's going to do it, but she is."

"You're saying I can start typing?" I said.

"You might wait a while longer."

Looking back on it, if you went strictly by the numbers, Ginger was in a four-way tie for the lead after nine holes.

She and Jan Dunn shot even par 35s on the front nine while Penny Cooper turned in a two-over 37, and Marian Hornbuckle, who started one stroke in back of Penny, went out in 36.

In real time, the four-way deadlock occurred over a period of thirty-five minutes.

What added to the chaos of trying to watch and keep up with things was the way the combatants were spread out. Ginger and Jan were playing two holes ahead of Penny Cooper and one hole ahead of Marian Hornbuckle, who was one hole in front of Penny.

All that's part of the deal if you're accustomed to watching golf tournaments.

The tenth hole, "Fatty Arbuckle," was a long par-four and was misnamed in my opinion. The fairway wasn't that wide and the green wasn't that big, or fat, I should say. But Ginger birdied it when she launched a big drive and rifled a five-iron onto the green and cozied a downhill putt into the cup from fifteen feet.

That birdie, and the two pars that followed, gave Ginger a one-stroke lead on the field, but only momentarily. Penny Cooper birdied the ninth to pull back even with her.

It was a three-way race at this point. Ginger Clayton one under on the round, Penny Cooper one over, and Jan Dunn even par, one shot back. Marian Hornbuckle had hooked a ride on the bogey train. She was now four over par and for all purposes out of it.

There's always a defining moment in a golf tournament—in any sports event, in fact—and I thought this one came at the thirteenth hole, the number one handicap hole on the course, a viciously long and crooked par-four. It was a 468-yard hole, dogleg right, palms lining both sides of the fairway, bunkers surrounding the green, narrow opening.

The hole was aptly named "Box Office Poison."

Ginger had bogeyed it three straight days by hitting a poor drive into the palms and two poor second shots into bunkers.

But this time she played it the way she played my laptop in New Mexico.

Off the tee, she hit a rocket fade of 275 yards around the corner of the dogleg. Then from roughly 190 yards she clubfaced a low, screaming three-iron that was on the flag like a laser beam. The ball ran right through the opening and onto the putting surface and rolled up to within a foot of the flag in the back of the green.

It was some golf shot, boy. Kick-in birdie at the toughest hole. It was like an eagle. It was like picking up two shots on everybody.

The shot caused the biggest roar of the day from the crowd, and the second biggest squeal of the week from the mom. Thurlene couldn't possibly have topped her ecstatic squeal at the sight of Tang Chen hitting it out of bounds on Friday.

But we didn't celebrate the defining moment very long.

Ginger stepped up on the next tee with a wedge in her hands and bogeyed the fucking lollipop.

The straightaway ninety-nine-yard par-three with no sand and no water. "Shirley Temple." It should have been a simple pitch shot, another potential birdie, and no worse than a par.

But she got cute and took it to the butcher shop. The pin was on the front and she tried a bump-and-run. The trouble was, her shot found a wet spot in the fairway some fifteen yards short of the green—and stuck.

She went with a lob shot from there but flew it over the flag and left herself a ten-foot putt coming back, which she missed. Left it short.

Thurlene stared at me, frustrated, baffled.

If I didn't look concerned, if I looked a little too nonchalant, it's because I could afford to be frivolous about the situation. While I was rooting hard for the kid in my gut, I had a story to root for first, and Ginger had already saved the story for me.

She'd fought back into the mix. I figured she'd nailed the *SM* cover for sure. I was thinking it'll be great if she wins, but it won't be too bad a thing if she loses now. No disgrace for an eighteen-year-old to lose a major on the last nine holes, in the final hour, to a player of the stature of a Penny Cooper or a Jan Dunn.

Now Thurlene said, "Okay, Jack. You're a big-time golf writer. You've been around. Will you kindly explain to me how in the name of God a player of Ginger's caliber, with her talent, can birdie the hardest hole on the golf course and five minutes later bogey the easiest hole in the whole goddamn world?"

I shrugged. "There's only one explanation."

"What?"

"It's Chinatown, Jake."

42

The easiest way to watch a golf tournament, it goes without saying, is at home in your comfortable chair with your dog and your clicker and something cold to drink and a handy bowl of Orville Redenbacher's microwave buttered popcorn.

But you need to keep in mind that TV distorts golf. Uphill or downhill never looks as severely uphill or downhill on the screen as it is in real life. A camera behind a player facing a 250-yard shot makes you think he or she can get home without much effort using a short iron. But if you're out on a golf course, you know that 250 yards looks like—and is—a long way off. At least it is for normal humans.

TV makes every golf course look beautiful, and this is okay. Every golf course *is* beautiful compared to a row of tenements in the Bronx. For an object to gaze at, even someone in need of cataract surgery would choose a burned-out public golf course with unraked bunkers, hardly any trees, and shaggy Bermuda greens over any downtown street in any industrial city.

Come to think of it, I grew up on a course like that—and thought it was perfectly swell.

As for watching a tournament up close and personal, out on the course, there are four basic ways that golf fans go about it.

One, they do the grandpa and grandma thing. Pick a spot by a green, in a grandstand, or on a gentle slope, and sit there throughout the day, groaning over missed putts and applauding those that drop, seeing every player in the field, and not minding that most of them today look alike.

Two, they have a favorite player for some reason or another, usually somebody who's not even in contention, and they walk the full eighteen with her or him, seeing every shot of the round, good or bad, and do this out of what a sane person would consider to be perverse loyalty.

Three, they couldn't care less about who wins. They're only out there to pick up swing tips that'll improve their own games, although the tips usually confuse them and they come away with funnier swings than ever.

Four, they're like me. Aware it's a war, an athletic event. Players competing against the course, the other players, and most of all themselves. You try to keep up by moving from one player in contention to another, then back again if necessary. Your eyes scan the scoreboards at each opportunity. You rely on your knowledge of the contestants, their histories in combat.

You know where to anticipate the birdies, where the danger lurks on the course. You've learned to interpret the distant roars and moans of the galleries. That was a birdie. That was undoubtedly a par. That must have been a chip-in. But you don't have to be a golf writer to watch a tournament like this. You can just be a golf nut.

Though it went against my journalistic tendencies, we made the decision to follow the kid the entire back nine, win or lose. But why not, in this case? Ginger was my story. Ginger was Thurlene's kid.

Thus, we were loitering behind the fifteenth green, waiting for Ginger and Jan to putt, when the numbers went up informing us that Penny Cooper had bogeyed the eleventh and twelfth holes and slipped to three over on the round.

There were two sounds as the numbers were posted. Moans from the fans of Penny, delirious whoops from Ginger's fans.

"My God, we have a two-shot lead," Thurlene said, mentally doing the arithmetic. It told her the kid was one under par and Penny Cooper was now three over. Ginger had started the day two back of Penny, but now she was two ahead.

"One," I said, correcting her. "She's two ahead of Penny, but only one ahead of Jan . . . who's still in the tournament, if I'm not mis-taken."

An instant later Ginger didn't even have a one-shot lead on Jan Dunn.

The two-time major winner rammed in a thirty-foot birdie putt on the fifteenth green to pull into a tie with Ginger.

Jan Dunn's long putt was a dagger in Thurlene's heart. But she took it with a calm display of sportsmanship. She nodded in a man-ner that said, "Good going, Jan—that was quite timely."

Of course, I knew she was really thinking: "How many more no-brainers are you going to make, you lucky bitch? You're a friend but this is a major, for Christ's sake."

It was now a two-chick race with three holes to go.

Jan's tie for the lead perked up her support group. We heard:

"You got the tits,
You got the ass!
Come on, Jan.
Step on the gas!"

"Aren't they wonderful," Thurlene said. "I'll sleep better tonight knowing those people are going to die someday."

Cy Ronack, my pal, the writer from *Golf World*, found us at "Mae West." We were near the sixteenth green, waiting for Ginger and Jan to play their shots to the 174-yard par-three, the hole with two big mounds on each side of the green and protected in front by a pond.

"Your office is frantic," Cy Ronack said. "Gary Crane has been try-ing to reach you for three hours. He left a message with Monique in the pressroom. She gave it to me in case I ran into you on the course. Am I running into you?"

"You are."

"Your boss says they want your piece tonight. They're going with Heather on the cover."

Thurlene said, "Did you say *Heather*?"

Cy read from his notes. "They want to go with it as a long 'lead takeout,' whatever that is. Their other 'missiles' have misfired. The tennis doping story has lost its momentum. The three crooked NFL zebras have retracted their confessions . . . and the college football coach denies knowing any of the fourteen women who've accused him of sexual harrassment."

"Gary's having a rough time," I said.

"They've received great shots of Heather from your shooter. What an amazing world we live in. It was only yesterday that photographers had to rush to the airport after an event and ship their film to New York overnight. Now a guy clicks off a series of shots, looks at them in a little window on his camera, presses a button, and they appear on somebody's screen three thousand miles away."

"In living color," I said.

"Who is *Heather*?" Thurlene said.

"Don't worry about it," I said. "We've got the cover. Heather is Ginger. Rhymes with danger."

43

Ginger's iron shot to the sixteenth grabbed a chair. The shot gave her an inviting eight-foot birdie putt. It prompted a loud "Oh, yeah, baby!" out of Thurlene, and an audible "All right!" out of me. Which drew a glance from Cy Ronack, who said, "I've always heard journalists are impartial."

I said, "We are—I'm rooting for my story."

After Jan Dunn two-putted from thirty feet for her par, Ginger took what seemed like far too long reading her putt. She kneeled and studied it from all four sides, walking patiently with Tyler Hughes from one position to another.

Thurlene said, "She's acting like the tournament's riding on this, but there are two more holes to play."

"Looks to me like she's thinking this is her last chance at a birdie," I said. "Don't be long, is what I'd tell her."

"Better long than short," Thurlene said. "Give it a chance."

"But you know a putt that's long didn't go in," I said.

Thurlene looked at me like I was Retardo Montalban.

I said, "Bobby Jones says it in his book. That's why he played his putts to die at the hole . . . and Ben Hogan always said he found more trouble going long than short, with a shot or a putt. Hogan said there was usually more trouble *behind* a green than in front of it. He lost an Open and a Masters by charging birdie putts. He three-putted the last green at Augusta *and* at Canterbury in forty-six."

"I'm glad Ginger is putting this instead of Jones or Hogan."

"Why? Because they're dead?"

"Hush."

Ginger backed away from the putt once, stood over it again, took two practice strokes, and finally rapped the ball into the center of the cup, having accurately read a slight break to the right, the ball dying at the edge and dropping.

The kid didn't even react. She ignored the explosion from the crowd. She was Downtown Focus City as she walked to the seventeenth tee, leaving Tyler to retrieve the ball from the cup.

The birdie moved her to two under on the round and gave her a one-shot lead over Jan Dunn with two holes to play.

As Jan Dunn staggered to a bogey on the seventeenth, "Sam Goldwyn," a four-hundred-yard par-four, Ginger nailed her drive long and straight, leaving herself a second shot of 120 yards, and she put that one on the green twenty feet from the flag, and easily two-putted for the four that hurtled her into a two-stroke lead over Jan Dunn.

"You know why she's doing this?" Thurlene said. "I promised her she can have a car."

"You promised her a car if she wins?" I said.

"I told her she can have a car regardless. She's thanking me."

Cy Ronack said, "There's your lead. 'She did it for the car.' "

I said, "I've been thinking more along the lines of, 'Call her Ismael if you want to, but her name is Ginger.' "

Cy said, "You might want to play around with 'In my younger and more vulnerable years . . .' "

"That was the time I said, 'Ginger, this could be the beginning of a beautiful friendship.' "

"Then you turn up the collar of your coat and walk back to the hotel in the rain."

"Isn't it pretty to think so."

Thurlene said, "If the two of you don't mind, can we get past this last hole? It's sort of important."

"We can," I said. "There's nothing left to do but win the war."

Ginger and Jan were standing on the eighteenth tee. "Tinsel Town." The 352-yard par-four with trees left and out of bounds right. It looked like Jan was talking to her. Ginger was nodding as she stared ahead.

We were walking along the ropes, working our way to the green.

I said, "Smart money would play this hole with three seven-irons— cinch a bogey five. She has a two-shot lead."

"That would leave it open for a playoff if Jan birdies," Thurlene said. "It's not Gin's nature to play safe. She has it wrapped, now she wants to tie a ribbon around it. She'll go with a three-wood. Besides, like she said, this course owes her one. She wants to kick it to death."

"Bring the monster to its knees."

"Where have I heard that?"

"Hogan said it at Oakland Hills . . . after he won the fifty-one Open with the sixty-seven in the last round. Evidently it was the world's hardest golf course that week. At the public ceremony, Hogan said he was glad he brought 'this course, this monster' to its knees. But I have it on good authority that in the locker room he said he was glad he brought 'the son of a bitch' to its knees."

Cy Ronack said, "Late in the summer of that year—"

But I nudged him into silence as Ginger ripped a three-wood center-cut, safe in the fairway, 125 yards short of the green.

"Merely perfect," I said. "I don't think there's anything she can do to screw it up from there."

"Not a chance," Thurlene said. "Not this kid."

The mom was right. Ginger lofted a high nine-iron onto the green. The ball settled in about twelve feet from the cup. As the two players walked up the fairway to the green, Jan Dunn gave Ginger a congratulatory hug, patted her on the back, then pointed to her and applauded, encouraging the gallery to join in, which it did.

"Isn't my kid something?" Thurlene said. "Isn't she *something*?"

With that, Thurlene smothered me with a hug and kiss.

I said, "It's proper training in the home, is all."

Ginger denied herself any show of emotion until after she drained the twelve-foot birdie putt for a finishing 67, a Hogan 67, the only sub-70 round of the championship, and a three-stroke victory in the Colgate–Dinah Shore Kraft Nabisco Le Grand Cheval et Petit Chien Classique.

. She leaped into the arms of her caddie, Tyler Hughes, and a moment later was being sprayed with bottles of reasonably priced champagne furnished by the tour for such occasions. Debbie Wendell, Suzy Scott, and Linda Merle Draper had dashed onto the green and were doing the spraying.

I helped Thurlene duck under the ropes, where it would be easier for Ginger to spot her. Cy Ronack came with us. We pointed to our press armbands to prevent three frantic volunteer marshals from throwing flying tackles on us and calling 911, the First Marine Division, and the CIA.

Ginger rushed over to hug Thurlene. A long hug. Tears.

"Well," Thurlene said to her daughter, "I don't know about you, but it's the most fun *I've* ever had."

"You get a hug too, Jack," Ginger said, and strapped it on me.

She turned back to Thurlene. "Mom, I want a Lexus. A champagne gold LS Hybrid. They start at over a hundred grand."

"You got it, baby."

She yelped with delight, hugged her mom again, and jogged to the scorer's tent, slapping the palms of fans along the way.

44

As soon as Ginger left to sign her scorecard and make the Horse Dog official, three familiar gentlemen approached Thurlene. They were the sports agents: Larry Silverman, Howie (the Dart) Daniels, and Smacky Lasher.

They were trying desperately to look sporty. Larry wore a maroon crew-neck golf shirt under his gray blazer. Howie wore a yellow crew-neck golf shirt under his black suit coat. Smacky wore a green soft-collared golf shirt under his brown checkered sports jacket.

Each agent attempted to give Thurlene an envelope, but she refused to accept any of them.

"Not yet," she said.

Howie Daniels said, "But you told us—"

Thurlene raised a hand that said, "Please . . . ?"

Smacky Lasher said, "I thought the deal was—"

She stopped *his* sentence with her own.

"Whatever I said before doesn't matter now, does it? I know you people can count. Ginger has won three tournaments in a row."

"You'll like my package," Smacky said, boring ahead. "My package includes a tax accountant, traveling companion, investment counselor, professional caddie. The numbers are—"

Thurlene said, "Gin likes the caddie she has . . . and I'm her investment person, tax accountant, and traveling companion."

Smacky shifted gears, breaking the speed of light. "That's why this offer sucks. I told my boss it sucks, but he said go with it anyway. What does he know? He watches poker on TV. You never saw this, Thurlene."

The agent stuck the envelope in his coat.

Thurlene smiled.

Smacky said, "Allow me to spitball for a moment." He started to punch on a pocket calculator.

Howie Daniels said, "I have it all laid out, Thurlene. Ginger needs a swing coach, a travel agent, and a fashion consultant. That's to start. I have them built in. Also, we need to talk about a sports psychologist, a schedule advisor, a one-fourth interest in a Gulfstream—"

"No motivational whisperer?" I said, interrupting.

"Good," Howie said. "Jack's here. Great you can be with us, Jack."

"I would think she'd need a motivational whisperer, and maybe her own massage therapist."

"Appreciate your thoughts, Jack."

Howie glanced at Cy Ronack. "Oh, *Golf World* is here too. Terrific. More financial help from the literary set."

Cy said, "I'm just here to help out with the performance clauses."

Howie's cell buzzed. He began scrolling.

Thurlene looked at Larry Silverman. "Nothing to say, Larry?"

"I suspect you have more to say," Larry said.

"I do," she said. "Ginger and I are going to Palm Beach from here. She's taking the next two weeks off. You guys have my phone number and my e-mail. I will expect to hear from you no later than a week from today. That's the deadline I've given the others."

"The others?" Smacky said.

"Do you think you're the only three people interested in Ginger Clayton?"

"Of course not," Larry Silverman said.

Thurlene said, "One more thing. I'm sure you remember three years ago when Tricia Hurt turned pro at sixteen . . . and signed with Walsh Goodman. She had never won anything, but she showed potential and she was a pretty girl, extremely photogenic. Walsh guaranteed her nineteen million dollars the first year . . . even if she never made a cut."

"You did read that," Cy Ronack said. "I wrote it first."

Howie said, "Very unrealistic on Walsh's part. That's why they're a theatrical agency."

"Nevertheless," Thurlene said, "I'd like for you gentlemen to keep that in mind as I leave you with two words that have become my favorite two words in the English language."

"What words?" Smacky asked innocuously.

It was a read-my-lips thing as Thurlene said:

"Bidding war."

After the agents drifted into the sunset—each guy nodding, frowning, sulking, faintly smiling—Thurlene gazed at the big scoreboard behind the eighteenth green.

"What a lovely sight," she said.

The final scores of the top ten read:

1.	Ginger Clayton	76–73–71–67—287
2.	Jan Dunn	72–75–73–70—290
3.	Penny Cooper	73–71–74–73—291
4.	Marian Hornbuckle	74–74–71–74—293
5.	Morgan Pressel	72–77–72–73—294
T5.	Paula Creamer	73–74–72–75—294
T5.	Natalie Gulbis	75–70–75–74—294
8.	Suzy Scott	71–78–72–75—296
T8.	Sophie Gustafson	74–74–70–78—296
9.	Lorena Ochoa	70–79–73–75—297

Cy Ronack said, "I'll have one of our photogs shoot it for you . . . for the scrapbook."

"That would be great," Thurlene said.

"I have to go type," I said.

Thurlene said, "I'll come in for Ginger's interview after the presentation ceremony."

Cy Ronack said, "Here's your lead, Jack: 'Outlined against a blue-gray March sky . . .'"

"That would never work," I said as I headed for the pressroom. "No sportswriter could make something like that work."

45

The laptop was open, the cup of coffee within reach, but the muse was taking her own sweet time coming to visit. She does that on occasion.

The other writers nearby were already grinding, going to the whip, or else they were leafing through interview printouts, browsing through record books and media guides, or cussing electricity.

Two-thirds of my piece had been written the first two days in Palm Springs. Two thousand words. All I needed was the top. Around 640 words.

I would write to fit, as usual. They were already closing in the New York office. This was good. You never want to give an *SM* editor too much time or any choices.

If you do, and you're out of town, and therefore unable to grab the editor by the necktie and drag him down the hall to a dark corner where you can choke him to death if he's jacked around with your piece, he's a mortal lock to lift out anything remotely humorous and possibly even turn it into a story about croquet.

I sipped coffee, yearned for a Marlboro, and thought about putting Ginger's three wins in a row—topped off by a major—in perspective.

No teenager had ever created such a stir on the tour. And she was joining an elite list of past winners of what I still call the Dinah.

Among others, the past winners included Annika Sorenstam, Juli Inkster, Nancy Lopez, Amy Alcott, Mickey Wright, Kathy Whitworth, and Judy Rankin. Neat crowd to hang out with in the record book.

And there was one more thing. Ginger was eighteen and two months. Which made her the youngest winner of a major in the history of women, ladies, teenage girls, or high school beauty queen homewreckers.

I finally gave up on the muse and went without her, comforting myself with the thought that, what the hell, I wasn't going for the anthologies here.

The fun part is always typing the byline. It's generally downhill after that. I wrote:

By Jack Brannon

Put a golf club in the hands of an 18-year-old babe who looks like she's climbed out of a centerfold and what you have is Ginger Clayton, the greatest thing that's happened to women's golf since Mary Queen of Scots picked up a shepherd's crook and drove a wee stain into a rabbit scrape on the links of Old Bagpipe.

An hour later I was done. Filed. Attached. Sent. Landed.

Ginger was still in the interview area. She was up behind a table and microphone. Up there with a replica of the $500,000 winner's check and the championship trophy. The trophy looked like a horse's head sitting on top of the world's largest can of dog food.

I walked over to catch the rest of Ginger's interview when Thurlene came out of the area.

She said, "We have to talk when you're finished writing."

"I'm finished," I said.

"Really? That quick?"

"Well, it wasn't *Anna Karenina*."

"Oh, no, not again."

We moved out onto a terrace off the pressroom. She lit a Capri.

"Jack, do you have to live in New York?"

"I don't have to," I said. "We have writers who live other places. But I like living in Manhattan . . . Why?"

"What if you lived in Palm Beach?"

"I would want to live in Palm Beach why? Because you're there?"

"Yes. Me and Lolita."

"I can't afford to live in Palm Beach. I can't afford to live in New York either, but I'm used to it."

"Maybe you wouldn't have to afford an apartment in Palm Beach. Our condo is big. Like, huge."

"So I do what? I grab my dop kit and my books and CDs and mosey on down?"

"There's a spare bedroom you could have for your office. The West Palm airport is convenient. The schedules are good. You can go everywhere pretty easily from West Palm to cover your slugs. We could go with you sometimes. You could go with us sometimes. And you'd have your own computer guru. Ginger. She wants you there too."

"She told you that with her own mouth."

"Her exact words were 'Don't let Jack get away, Mom. If you do, you'll die too young in a strip mall.' "

"Is this a proposal?"

"We're in love, right? We should do something about it."

I said, "Thurlene, two weeks ago your daughter and I were alone and she talked about you. She described you as gorgeous, intelligent, witty, energetic . . . but especially gorgeous and intelligent. That's all true. Lord knows, it's true. And it's great she recognizes it. But I've got to tell you. I'm afraid you might be too much woman for me."

She put her arms around my neck, drew me closer, and said:

"I can scale back."